BITING WIND

BITING WIND

A Salt Creek Novel

Phil LeMaitre

This novel is a work of fiction. The names, characters, and exploits are the author's imagination and are used fictitiously. Any resemblance to actual persons, living or dead, businesses, and companies are entirely coincidental.

Biting Wind: A Salt Creek Novel by Phil LeMaitre Copyright © 2019, 2021

Second Edition

Published by Salt Creek Tales-Phil LeMaitre, Rockledge, Florida
ISBN:978-1-7379585-4-3 (Paperback)
ISBN: 978-1-7379585-5-0 (eBook)

Cover photography by Phil LeMaitre

phillemaitreauthor.com

Dedicated to everyone that has lived or is still living within the Salt Creek community...GO OILERS!

Wednesday, January 1, 1992

Gas Plant Camp, Midwest, Wyoming

10:45 p.m.

Young Wesley Corbin stood on his bed and peered through his frost-covered bedroom window in his family's home on the corner of Ash and Aspen streets in Gas Plant.

It was hard for him to make out any objects in the backyard because of the waning moon. However, he could make out things like the swing set and the garage since whatever light was present reflected against the fresh powder snow.

It was cold outside, but that didn't bother him since winter brought new opportunities like sledding. However, it was hard to find a grass-covered hill in the middle of the oilfield. Hills around his home were most often barren with exposed tracks of clay-like bentonite instead of topsoil.

Wesley was on Christmas break, and the next day would be his last day of vacation. He thought it was strange that school would start up again the upcoming Friday instead of waiting to begin on Monday after the weekend. Wesley went so far as to express his misgivings to his parents, who promptly reminded him that an extended vacation would keep him in school until the middle of June.

The boy sighed heavily at the thought of being trapped behind in his desk in Mrs. Morgan's fourth-grade class once again. He longed for freedom from school though he relished the idea of playing junior high football in two years as a sixth-grader and later as an Oiler on the high school team.

The boy's breath instantly froze upon the window glass, which made a thin layer of frost. It now obstructed his view of the backyard, which irritated him. So, he held his breath to prevent more icing, and then he scraped it off of the window with his thumbnail. Finally, Wesley ducked his head and expelled his lungs, and drew in another breath so he could finish. With the window clear on the inside, he saw nothing but an endless blanket of darkness beyond the backyard.

As he turned his head to climb down from his bed, something caught Wesley's eye. He looked out the window once more, and he spotted a small greenish-yellow light that floated somewhere well beyond the back of his house toward Castle Creek. He watched the orb float slowly, and it appeared that it bobbed along like someone carrying a lantern. Then it hit him: it was a ghost light!

The boy quickly reached over to his bed stand and nearly toppled off of the mattress. Then, he regained his balance and picked up his two-way walkie-talkie. The transceiver was a part of a twin set that he received seven days earlier on Christmas morning. Wesley kept one and gave the other to his best friend, Stewart Jenkins, who lived a few doors down on the corner of Ash and Pine Streets. On every night since Christmas, the two boys secretly talked back and forth and inserted the words *over* and *roger* to sound like they were in the military.

With the walkie-talkie in hand, Wesley looked back out his window and again spotted the glowing orb moving slowly through the darkness.

He pressed the talk button on the side of the unit, "Hey Stu! Are you up? *Over.*" Silence.

The boy tried again, "Stu, this is Wes. *Over.*" While Wesley looked through the window once again, his hand-held radio squawked.

"Wes? Did you call me? *Over.*"

"*Roger*, I did call you. *Over.*"

"What's up? *Over.*"

"Meet me now in front of my house, *Over*," insisted Wesley.

"Roger, wilco."

Wesley quietly got off his bed and then walked over to his closet to put on his coat and snow boots. Next, he opened his door and looked out into the living room, which was dark and intimated to him that his parents had gone to bed. Then, ever so quietly, Wesley stepped into the short hallway, tiptoed across the living room and kitchen, and then walked out of the back door. He eased the door back into place and held the screen door steady until it gently latched into place with a small audible click.

The snow underfoot made a squeaking sound as it crushed under each of his footsteps as he made his way to the front of his house. Stewart was already in front of the house on the street and waited patiently for Wesley to join him.

"What's going on, Wes?" Stewart asked.

"I want you to see something?" Wesley whispered.

"What?" he shouted.

"Keep your voice down. I don't want my parents to hear us. Just follow me."

Wesley led the way to the end of the street that emptied directly into the surrounding oil field. Though the orb was no longer in view, he hoped it was somewhere over the slight rise to the east.

After walking fifty yards east, the boy stopped and said to his friend, "look straight ahead toward Castle Creek."

It didn't take Stewart long to find what his friend wanted him to see. The bright green and yellow orb floated just above the ground and seemed no farther than a hundred yards away.

"Wes, do you know what that is?"

"Yes, it is a ghost light, Stu."

The two boys watched the glowing orb for another minute when it simply vanished. The boys continued to watch in utter silence and hoped that the luminescent sphere would show itself once again. But, unfortunately, the only light the boys could see was the thick band of stars that made up the Milky Way galaxy, glowing unspoiled by light pollution from a city.

After another ten minutes passed by, Stewart suggested, "how about we come out here in the morning and look around where we saw the Ghost Light?"

Wesley nodded. "Cool, let's do that. But, come on, I am getting cold out here in my pajamas, and I had better get inside before my parents know I am gone."

* * *

Thursday, January 2, 1992

Corner of C Street and Navy Row, Midwest, Wyoming

Sheriff Deputy Eddie Crandall walked out of his bedroom after he finished putting on his uniform. He moved over and sat down on his couch in the living room to pull on his cowboy boots. As he tugged the first one on his foot, he completed an inventory of things he wanted to say in his new trainee. Recently, his boss, Sheriff Doan, telephoned Eddie to inform him of the decision to increase the number of deputies in the Salt Creek community to two full-time positions. The Sheriff then told Eddie he selected Deputy Tracy James for the new role.

As he tugged on his second boot, it occurred to him that he knew very little about his trainee. He only got what Sheriff Doan relayed to him and the tidbit of information in her personnel file. First, he knew she was 23 years old, single, originally from Cheyenne, had spent four years as an Air Force security forces member. Second, Tracy's employment with the Sheriff's department began about three months before. Her job entailed transporting inmates from the county jail to the courthouse. Third, Eddie was puzzled why the Sheriff would assign her to work with him because the Salt Creek community had always been a single deputy district.

He stood up from the couch and walked over to the coffee pot next to the sink on the kitchen counter. Eddie reached up to the cupboard above the coffee maker, retrieved a mug, and then filled it with coffee. The clock on his stove displayed *07:15*, which told him it would only be fifteen minutes until his trainee would arrive. He then took the cup in his right hand and walked to the front door, opened it, and stepped on the deck he built the previous summer.

The Sergeant looked east from his place over the empty lot behind the town hall. That morning, the only thing in the sky was the sun, and not even a stray cloud or airplane contrail spoiled the vast light blue sky. The early morning sunlight felt warm on his face despite the cold temperature. He raised the steaming cup of coffee to his lips and took a sip, and then looked to his left upon a little house at #6 Navy Row as he often did. A married pair of teachers and two little girls lived in that house, and they were great neighbors. But, then, a thought occurred to him like a thunderclap about all the changes that have taken place since the house's former residents had left town.

The tiny house used to be the home of Rob and Sara Anderson and their son Josh and his little sister Cindy. Josh left town in 1985 to attend the U.S. Coast Guard Academy. Then, after Cindy graduated from Midwest High School in 1987, Rob and Sara decided to move into Casper, where Rob took a similar position at a junior high school.

Eddie always liked the family and respected them much. In the 1984-1985 school year, he got to know them exceptionally well due to an event that shook the community. But the Andersons moving into Casper was only the tip of the iceberg of changes at the school. Since then, six other teachers had left Midwest between 1986 and 1989.

Additionally, the Salt Creek area went through tremendous changes that started in late 1985 when oil prices plummeted to the point that it cost more to produce oil than to sell it. As a result, the two small grocery stores in Midwest and Edgerton had closed down, forcing area residents to shop in Casper 40 miles to the south. The small school population reduced even more. Due to declining enrollment, the Wyoming High School Athletics Association forced the high school football team to drop from the 11-man classification down to the newly created 9-man division.

The recent 1990 census revealed that citizenship in the Salt Creek communities of Midwest and Edgerton had reduced by 22% compared to 1980. As a result, some of the people lost their jobs, which forced them to move. While still others resigned their positions and moved to another place and started another career.

During that timeframe, Eddie had his fill of assisting landlords evicting renters who could not pay the rent or serving court summons in divorce cases. He even detested the time when he had to arrest an area resident for drunk driving. It turned out that the man was one of many that particular day who drank too much after losing his job when the company handed out layoff notices. Though everybody in the community agreed that Eddie was right in doing his job, it didn't make him feel any better.

Four years before, he had bought his home from Mrs. Fortney. She decided to move in with her daughter in Phoenix, Arizona, due to her declining physical health. The house itself was a modular home set upon a solid concrete foundation. It was complete with three bedrooms, two bathrooms, a fenced-in yard, and a carport. Eddie liked the house so much that he offered Mrs. Fortney an extra thousand dollars over her asking price, to which she refused. Yet, he loved living in the Salt Creek community so much that he had turned down other department positions in the previous seven years because it meant moving to Casper.

He took another sip from his mug, but the coffee had already turned ice-cold, so he poured it out into the snowdrift next to the porch and went back inside.

Fifteen minutes later, Deputy Tracy James pulled up in front of the Sergeant's home in her Sheriff's Department sedan cruiser and placed the transmission into the PARK position. Then, she reached over to the seat next to her and grabbed her green Sheriff's Department ball cap and put it on top of her head, and carefully pulled her short ponytail through the opening above the adjustment tabs. But before exiting the vehicle, Tracy looked one last time at herself in the rear-view mirror to make sure her look was professional. Then, she reached out with her left hand to open her door and told herself, *"make a good impression,"* and, with that, she stepped out of the cruiser and shut the door.

Inside his home, Eddie heard the car door shut, and he stood up from the couch and walked over, and opened the door. He watched his trainee walk carefully up the salted sidewalk. With each step, the salt granules crunched sharply under the soles of her boots. She had a slim athletic build, stood approximately 5'5" tall, had light brown hair high-lighted with a few natural streaks of blond. Even at that distance, he could see her pale blue eyes.

Eddie opened the storm door and held it open with the back of his right leg, and he welcomed, "Deputy James, it is good to meet you."

In a blink of an eye, Tracy scanned her new supervisor from his head to his feet. She met her trainer's eyes and saw that he expressed a warm and welcoming spirit that countered her expectation of how he would receive her. To Tracy, he looked about 6' tall, 190 pounds, short-cropped red hair, and many freckles.

Deputy James replied, "Good morning Sergeant Crandall. It is good to meet you at last."

Eddie smiled and motioned for her to come inside.

Once Deputy James entered his home, she appropriately wiped her feet on the doormat and began to take off her gloves first and then her coat. Meanwhile, he stepped behind her and closed the door.

Eddie offered, "here, I will take your coat, and you can make yourself at home."

He took the coat over to a rarely used chair near the front window and placed it neatly across the seat. Eddie turned and motioned for his trainee to sit down on the couch, which she complied with, and he took a seat in the lone recliner in the room and started his introduction.

"Deputy James, my name is Eddie Crandall, and you may call me Eddie since I like to keep things informal around here."

"Thank you, Eddie, I am Tracy James, and I prefer Tracy if that is okay?" she asked.

"Alright, Tracy, it is. Welcome to my home, which also serves as my office. Would you care for a tour?"

"Sure, lead the way."

After they both stood up, Eddie showed Tracy his kitchen. He welcomed her to bring any particular snacks or other food that she wanted to keep on hand while working in the office. He explained that behind the kitchen was his bedroom and bathroom and stressed that she had open access to the rest of his place. Eddie also showed her the location of the second bathroom next to the spare bedroom door, which contained only a tiny twin bed surrounded by boxes.

Tracy took inventory of what she saw and noticed a glaring absence of photos of either Eddie or other family members. For the most part, the walls were bare except for the two Charles Russel framed prints that hung on opposite walls in the living room.

Next, he led her into the other bedroom that he converted into an office. An antique oak desk dominated one side of the room, and the closet contained a file cabinet and a gun safe equipped with a combination lock. On the other side of the room was a smaller gray metal desk complete with a matching chair.

"I picked up a desk for you yesterday from Reed, who is the head custodian at the school. I bought it for a reasonable price of $25 so that you could have at least a little space to call your own. The Sheriff's department is also paying to put in another phone line that will ring directly to your desk."

"Thank you, Sergeant. Unfortunately, I don't know what to say since I won't be out here that long or just long enough to complete my field training."

Eddie took a deep breath and had quietly dreaded to be the one to tell Tracy, but he exhaled and started to speak.

"Tracy, why don't you take a seat at your desk," and as she turned and sat down, he moved to the front edge of his desk and sat down on the side of it.

He said, "Deputy, I hate to be the one to tell you this. But, quite frankly, it should have been made clear a week ago when the Sheriff made the decision." Eddie paused for a few seconds but then continued, "you are not just assigned to receive training from me. Rather you are also permanently assigned to help me district this area."

Tracy's face flushed bright red, and tears started to well up in the corners of her eyes, but just as quickly as her shock came to the surface, it disappeared even faster.

She looked up at Eddie. "Well, I am not surprised by how they handled it," then trailed off her words.

"Handled what exactly?"

Tracy shook her head. "Oh, never mind, it is in the past and doesn't matter now. So, I guess this is it, and I will have to make the best of it, huh?"

"If it makes you feel any better, I was assigned out here by myself with no field training and with only six months on the job at the county detention center."

Tracy shrugged her shoulders apathetically. "No, it doesn't make me feel any better, but it is what it is."

Eddie stood up from his desk and walked a couple of steps closer to Tracy, still seated.

He asked her, "would you like any coffee, or if you haven't had any breakfast, we could drive over to Edgerton and eat at the Café, my treat? It would give us a chance to get to know each other and allow me to show you around a little, so what do you think?"

"Now that you mention it, I am a little hungry since I skipped breakfast in my rush to get out here this morning from Casper."

"Okay, it is settled. Grab your coat and follow me to my unit."

Tracy complied and put on her coat and pulled on her gloves, and stepped through the open door held by Eddie.

When he closed the door, Tracy turned around and asked, "aren't you going to lock it?"

Eddie's face broke into a broad smile. "No, we don't have much of a problem with an unlawful entry around here, but don't worry, I have all my firearms locked away in a safe in my office."

Tracy furrowed her brow while trying to understand the premise. She hadn't ever left any house without locking the doors, even as a child.

They walked across the porch away from the front steps toward a brand-new department issue, Chevy Blazer, sitting under a carport next to an older Red-colored Ford F-150 pickup. When Eddie reached the vehicle, he walked to its front and unplugged an extension cord under the front grill.

"What is that for?" Tracy asked as it intrigued her to see such a thing.

Eddie held up the plug with his hand. "What this?"

Tracy nodded her head.

He continued, "the power cord is for the immersion heater, which is attached to the cooling system that keeps the engine block warm during cold weather. Sometimes the heat from the immersion heater will rise through the defrost vent on the dashboard, which warms the inside of the windshield, preventing ice from forming."

He then walked around his unit and opened the driver's side door, and without getting behind the wheel, he started the Blazer. Instead, Eddie grabbed the ice scraper from under the driver's seat and quickly scraped off the soft ice. Meanwhile, Tracy sat in the passenger seat and watched as he cleared the windshield. She remained quiet until long after he had climbed in and backed the Blazer out of the driveway.

Eddie looked over at Tracy and asked her, "how about I give you a little tour of our community on our way over to Edgerton?"

"Sure, that would be nice since I don't know my way around. In fact, until today, I had never been off of the Interstate north from Casper up to Sheridan," Tracy explained.

"No problem, my house is C Street, as you already know, and we are now on Navy Row heading west. At the corner, we will turn left on Fitzhugh, which forms the western edge of the town of Midwest."

Eddie turned his Blazer on to Fitzhugh and called off the east-west street names in order starting with Peake, Watson, Lewis, Stock, and then turned left onto Ellison and pulled to a stop overlooking the football field.

"Tracy, look out in the distance to the south over the football field and across the Salt Creek. Do you see those houses of there?"

She pointed in the general direction and asked, "Umm, do you mean that little town over there?"

"Yes, that 'little town' is called Gas Plant, and it is a part of Midwest too."

While she looked at the football field, she asked, "is this one of those small towns that revolve around the school?"

"It is, and you will see that the school's sports and other activities are often the glue that binds this place together like a big family."

* * *

3

While driving through the town of Midwest, Eddie pointed out various places such as the Post Office, the Methodist Church, and the mayor's house. Then on Lewis Street and heading toward the junction of Highways 387 and 259, he pointed out where to turn to go to the school parking lot.

After they crossed over the cattle guard, Tracy said, "I know where I am now; this is where I came into town." At the stop sign, Tracy looked south along Highway 259 and asked, "where does that road go?"

Eddie grinned as he crossed over the junction. "It goes to Casper." He shot a quick look at his trainee, who seemed confused. Then, he offered, "I bet the directions you received at headquarters told you to go up I-25 until the Midwest exit at Smokey Gap Junction, didn't they?"

Tracy looked over at him and eked out a simple "uh-huh."

He laughed. "Okay, when you head home today, do me a favor and take Highway 259, and you will see that it is quicker."

The Sergeant then began to talk about Edgerton as they crowned the hill that separated the two towns that stood one mile apart from one another. When the café came into view, he turned his rig off Highway 387 and into an empty parking place to the right of the building.

The deputies exited the Blazer and made their way inside the café door. They sat down at the counter after hanging up their coats on a rack at Eddie's suggestion.

Instantly, a waitress appeared in front of them wearing a pair of high-waisted jeans and a tan button-down blouse with a name tag above her right breast pocket that read "Liz." Without asking, she placed two empty mugs in front of them and poured coffee into each.

Liz Duggan was in her thirties and had chocolate brown eyes and sandy blond hair that framed her cherubic face.

She looked up at Eddie and asked, "do you want your usual pancakes and bacon, hon?"

He smiled. "Yes, but make it a short stack this time."

She turned her attention to Tracy and asked, "do you know what you want, sweetie, or should I give you some time?"

Tracy lifted her eyes off of the menu and looked up at Liz. Then she returned Liz's welcoming smile with one of her own, and said, "I will have the same as the Sergeant."

As soon as Liz spun on her heels to walk back to the kitchen, Eddie mentioned to Tracy, "that was Liz Martin, and before you ask, she is just as sincere about her kindness as she sounds."

Tracy nodded her head that she understood and replied a simple, "she seems nice." But curiosity overcame her and asked her new boss a follow-up question, "you seem to know her well, so what is her story?"

Eddie reached out with his right hand, grabbed his coffee cup, raised it to his lip, and took a long sip. Then he turned to Tracy and said, "she is a model of resiliency, and she is someone you should get to know."

"Resilience? I don't understand. What happened to her?"

"Five years ago, her baby boy of four months died of sudden infant death syndrome. Then a year later, she lost both of her parents months apart to cancer."

He paused briefly and then leaned forward toward Tracy. Then he whispered, "her husband died two years ago."

"Oh, no!"

He nodded. "Yep, it happened just east of Shoshoni. He was driving his flatbed tractor-trailer toward Casper when a westbound truck skidded out of control into his lane. It killed him on impact."

Tracy's face flushed at the news, but Eddie kept talking.

"Then, to top it all off, her brother Earl, who was in the Marines, died almost a year ago in the initial wave to push Iraq and Saddam Hussein out of Kuwait."

The news shocked Tracy, but she managed to ask, "how on earth does she find the strength to ever smile again with such tragedies?"

"Good question, the insurance settlement from the other truck driver coupled with her husband's life insurance policy, and her brother's serviceman insurance, helped her become debt-free. She now has money saved in the bank to send all of her kids to college. She also bought up a few empty homes in the area as an investment and to generate a stream of steady income."

"That's nice, but what I meant is, how is she doing inside her, emotionally?"

"As I said, she is resilient. She did receive some grief counseling at the church, which helps her get up every morning with gratitude. Then Liz comes here to work both the morning and lunch shifts, and then in the afternoon, she runs the after-school care center in the school cafeteria. She is a remarkable woman whom I have the privilege of getting to know at church. But, more importantly, for you, if you decide to move and live out here in this area, she has a trailer for rent here in Edgerton and a house available in Midwest."

Tracy let the suggestion sink in. Her thoughts were interrupted when Liz came around the corner while carrying two plates of pancakes and bacon. She placed them in front of Eddie and Tracy.

Before she left, Liz looked at both of them and said, "let me know if you need anything," and with that, she turned and met with another customer who had just arrived.

Eddie and Tracy began to eat their breakfasts, and he decided to break the ice with Tracy.

So, he asked, "now, before we get into the training piece of your assignment out here, I have to know one thing: why did you get sent out here to me, of all people? It is not that I mind since I am kind of excited to train and work with you, but it just seems odd that Doan sent a rookie out here of all places."

Tracy had anticipated that particular question to come up. She even practiced her response on her drive north from Casper that morning.

However, instead of her rehearsed line, she opted only to say, "I don't want to talk about the reason, and I want to put the situation behind me. I love law enforcement, and when they offered me this opportunity, I readily accepted it."

Eddie instinctively knew there was more to the story and knew that as her trust grew in him that someday she would tell him, but until then, he decided to leave it alone.

After breakfast, Eddie described the training plan and their duty schedule. He also explained that there was one other law enforcement officer in the area and that his name was Chief Wyatt Traynor. The latter was the Chief of Police in Midwest. Eddie also explained that Chief Traynor used to have a deputy, but the 1989 budget cuts removed the position. Finally, he told her that the Chief served as his mentor in his first few years in the Salt Creek community and was still a close personal friend.

Tracy took in every word and started to relax a little, though deep inside of her, she didn't know how much she could trust Eddie. She thought he was courteous, professional, and well-mannered by how he greeted her at his place. Additionally, Tracy was also shocked to see how neat and orderly his house was and wondered if there was ever a Mrs. Crandall? Her question went both unasked and unanswered for the moment because Eddie asked if she was ready to go back to the office.

Then, following Eddie's lead, Tracy stood up and retrieved her coat off of the coat rack and donned it and followed him out of the door. As she breached the front opening, she looked to her right and spotted a bank building.

She remarked, "that is nice, Eddie. So you have a local bank out here instead of driving into Casper to cash a check."

Eddie looked toward the building that Tracy mentioned and the accompanying empty parking lot.

He replied dryly, "yes, it was nice for a time, but the bank has been closed for years now."

It served him as yet another reminder of how much change had occurred since he first arrived in the community.

* * *

4

As they turned toward their vehicle, the blustery Wyoming wind hit their faces with a biting sting. The gale forced Eddie to hold his cowboy hat with one hand as he and Tracy quickly climbed into the Blazer. Once inside the car, he murmured something about the wind while turning the key in the ignition switch to start the Blazer. Eddie then backed out of the slot, and they made their way back toward Midwest.

While he explained the intricacies of the Salt Creek community to Tracy, the Motorola radio in his unit squawked. So he silenced the conversation so he could hear the transmission. Then, without taking his eyes off the road, Eddie deafly reached out with his right hand and adjusted the volume on his speaker. Then he waited for the call to repeat if the dispatcher intended to contact him. Then it did.

"Sheriff 36-Dispatch."

Eddie grabbed the microphone from its cradle mounted on the dashboard, pressed the microphone button, and replied, "Dispatch, this is Sheriff 36," and waited for a response.

"Sheriff 36- Chief Traynor Midwest PD has requested your assistance on the east side of Gas Plant, copy?"

"Dispatch- Sheriff 36 en route."

After coming to a stop at the crossroads of Highways 387 and 259, Eddie replaced the microphone in the cradle. He looked over at his trainee and said, "something is up, or Chief Traynor would have called me directly."

"Do you want me to switch on the lights and the siren?" Tracy asked.

He grinned. "Just the lights; we don't need to alarm everyone as we pass through town on our way out to Gas Plant."

The dyad rode in silence as they proceeded down Lewis Street in Midwest. They continued west on the street until it ended at Fitzhugh, where he turned left. The Blazer descended the hill on the south side of town and traversed over Salt Creek via the bridge.

When they arrived at Gas Plant, Eddie turned left onto Ash Street. From there, they followed the road to the end of the houses, where they spotted Chief Traynor's late model Ford Bronco 150 yards due east of the last street.

Before leaving the pavement, Eddie came to a stop.

Then he instructed Tracy, "wait here while I lock in the front hubs."

Next, Eddie climbed out of the Blazer and walked to the front of the vehicle. He then turned the dial on each front axle hub from the 2X4 to the 4X4 positions and returned to the driver's side door. Once inside, Eddie moved the transfer case shifter to put the truck in four-wheel drive.

After Eddie parked the Blazer alongside Chief Traynor's department Ford Bronco, the deputies got out of their unit. They walked down the shallow slope toward Traynor, who stood next to a bulging sheet on the ground just a few yards from Castle Creek.

"Hey Wyatt, I just got word on the radio that you needed some help. What can I do?"

The Chief turned his head at the sound of Eddie's words and replied with a curt "hey" and waved at him to come closer. However, Traynor's eyes turned toward the female deputy that walked behind Crandall and offered an introduction.

"Deputy, I am Midwest Police Chief Wyatt Traynor," and he offered her his right hand to shake.

Eddie's face blushed in embarrassment and interjected, "I'm sorry, Wyatt, this is my new trainee, Deputy Tracy James."

Tracy stepped forward and took the massive paw of Traynor's, and shook it.

"It is a pleasure to meet you, Deputy James. First, I must say that your assignment to work with Sergeant Crandall is perhaps the best decision Sheriff Doan has ever made. But, believe me, the Sheriff has made some bad ones over the years."

Eddie brushed off the backhanded remark about his boss. He then cautioned, "come on, Wyatt, how about you refrain from filling Deputy James in with all your strong positive sentiments toward Sheriff Doan."

Traynor let out a laugh and then turned and knelt to grab the edge of the plastic sheet and exclaimed, "well, the Sheriff is not going to like this," and then he jerked back the sheet back to show a dead male human body.

Instinctively, Eddie stepped forward and carefully knelt to look at the man's face turned to one side, and he thought the man looked familiar. However, after further study, he determined that the man was nobody that they had ever seen around the Salt Creek area before. Though behind both of the men, they heard the sound of someone violently regurgitating their breakfast, and they turned in unison to see the source of the noise. They saw Tracy bent over at her waist with her right hand on the hood of the Blazer while she emptied her stomach.

"Better get some water in her to stop the dry heaves that are soon coming," Traynor suggested.

Eddie stood up and walked over to the Blazer and opened the driver's side door and pushed the seat forward, and retrieved a green water jug from the floorboard in the backseat. He also grabbed a roll of paper towels from the rear cargo area and walked around the truck toward his trainee.

"It is okay, Tracy, I got sick the first time I saw a dead body, but you need to trust me and stand up now, please."

Tracy slowly stood, and the urge to vomit slowly started to leave her. Eddie handed her the roll of paper towels, which she took without instruction and tore a few sheets off to wipe off her mouth and then the tiny splatter that fell on her boots.

"This isn't my first dead body," Tracy protested.

Eddie smiled and handed her the jug of water. Tracy opened the spout and lifted the container for a mouthful of water, and quickly spat it back out again.

"Tracy, swallow some mouthfuls of water, so your stomach has something on it to keep you from feeling sick. Then come back down to help us look around the body...okay?"

She looked up to him and responded with a few quick nods of her head.

By the time Tracy had rejoined the two other law officers, they had already gone through the deceased man's exposed back pockets. They failed to find any kind of identification on the mystery man. Since the body was lying face down, they determined to check the front pockets and inside the coat once the forensics team arrived to move the corpse. All they knew of the dead man was that he had brown hair, brown eyes, approximately 5'7", a thin build, and a small hatchet-like face.

Eddie looked over to Tracy and asked her to call Dispatch and inform them about the dead body found just east of Gas Plant. Additionally, he instructed her to request a forensics team to remove the body. She opened the passenger door of the Blazer and grabbed the radio microphone from the cradle, raised it to her mouth, and then froze.

She looked over to Eddie and asked, "Sergeant Crandall, what is your call sign again?"

Eddie grinned and replied, "Sheriff 36." He then turned to Chief Traynor and asked him, "who called in the body?"

Traynor turned his body completely around and said, "it was two boys that live in Gas Plant, and their names are Wesley Corbin and Stewart Jenkins."

"I know those boys; I coached them last year in the youth basketball league."

Tracy interrupted the conversation when she relayed that "a forensics team will arrive around 10:30 a.m. but...." her words trailed off.

"But what Deputy?" Eddie asked.

"Sheriff Doan interrupted my transmissions back and forth to the Dispatcher from his mobile unit and said that he wants you to call him on a landline ASAP."

Eddie let that sink in, though Chief Traynor rolled his eyes.

"Oh, I bet he is planning another press conference so he can wear his Stetson hat," Traynor said, and then added, "I'm sorry, did I just use my inside voice?"

Eddie didn't hear all of Traynor's comment since he was already deep in thought about the mystery man under the plastic sheet a few feet in front of him. Instead, he walked back up the shallow creek bank and waived at Tracy for her to follow him to the back of the Blazer, where he opened the back latch.

Without uttering a word, Eddie handed Tracy a Polaroid camera. He then grabbed a stack of self-standing and numbered evidence tags. While closing the back hatch to the Blazer, Eddie informed Tracy that they would begin a sweep of the area for evidence. Perhaps they would find something to explain the dead man's death since he assumed the mystery man succumbed to the elements. Tracy nodded and understood.

Sergeant Crandall placed the #1 tag next to the body and instructed Deputy James to take four photos from four different angles precisely as they found the body. She also took one image that showed the man's face. Next, with help from Chief Traynor, they began an arching sweep of the area from the body and increased their circles as they arched outward.

On his second arc, Eddie looked up along the edge of Castle Creek and traced the small stream across the wide-open expanse in front of him to the south and west. Only when his eyes descended off of the horizon and back down the creek's edge did he notice something. It was a single set of footprints in the snow. Without a word, Eddie walked toward the only trail of prints 20 yards away, and Tracy followed along behind him.

The tracks, made by a human and only five of them in total, were headed in the same direction as to where the deceased man fell. Eddie continued his march along the edge of the creek for another 50 yards. Still, they found no other indications of the mystery man's tracks.

Then Tracy walked up beside Eddie and asked, "what are we looking for?"

Her voice spooked him because he did not hear her walk up behind him due to the noise of the wind, and he physically reacted in a jolt.

Eddie turned his head to Tracy and said, "those tracks behind us belong to the deceased man since the sole impression is a spot-on match to the pack boots the man is wearing. I think he was following the creek bed."

Tracy asked, "but where are the other tracks?"

The wind gusted suddenly, and tiny ice particles like grains of sand blew across the open ground and stung the officers' faces.

Eddie squinted his eyes and replied, "that is why we don't see any other tracks. The wind erased them." He took a deep breath and let it out into a small cloud of steam. Then he added, "how about we take a few photos of the footprints, and then let's go back to the Blazer and warm-up because it is starting to get cold out here.

While retracing their steps back to the original scene, they observed the wind covering their fresh tracks in the snow with each gust.

As the deputies approached the body and Chief Traynor, Eddie asked, "Wyatt, have you interviewed the boys, Wesley and Stewart, yet?"

"I haven't, considering that the body is not within Midwest town limits; the jurisdiction is yours."

Eddie nodded in agreement. "I thought that was the case." Then the Sergeant added, "Wyatt, would you mind hanging out here while I take my trainee up to the boys' houses to interview both of them?"

"Nope, I don't mind, but I will wait here inside my Bronco. The wind chill has to be in the low teens or single-digit temperatures by now."

Eddie could hardly crack a smile because his cheeks were frozen but managed to say, "no problem," and then waved at Tracy to join him in the Blazer.

It took a couple of minutes before any resemblance of warm air to flow out of the Blazer vents, but just being out of the wind had helped them warm up considerably. But the ride was brief and they soon arrived at the Corbin home on the end of Ash Street. They simultaneously stepped out of the Blazer, walked up to the front stoop, and knocked on the door.

Twila Corbin, Wesley's mother, answered the door and instantly welcomed the two law officers into her home. Eddie came in and stomped the loose snow off of his boots, and looked around. From his vantage point, he saw that the front door emptied into the lone family room in the house. As luck would have it, both Wesley Corbin and Stewart Jenkins were seated side-by-side on the sofa watching television.

Twila turned to Eddie and said, "Sergeant, we were expecting you. I took the liberty to call both of Stewart's parents who are at work now, but they are fine with you asking their son some questions as long as I am present."

"Thanks, Twila, but I assure you that my questions are pretty harmless," he explained. Then he introduced Tracy to her.

Before entering the living room, Eddie turned to his trainee and spoke in a soft tone, "get your notebook out, Tracy, and record the boys' responses if you would. Then, we can compare notes later, and by doing this in this way, you will see me demonstrate how to question a witness. Are we clear?"

Tracy nodded. "I got it, Sergeant."

Both Eddie and Tracy walked over toward the couch where the boys sat. Meanwhile, Twila brought in two chairs from the dining room for the Sheriff officers to sit upon, and then she turned off the television.

Wesley spoke up first, "Hey Sergeant, are you going to coach us again in basketball this year?"

Flummoxed for a second, Eddie offered, "I, uh, planned on it, but that means Stewart here has to play as well."

Stewart looked up to his wind-burned face and said, "that sounds fun."

"Okay, now that is settled, tell me, boys, how is it that you two found the man lying down by Castle Creek this morning?"

The boys exchanged nervous glances. Finally, however, Wesley broke the momentary silence by explaining what he saw the night before. First, he recalled seeing a greenish-yellow light floating above the ground in the direction of Castle Creek. Next, he revealed how he and Stewart snuck outside their houses to watch the orb for a minute or so before it vanished. Finally, Stewart interjected that they went down to the creek after breakfast and walked to the exact spot where the "Ghost Light" disappeared, and that is where they found the man's body.

Eddie looked at Tracy, and her facial expression must have matched the one of his own when the boys uttered the term *Ghost Light*.

Before Eddie could ask a follow-on question, Twila interrupted him.

She said, "I know what you are thinking about Ghost Lights, and since you are not originally from around here, I am not sure you know the story behind it?"

Eddie shook his head. "No, I do know about it. Legend has it that a Ghost Light is a lantern belonging to one of the area's original settlers, an Irish farmer named O'Rourke. The same legend says that whenever Ghost Lights appear, it means that O'Rourke is wandering around looking at his fields. I also know that scientists have offered that the

Ghost Lights are nothing more than luminescent balls of gas of some kind. Still, I have never seen the phenomena myself."

"Seems to me, Sergeant Crandall, that you are getting more OFT every day," Twila quipped with an approving sparkle in her eye.

Eddie turned back to the boys, "so when you found the body, what did you do next?"

"We ran here as fast as we could, Sir, and we told my mom," Wesley explained, and Eddie looked over to Twila, who confirmed the lad's statement with an affirmative nod of her head.

Eddie stood up and reached his right hand out to both of the boys and shook their hands. He thanked them for providing a statement and then turned to Twila and thanked her as well.

Tracy spoke for the first time only to say, "thank you all for your help," and then followed her partner back outside and into the department vehicle.

As Eddie drove across the two-track lane in the snow back to Castle Creek, he could see that the Sheriff's Department forensics team had arrived. The team was busy breaking their gear out of the back of their Chevy Suburban. Eddie pulled up along Chief Traynor's Ford Bronco once again. Then he and Tracy quickly exited his rig and walked down to the frozen body.

The forensics team looked around the immediate vicinity of the body. However, they came up just as empty with clues as had Chief Traynor, Sergeant Crandall, and Deputy James. Eddie then handed over the Polaroid pictures that they had taken earlier to the lead technician but kept one for the file. Tracy also pointed out where the boot tracks had been as well. But now, all the footprints had disappeared from the blowing snow. Lastly, the technicians turned and reached down and grabbed the dead man by his coat. When they tried to lift him off the ground, the body remained frozen to the grass beneath him.

"Man, this guy is as frozen as a popsicle," the lead technician said.

The other technician remarked, "I know, it is going to take this guy 24 hours to thaw out enough for a proper examination to determine a cause of death."

The technicians re-gripped their hands on the man's coat and used their legs to help lift the body. Then, with a grunt out each of them, the body broke loose, which made a sound like breaking a bundle of dry twigs.

The technicians checked each pocket in the man's clothing with the body rolled over but did not find anything. Next, they placed the corpse inside a large plastic bag and zipped it shut. Lastly, the lead technician affixed an identification tag to the outside zipper that read: *John Doe*. Afterward, Eddie and Tracy helped the forensic technicians pick up the heavy body bag and lifted it into the back of their Suburban.

The lead technician turned and said, "see you later, guys," and left the scene as quickly as they had arrived.

Chief Traynor, Sergeant Crandall, and Deputy James remained huddled close in the wind and watched the Suburban drive into Gas Plant. Then they turned their heads toward one another. But, before they spoke, Tracy suddenly stepped over to where the body had been on the ground and grabbed a folded piece of paper before the wind blew it away.

She handed the article to Eddie. "This might be a clue."

Eddie nodded but then suggested, "let's get out of the wind and look at this in my Blazer?"

Tracy opened the passenger side door, lifted the seat forward, and swiftly climbed into the back seat over the objections of Chief Traynor, who volunteered to do so himself. Meanwhile, Eddie slid into the vehicle behind the wheel. After he took off his gloves, he unfolded the paper, and to everyone's surprise, it contained a poem of sorts.

It read:

MUTTS FALL EASILY INTO INIQUITY
INKLINGS ADHERENCE BECOMES NECESSARY
DISAPPEARING TREES GIVE WAY TO GRASS
WELL DOWN THE COURSE OF PILGRIM'S PASS
EVER STEAMBOAT STANDS IN FROZEN POSE
SURMOUNT THE FLOW AT GHOSTLY PROSE
THE OMNIPRESENT BEAR POINTS THE WAY
WINCHING THE TACK TO YOUR SURVEY
YONDER IS THE ROCK OF TWENTY NINE'S BANE
OASIS APPEARS AT THE END OF THE WANE
MANAGE PORT TILL POINTING THE CRAFT
INTERSECT THE LIP NOT SLOWED BY DRAUGHT
NEIGHBORLY TEA STEEPS INTO BRINE
GUAGE A CRYPT ALONG THE SPINE
UNDER WHOM ENTERS SHOULD KNOW THE COST
SEARCHING COMES EASY ON VIPER'S HISS FROST

"What is this?" questioned Chief Traynor.

"I don't know yet, but when we find out, it could tell us why this man came to Midwest," Eddie surmised.

Traynor remained stoically quiet in thought, and after a minute of silence, offered, "or not, I mean, the man has no identification, nor have we found his vehicle. Moreover, the man is not an oil field worker by how he dressed. So I am afraid we have another mystery without a whole lot of answers on our hands again."

Tracy asked inquisitively, "what do you mean again? Does this sort of thing happen a lot out here?"

"No, it doesn't. I will brief you later about the case the Chief is referring to," Eddie replied.

* * *

5

It was only noon when Sergeant Eddie Crandall and Deputy Tracy James arrived back at Eddie's house and office, but it felt like it was much later. Both felt chilled to the bone from standing outside in the gusting wind along Castle Creek. So, they each quickly took off and hung up their coats at the front door along with their boots. Eddie then walked into the spare room next to the office, where Tracy heard him scrounge through a cardboard box. When he returned to the living room, he tossed her a clean pair of wool socks.

"Take your other socks off and put those on to start warming up your feet?" he said.

"How did you know my feet were cold?"

"I didn't, but I figured that since my feet felt like blocks of ice that yours were no better."

Eddie secretly dreaded his upcoming phone call to Sheriff Doan. It was not that he feared to speak to his boss. It just came down to the simple fact that Eddie didn't exceedingly respect his boss. His first sign of uneasiness went back as far as the fall of 1984 when he was working on the Tim Savolt case, and his boss took personal credit for each break that followed. Since then, Eddie had also witnessed many fellow deputies come under the wrath of Sheriff Doan when they openly disagreed with the department's official conclusions toward their investigations. As a result, those deputies were all fired for insubordination. Eddie had learned long ago that it was best to keep his head down, work hard, and always follow through.

Tracy, meanwhile, thought long and hard about the ode of sorts that they had just found and studied the paper relentlessly to find a new meaning.

"Well, I had better get this over with sooner rather than later," Eddie announced and got up out of his recliner after putting on the wool socks and walked into his office.

Tracy instinctively followed behind him and took a seat at her desk. Eddie picked up the phone and dialed Sheriff Doan's direct line, and the other end picked up after three rings.

"Sheriff Doan," said a harsh voice.

"Good afternoon Sheriff, this is Sergeant Crandall."

"What is going on, Crandall, and how come it took you so long to call me back?"

Eddie paused to refrain from taking the Sheriff's bait. "First, we have a dead body that was found this morning by a couple of boys just east of Gas Plant, and second, this is the first opportunity for me to call you since I arrived on the scene."

"Who found the stiff?" Sheriff Doan said with a self-amused chuckle.

"A couple of boys saw what they understood as a Ghost Light last night, and then when they went out this morning to where they saw the Ghost Light disappeared and they found the body."

"Crandall, you cannot be serious, a Ghost Light? That is just a legend, and I don't see how it matters to this case?"

"Sheriff, I am just reporting what the boys witnessed concerning how they came across the frozen body. You, of all people, should know how it is. Why, everyone knows that when you were a deputy, you became the lead officer that wrote down all of those eyewitness reports of UFOs near Casper Mountain back in the 1970s."

Sheriff Doan took a deep audible breath and let it out in another question, "do you know the deceased; I mean, is he from around there?"

"No, I don't believe he is since I don't recognize him, but that doesn't mean that he isn't a new addition to the community."

"Community," snickered Sheriff Doan. "Come on, Crandall, I could pass through both Midwest and Edgerton on my way to Gillette and see every single person in either of those towns."

Eddie refused to allow himself to become goaded into a useless debate. But, conversely, Eddie stayed on point by informing the Sheriff of his plan to show a Polaroid picture of the mystery man's face to local business owners. With any luck, someone could recognize and identify the man.

Sheriff Doan breathed heavily into the phone. "Good, and while you are doing that, forensics will run the man's fingerprints, and I am 100% certain we will get a hit on him."

"Why are you so certain, Sheriff?"

"Why? I will tell you why Sergeant, it is because the guy is probably just oil field trash like everyone else out there and probably has a record."

Eddie desperately fought the urge to rebuke his boss. Sheriff Doan had long made it known that he despised all communities outside of Casper.

Instead, Eddie replied, "come on, Sheriff, if you spent some time out here like at high school sporting events or even Salt Creek Days, you would find a lot of down-to-earth and pleasant people. Better yet, they are your constituents."

"Sergeant Crandall, I don't want to get to know them, and I don't need their votes." He then paused for a few seconds and continued, "I want you to sum up this case in two weeks starting from today. I don't want any excuses either. I don't want this to turn into another Tim Savolt fiasco. So you will also give me a progress report every two days, got it?"

"I got it, but when do we expect the forensics team and the coroner's office to finish their work?"

"I thought I just told you I don't want any of your excuses, they will finish when they finish, and you will need to take Miss Tracy with you and do some real detective work."

"I understand, Sheriff, and I will take Deputy James with me throughout the investigation."

"Good," barked Sheriff Doan, and he abruptly hung up the phone.

Eddie gently removed the receiver from his ear and placed it back in its place atop the phone. He put his face into both of his hands and began to rub his eyes, cheeks, and neck methodically. When he lifted his eyes back toward Tracy, he wondered if she overheard the entire phone call.

Tracy met his eyes and asked, "what is a Tim Savolt fiasco?"

Eddie physically reacted in a jerk and asked, "did you hear all of what Sheriff Doan said?"

She nodded her head and offered, "by the way he yelled through the receiver, I heard everything plain as day."

"Okay, let me get the file." Eddie stood up, walked over to the file cabinet in the closet, and dug out a brown manila folder. He carried the file over to Tracy and handed it to her, and she opened it immediately.

Eddie explained, "Tim Savolt was a very well-respected science teacher at the school. Unfortunately, he went missing back in August of 1984, and when I say he went missing, it was like he vanished. His apartment was tidy when Chief Traynor conducted a welfare check, but then a few days later, Savolt's place got tossed. All I know is that the teacher was conducting a field study on the water quality of Salt Creek since it flows through the entire oil field. Now, if you listen to Sheriff Doan's claims, he will say that it was the Sheriff's Department that found all clues, but in reality, it was a boy named Josh Anderson and a few of his friends."

Eddie got up and walked over to the window and pulled back the curtains, "Do you see that house there at #6 Navy Row?" he asked.

Tracy got up from her desk, walked over to the window, and looked at the small house. Then, she replied, "yes, I see it."

"Josh Anderson used to live there with his parents, who also worked at the school. His little sister is named Cindy."

"Wait, Cindy Anderson, the basketball player?"

"Do you know of her?"

"Of course, she was a four-year starter on the University of Wyoming women's basketball team. She and I graduated high school the same year, and I remember watching her play at the State Basketball tournament. I thought she was the best player I ever saw. She would have dominated Class 4A as well."

Eddie smiled and went back to informing Tracy about the Savolt case. "Josh went on to publish Savolt's field study, and you will find a copy of that in the file as well. In addition, there are some other particulars in the file, like the two men who drove the mysterious 1978 dark green Ford F- 150. One of the men died, while the other one fled after they tried to take out Josh Anderson and a couple of his friends one fateful day north of town near the old Light Plant."

He then added, "if you would like, you can look over that case file whenever we have some slack time. Maybe you could provide another perspective that has eluded all of us involved?"

She shrugged. "Okay, it sounds like fun, actually."

* * *

6

Later that afternoon, Eddie and Tracy left the office and drove over to the Salt Creek Inn on the eastern outskirts to Edgerton on Highway 387. The law officers parked their department Blazer outside the hotel office, entered the door, and walked up to the counter where they met the establishment's owner, Clare Olsen.

"Good afternoon, Clare," Eddie offered.

"Hello, Deputy, I mean, Sergeant Crandall, congratulations on the promotion, by the way.".

"Thanks, Clare, and the person next to me is my new partner, Deputy Tracy James, who is new to the area." Eddie paused while he reached into his shirt pocket, then said, "I have a favor to ask. I want you to look at this Polaroid and tell me if you have seen this man before?" Eddie then handed the photo over to Olsen.

Olsen dropped his head and looked over the top of his glasses at the photo and held it about two inches from his face. Then, he lifted his head and said, "nope, I haven't seen him."

"Are you sure?" Eddie asked.

"I'm pretty sure, but we did have a guest check in a couple of days ago. So maybe it is him.?"

"Well, Clare, wouldn't you recognize him by the photo then?"

Clare tilted his head and shrugged. "The guy checked in when my nephew operated the counter for a few days during his break from college."

"Where is your nephew now, and could we speak with him?"

"Sorry, he left yesterday to go back to Spearfish, South Dakota. He studies at Black Hills State College." Then Clare got a thought and picked up the hotel registry folder from under the front desk and placed it on top of the counter. "Let me look over the registrations and see who arrived during my days off."

Neither Eddie nor Tracy said a word; instead, each nodded their heads in agreement. Olsen looked over the registry and noted three check-ins, two of them were just for one night and had paid with a credit card, but the other was a man who paid cash for an entire week.

"Sergeant, this guy in room 210 might be who you are seeking. His name is Jim Hawkins, who lists his hometown as Steamboat Springs, Colorado. Unfortunately, he did not list a license plate number on his vehicle. However, my nephew wrote down the make and model of his vehicle as a maroon Subaru Brat. You know, that goofy half-car and half-pickup that had seats mounted in the bed?"

"I have seen a few Subaru Brats, and I do agree that they are a little goofy. But, have you seen any activity from room 210?"

The hotel owner scratched his three-day whisker growth on his chin with his left hand while he thought, and then he replied, "no, I can't say that I have. The door has a *DO NOT DISTURB* tag posted on the doorknob, so again I have no idea. But if you want to search it, you had better let your Stetson-wearing dime store cowboy boss of yours know that he needs to go and get a search warrant. I know my rights."

"Thanks, Clare, I will let you know if we need to search the room, but of course, that will require a signed warrant."

"You are welcome, Sergeant. And Deputy James, if you need anything, you can come back and visit my little store here in the lobby. I think you will find more things around here than an ordinary 7-11."

Tracy nodded. "Thanks. I see that you have quite the selection."

The law officers turned in unison and left the lobby. Once outside, they both looked up to the hotel's second-floor balcony and noted the door marked 210. Yet when they scanned the parking lot, they did not see a Subaru Brat parked anywhere nearby. So they climbed back into the department Blazer.

As Eddie backed up, Tracy asked, "so where to now?"

"We are going to start by going down to the café, then the area bars, and then the convenience store over at the junction. We will see if anyone has seen this 'Jim Hawkins' around."

Tracy furrowed her brow. "That name, 'Jim Hawkins,' I don't know why but I have heard of that name somewhere?"

Two hours later, Eddie and Tracy had visited with workers at the café, the two bars on Second Street in Edgerton, and stopped at the convenience store in Midwest at the junction of Highways 259 and 387. Nobody reported seeing the man before.

"It looks like a dead-end, pardon my pun, but it seems nobody has seen the deceased man," Tracy offered.

Eddie nodded but added, "we still have one place to go."

"Where is that?"

"We are heading to the Castle Rock Bar located south of here on Highway 259."

Eddie maneuvered the Blazer away from the junction store, over the cattle guard, and turned right at the stop sign when he exited Midwest. He drove over the bridge that spanned the Salt Creek and over the other side. Tracy mentioned that she just got a whiff of a rotten egg smell. Eddie then explained that it was sulfur, a natural by-product from oil production. He also mentioned that the odor had made Midwest infamous for being ever-present in years past. Now, it was only an occasional nuisance due to changes in oil production techniques.

Eddie exited off Highway 259 and into a gravel parking lot with six vehicles as the sun had started to set in the west. The law officers got out of their department vehicle and entered through the front door. Once inside, they entered an expansive, dimly lit room, which made it difficult to see the patrons' faces both at the bar and at the tables near a small dance floor. Tracy detected the smell of stale beer mixed with thirty years' worth of cigarette smoke that hit her as soon as she entered the door, but she did not remark about it.

The deputies made their way to the end of the bar and waved for the bartender named Skip Tuggle to come over to them. Skip finished wiping the bar top with his towel and walked down toward the Sheriff's officers.

"Hey Skip, this is Deputy Tracy James, newly assigned to this area," Eddie introduced.

Skip's face broke out into a wide grin that revealed a missing canine tooth on the right side of his mouth. He said, "Hey Eddie, and it is nice to meet you, ma'am." Then Skip looked back at Crandall and asked, "I never thought I would ask you this, Eddie, but do you two want a drink?"

"No, Skip, that isn't necessary, but thank you. What we do need is for you to look at this photograph and tell me if you have seen this guy?" Eddie asked and handed over the Polaroid picture of the deceased man.

Skip's face went from a friendly look to one of shock and astonishment in a matter of a second. Skip's eyes hardened, and he handed the photograph back to Eddie.

"Have you seen him Skip?"

"Yes," Skip said dryly.

Tracy asked, "when did you see him last?"

Skip turned around and looked over at the other customers to see if anyone was paying attention to their conversation. When the bartender was satisfied that the patrons were not listening in, he turned his body back towards Eddie and Tracy.

"Skip?" Eddie asked.

The bartender searched for the words to say in his mind, made evident by his raised forehead and eyes looking at the ceiling rafters covered with dollar bills tacked to them.

Finally, he then looked directly at Eddie and said, "that man came in here yesterday at noon and ordered a Coors beer. I asked him if he was new to the area, and he said 'yes' but also mentioned that he wouldn't be around long because he found the 'oasis' whatever that means."

"What else did he say, Skip?" Eddie inquired.

Skip shrugged. "The guy asked about any rock formations in the area, which I laughed and pointed across the road at the Rimrocks, which you know are the largest in the area. But the guy wanted to know about formations to the west of the highway and how to get there. So I told him that he could take just about any oilfield road from Highway 259 near the bar, and it would lead him to Castle Creek. From there, I suggested that he follow the creek for a few miles to the southwest, where he would find a few sandstone outcroppings along some of the ridgelines. When I asked him why he wanted to know, the guy only said he was looking for 'lost treasure,' which is nuts because there aren't any stories or even legends like that in the Salt Creek area."

When Skip finished talking, Eddie looked over at Tracy, who was busy taking down notes.

Eddie looked back up at Skip and asked, "did he give you a name?"

The bartender thought for a second and said, "no, he didn't."

"Did you see where he went after he left?" Tracy asked.

"No, ma'am, I did not, and I didn't see a vehicle pass by the front window after he left either, sorry."

"Thanks for your help, Skip, and I will see you tomorrow night."

Skip replied, "will do, Sergeant."

Eddie turned to Tracy and motioned with his head for the two of them to leave.

Once back inside the Blazer and en route again toward Midwest, Tracy asked, "you mentioned to Skip about seeing him tomorrow night. What was that all about?"

"Oh, that? Skip and I are scorekeepers for the high school girl's and boys' basketball games. If you count both the junior varsity and varsity, there will be four games tomorrow night, starting at 5 o'clock. You are welcome to come along if you like, and maybe you'll get to know a few people too?"

Tracy tilted her head and thought about the suggestion for a few seconds. "I could probably watch a game or two, but I would need to leave by 7 p.m. to drive home to Casper."

"I understand about having to drive home, so have you thought about moving out here at all?"

"I have, but I don't think I can afford the first and last month's rent, considering I just paid the rent for my apartment in Casper."

"Okay, but if you want to check out any of Liz Martin's properties tomorrow, I can work out a deal with her so that you can afford your deposit and rent if you like?"

Tracy's eyes narrowed. "You would do that? Why?"

"Yes, I would, and it is because you are not only my trainee. You are also my new partner, and partners look out for one another."

"Okay, I will think about it tonight, but my roommate is not going to like it," Tracy said with a slight giggle.

Eddie pulled into the carport outside his home on C Avenue in Midwest. He then grabbed the extension cord and plugged it into the immersion heater cord when they exited the vehicle. He also suggested that Tracy start her department sedan and warm it up before driving back to Casper.

Once inside the office, the deputies went over the notes that Tracy took throughout the day. Then they made plans to drive along Castle Creek in the morning to search for the Subaru Brat. Lastly, the deputies reflected that they felt that the deceased man from that morning was Jim Hawkins. But that meant finding his vehicle or identification to solidify their suppositions.

When Tracy got up from her desk to put on her coat again, she told Eddie, "I copied down that poem that we found, and when I get home, I will see what I can do to crack the code of its meaning."

"Good idea, and I will do the same," Eddie replied.

As Tracy zipped up her coat, a thought crossed her mind, and she asked, "how come you didn't take down any notes today when we interviewed the people from the area businesses we stopped at?"

Eddie smiled and reached up with his left hand to his uniform shirt's right breast pocket, lifted out a small micro recorder, and held it up for Tracy to see.

Then he explained, "I learned this trick from a game warden friend near Sheridan to record inquiries mainly because it saves the time of writing everything down."

Tracy smiled and reached down to the doorknob and opened the door, and before she exited, she turned around and said, "neat trick. I will see you in the morning."

Eddie grinned and said, "goodnight, Tracy, and drive safe," and then she closed the door behind her.

Five minutes after Tracy left for Casper, Eddie put on his coat and then picked up the paper containing the poem they had found. He walked off his porch and marched across the street to # 6 Navy Row to talk to the new English teacher, Clint Morris. Eddie thought that having Clint look over the poem and ask him for any insights to shed light on what it meant and where it originated.

* * *

7

Friday, January 3, 1992

Deputy Tracy James arrived at the home office of Sergeant Eddie Crandall in Midwest precisely at 7:30 a.m., which was the established start time of her shift. When she stepped out of her vehicle and glanced over to the front door, Eddie already stood behind the storm door glass, watching her walk across the top of his deck.

His professionalism and outright courtesy toward her were a severe departure from the behavior of others in the Sheriff's Department. During the drive to Midwest that morning, Tracy thought that a uniform would become optional if she had a home office herself and worked relatively alone in the Salt Creek area. But, once again, Eddie appeared at his door dressed in a clean and pressed uniform.

He welcomed her, "Good morning Deputy James; I hope your drive was uneventful this morning."

Tracy walked through the door, instantly took off her coat, and hung it up on the coat rack next to the door. She then pulled a pair of neatly folded socks and handed them to Eddie. He took them from her, and he could smell the fresh scent of fabric softener on them.

She turned toward Eddie and said, "thanks, the drive was uneventful. I did as you said, and I took the exit from I-25 onto Highway 259, and I was shocked by the scenic view in the early morning light."

Eddie nodded his head and mused, "ya, I remember my first trip to Midwest, and I could not believe the scenery myself. When I crossed over 40-mile hill and saw thousands of pump jacks as far as the eye could see, I was so captivated by this land."

"Well, this morning, I saw Teapot Rock for the first time in my life. It looks so different from the pictures in my high school history book," she offered.

"Ah, the infamous Teapot Dome Scandal. You will find that almost every kid in town knows the story about that piece of history. But, as to Teapot Rock, it looks different because it is eroding fast, and pretty soon, it won't even resemble a teapot at all. So, do you want some coffee? I have a fresh pot in the kitchen."

"I would love a cup, but don't bother, I can get it myself," she said and walked by him and into the kitchen. She spied the Mr. Coffee coffeemaker, which sat on the countertop to the right of the sink. Then she asked, "where do you keep your cups?"

Eddie shouted from the office, "look in the cabinet above the coffeemaker. After that, come to the office."

She spun around and retrieved a mug, then seconds later, walked into the office with a steaming cup of black coffee in her right hand and set it down on her desk. Her desktop had changed overnight, and she saw that it now had a freshly engraved wood nameplate that read:

DEPUTY TRACY JAMES

Astonished at the small gesture, Tracy looked up at Eddie and asked, "where did the nameplate come from?"

"Oh, that. Do you like it?"

"I do thank you, but when did you have time to do that?"

"I didn't; rather, it was a high school boy who needed some extra credit work. So, I bought the material and talked with the industrial arts teacher for the boy to make it for me. Then, I went over to the school this morning and picked it up just before you arrived."

Tracy honestly did not know what to think. Again, her experience with the Sheriff's Department in Casper was not as courteous as Eddie had shown. Instead, she received an icy welcome from other deputies and an even colder reception from her supervisor that barely took the time to train her properly. That is, everyone ignored her except Sheriff Doan and a couple of his underlings. Her experience with them was not one she wanted to unpack mentally and did not want to talk about it.

She reached out and lifted her coffee and took a sip and, in her mind, ran a series of questions: "What was Eddie's motive for being so nice to her? Was he hitting on her? Was he...?" Her silent thoughts were interrupted by a repeated question directed toward her from within the room.

"Tracy, are you okay?" Eddie repeated.

She realized that her mind had drifted too long, and her cheeks blossomed red with embarrassment.

Turning toward him, she said, "yes, I am okay. I was just thinking about something. I'm sorry."

"That is alright. I do that myself sometimes. What I had asked was, did you come up with any ideas over the poem we found?"

Tracy retrieved her notebook from her breast pocket and flipped it open to the last entry she made the night before.

She reported, "I can only make out one connection. The word *oasis* is in the poem is the same word that our mystery man, Jim Hawkins, said to the bartender named Skip."

Eddie raised his left hand and rested his forefinger atop his upper lip, and thought about the information that Tracy had just revealed. Then, after a moment, he said, "that is good work. I didn't make that connection at all. But from what I found out last night, we are a long way from solving this case."

"Why? What did you find out?"

"Nothing much." Eddie said and took a sip of his coffee, and when he set the cup down on his desk. Then he continued, "I went across the street last night and talked to the English teacher, Clint Morris, at #6 Navy Row. I asked him to look over the poem."

Tracy sat up excitedly and asked, "Really? What did he say?"

"Well, it is complicated. Clint told me that the writing style is basic, but it is also cryptic. From what he could discern, the poem was a map of some sort by the clues left in each line. He said that while in college, he and a couple of his friends tried to crack the treasure codes in the 1981 book by Byron Preiss called *The Secret.*"

"Really? That is fascinating, was the book about real treasures, or was it just fantasy?"

"From what Clint said, that book gives clues to the locations of 12 separate treasures buried in 12 different cities in the United States. However, Clint said that someone did find the treasure in Chicago, but nothing from other locations so far."

"Did Mr. Morris say anything else?"

"Yes, he did. He said that he remembered reading an article once about an oil executive named Arthur Daniels, who left a treasure behind in a box of money along with a poem to guide people to it. But the teacher couldn't recall any other details."

"So, what do we do now?"

Eddie grinned. "How about we go to the library?"

Sergeant Crandall navigated the Chevy Blazer through the streets of Midwest on their way to the county library extension, located in Edgerton. While they rode in silence, Tracy processed all the things she had seen in the community over the last two days.

When Eddie came to a complete stop at the stop sign on the eastern edge of Midwest, Tracy finally spoke up and asked a question, "Sergeant, what is O-F-T? I ask because I heard someone say that to you yesterday, plus there are yard signs with O-F-T written on them in maroon and white paint?"

Eddie's face opened up into a wide grin, and without taking his eyes off of the road, he explained, "O-F-T is an acronym for Oil Field Trash. The moniker began back in the fall of 1984 when David Proctor, Ricky Fleming, and Josh Anderson, and a few others came up with it and used it during that fabled football season."

"I don't understand? Why would anyone celebrate a derogatory term like oil field trash? It just doesn't make sense?"

"I know, but since you are new to the area, you haven't witnessed how people in Casper or any other part of Wyoming react toward people in this area. I mean, even Sheriff Doan openly disparages the community. What those boys did in 1984 was to call out that, yes, they were oil field trash and were proud of it."

"I think I am tracking you now. OFT is disarming by removing any possible negativity associated with the term, am I right?

"Yes, you are correct, Tracy."

"Hmm, I saw some of that too when I was in the Air Force."

Soon afterward, Eddie turned the Blazer onto Second Street in Edgerton and then pulled up next to the library, which had just opened. The duo exited their department vehicle and carefully walked down the icy steps, and entered the building through the front door. They made their way to the checkout counter, and Katrina Alvarez, the head librarian, greeted them.

"Hey, Eddie," Katrina said. But before Eddie could return the salutation, Katrina focused her eyes upon Tracy standing next to him. She said, "and hello, Deputy James."

Taken aback that the librarian already knew her name, she replied, "Hi, I'm Tracy. Have we met before?"

Katrina laughed aloud and shook her head to say no, but then offered, "the Salt Creek Pipeline told me who you were."

"What is the Salt Creek Pipeline? Is it the local newspaper?"

"Oh no, darling, it is nothing like that. No, the pipeline is just your average word of mouth talk around a small town like this, that is all. But believe me when I tell you that a few of the single men in this area are very interested in meeting you too."

"Thanks, but I am not interested in any relationships now."

"Neither are they," Katrina quipped. Then she turned her focus back to Eddie, who had observed their back and forth exchanges like he was watching a tennis match.

"What can I help you with Eddie? Does this have anything to do with the unidentified man you found near Gas Plant yesterday?"

Eddie assumed that the news of the deceased man had also made its way through the Salt Creek Pipeline as well. He looked around the empty library and then leaned forward on the countertop. Eddie then asked Katrina if she could research an oilman rumored to leave a treasure behind after his death, with clues written in a poem? He explained how Deputy James had found a poem under the deceased man whom they believe could be going by the name of Jim Hawkins."

"So, the dead man's name is Jim Hawkins, the treasure hunter?"

Eddie shook his head and said, "we don't know for a fact that he was treasure hunting, but we have good reason to believe that the deceased is the same man who checked into the Salt Creek Inn. Nobody has seen him since."

Katrina grinned and bent over toward Eddie, who still leaned on his forearms on top of the counter. She said, "Jim Hawkins is the name of the treasure hunter in Robert Louis Stevenson's book *Treasure Island*."

Tracy's eyes opened wide, and she exclaimed, "that is why the name sounded so familiar."

"Correct, Tracy, I'm impressed. Now, Eddie, I believe the man that you want to find information on is Arthur Daniels."

"How did you know his name?"

Katrina smiled and teased in her reply, "because I can read. But, seriously, I read something about him one time, though I can't remember where? What I do remember is that the article stated that he left behind some treasure with a poem that guided the way, as you said."

Eddie nodded. "Can you help us find some old newspaper or magazine articles on him? We would appreciate your help, and perhaps the information will help us understand why Jim Hawkins showed up here in the first place."

While Eddie and Katrina filled out the research request form, Tracy turned around and began browsing the "Newly Released" bookshelf. She was intrigued by a copy of *Friday Night Lights: A Town, a Team, and a Dream* by H.G. Bissinger released in 1990. She became engrossed with the book's description on the back cover. When Eddie sidled up close and asked what caught her attention, Tracy turned the front cover over and showed it to him.

She asked, "so, is this book like what goes on around here in this area? I mean, you said the area residents have glued themselves to the sports scene at the high school after all."

Eddie handed the book back to Tracy. "I have read it already, and yes, in some ways, the book portrays this area in the same light, but it also highlights how people from different towns view each other. Do you remember what we talked about with OFT? Well, this book involves opposing views between citizens of Odessa and Midland in Texas in much the same way. But, unlike how things are in that part of Texas, our football players here are less into the party and womanizing scene. So, you should give it a read."

"Thanks, I think I will," she said and walked up to the counter and produced her library card to check the book out.

A few minutes later, as they began to leave out the front door, Eddie stopped and pointed to the faded black and white photograph of a football team that hung over the door.

He said, "While Texans claim the title of Friday Night Lights, it was that team up there that started the tradition. That Midwest team played the first nighttime high school football game in the USA against Casper right here in the Salt Creek community in 1925."

Tracy stood there looking at the picture in wonderment, and all she could reply was: "wow."

Upon returning to their office, Eddie began a training session with Tracy on suspect questioning techniques. He openly admitted to her that questioning people was something he fretted because nobody ever demonstrated how until Chief Traynor was kind enough to train him. In one exercise, Tracy practiced interviewing Eddie, who played an eyewitness to a crime. After each question, he changed his story slightly, which caused her to backtrack and repeat the interrogation. Afterward, Eddie emphasized that suspects who are not telling the truth will unwittingly change parts of their story. It then became the deputy's responsibility to catch those instances.

Eddie got up from his desk chair following the exercise and stated that he would make some soup for lunch and inquired if Tracy would want some too.

"I appreciate your constant hospitality, but you don't need to put yourself out at my expense. I brought a sack lunch today, so I am fine."

If her comment offended him, he didn't show it; instead, he shrugged. "Okay, suit yourself, but if you need to use the kitchen, you are welcome to do so."

While he was busy in the kitchen, Tracy began to eat her lunch and looked over the old Savolt missing person's case file. Her attention waned, though, because she ruminated about why Eddie was so friendly to her. Tracy admitted to herself that it was refreshing being treated so well and as an equal professional. She knew from experience that men did not operate on the same level of niceness that Eddie had displayed.

Her wayward thoughts vanished when Eddie re-entered the office carrying a steaming bowl of vegetable beef soup, and it smelled wonderful. Unfortunately, the scent of the soup caused Tracy's stomach to grumble, and it made her peanut butter and jelly sandwich taste insufficient. Before she started to ask him some specific questions to answer her doubts about his sincerity toward her, the telephone rang on his desk.

Eddie answered the phone after the second ring. "Sheriff's office, this is Sergeant Crandall. How may I help you?"

"Hey Eddie, this is Carlos Mondragon calling from the convenience store at the junction."

"Hi Carlos, what can I help you with?"

"I just got back into town after checking on the forty head of steers that I am pasturing on Mrs. Jewett's land. The reason I am calling is that I found an abandoned vehicle in a snowdrift next to the old railroad bed that snakes through that area."

"How do you know the car is abandoned and not parked?"

"Well, I don't know for sure. But I didn't see it when I was out there early on Wednesday morning, but I saw it today covered in snow."

"Do you have a description of the car?"

"Yes, it is a Subaru Brat."

Eddie's eyes opened wide, and he asked, "Carlos, can you do me a favor and lead us out to where you found it?"

"Sure, I can do that, just meet up with me at the store."

"Thanks, Carlos. I will see you in a few minutes," Eddie said and hung up the phone.

He turned to Tracy and said, "do me a favor and go into my living room and use my house phone."

"Okay, do you have a person and a number for me?"

"Yes, I want you to invite Chief Traynor to come with us, and his number is 8111."

Tracy looked confused. "So all I do is dial those four numbers?"

"Yes, all phone calls within the Salt Creek community only require the last four numbers. So, while you are calling the Chief, I am going to call Steve Otten."

"Why are you calling him?"

"I am calling Steve because he owns a backhoe service, but more importantly, he also has a winch truck that can tow the abandoned vehicle."

"Okay, I am on it," she assured.

While they both grabbed their weapon belts and put on their coats once again, Tracy generated enough courage to ask him another question.

"Eddie, why did you invite Chief Traynor? I mean, isn't everything outside of the Midwest town limits our jurisdiction?"

He nodded and understood that she had made an astute observation. "It is not that clear. In that part of the oilfield, you will find a private, state, and Bureau of Land Management (BLM) mixture. If that vehicle is on BLM land, we will involve the local BLM law enforcement officer. But the reason I am asking for Chief Traynor's assistance because he lends an enormous amount of experience. Plus, we could use another set of eyes to find a clue as to whom the vehicle belongs to."

Tracy took a deep breath but mumbled out in her exhale, "somebody should show Sheriff Doan what cooperation is all about."

Her derogatory comment did not evade his ears, and he turned to face her. "Deputy James, I will remind you that Sheriff Doan is our boss, and we follow his orders, period. I am not saying that you cannot disagree with him, whether professionally or personally, but we respect his office. That goes even if we cannot respect the man or woman who resides in that office."

Tracy nodded and walked out of the front door as requested. Yet, in the depths of her thoughts, she screamed out on the inside. Most of all, she wanted the world to know why she did not respect the Sheriff. Tracy vowed that when she knew that she could trust her new Sergeant and partner, he would have a whole new perspective on Sheriff Doan.

* * *

8

The once cold morning with such a sunny promise had turned into an overcast disappointment complete with a 20 mile per hour wind. The gale blew steady out of the west, making the wind chill just a degree or two above zero. Tracy stared out of the window into a vast landscape that looked like an artist's abstract using only white and black paint. Wherever the snow gathered, it was white, and it was dark where the wind blew the snow off.

Her exasperated breath frosted the passenger side window of a dark blue Chevy pickup. The emblem on the truck door read in rancher language as a Rafter M, signifying the Mondragon ranch. Carlos, the pickup's driver and Chief Operating Officer of his family's ranch, led the small caravan with Sergeant Crandall and Chief Traynor together in the vehicle following them.

Carlos had already explained to Tracy that his family came to this area over 150 years ago. He also told her that he and his wife had transitioned from pure ranching toward a guest ranch operation.

Tracy nodded, but she asked Carlos the most curious question while the truck rambled down the dirt road next to Castle Creek. "So, are you an original *OFT* as well?" she asked with a smile.

Carlos smiled wide enough to expose his near-perfect white teeth. He looked at her and inquisitively asked, "so, you have been here for what, two minutes, and you already know about OFT, huh?"

She continued her chiding of Carlos by replying, "yes, I heard about it in the Salt Creek Pipeline."

Carlos laughed out loud and long enough for him to cough a few times as well. After a few seconds, he regained composure. Finally, he answered her question, "yes, I am OFT, and I was one of the original members. The concept of OFT came about while riding in a car with my friends one night coming back from Casper during high school."

Tracy used her newly acquired questioning technique by remaining quiet and maintaining eye contact long enough to elicit more information. It surprised her that the tactic worked because he opened up about how much he missed his buddies. Plus, Carlos emphasized that half of the original OFT members, namely Ricky, Josh, and David, had left town for college and were now well into their careers elsewhere. However, he also revealed that he, Pete LaRoche, and Steve Otten remained in the community.

Upon hearing Steve Otten's name, Tracy commented, "I have heard of Steve. He is the one with the winch truck, right?"

Carlos nodded and told her how close he felt to that band of friends and how it also served as the core of a once-great football team. She rolled her eyes at that comment, though he reassured her that in this community, at least, all school sports, school dances, school plays or concerts, were town events. Tracy looked out the window once more and recalled her playing days as a reserve basketball player at Cheyenne Central High School. She remembered that her games barely had enough people in the stands to be called a crowd. That was true until they played their crosstown rival, Cheyenne East, and then Storey Gymnasium would be packed to the rafters.

Tracy snapped out of her thoughts when Carlos slowed the pickup truck and drove off the dirt road and onto a two-track trail that cut up and over an old railroad bed. Once on the other side, he stopped and placed the truck's transmission into the PARK position. They remained seated in the vehicle until Eddie's Blazer and Steve Otten's GMC winch truck had crowned the railroad bed and stopped near Carlos' pickup.

Eddie stepped out of his unit, walked over to Carlos, and said, "okay, Carlos, where is the vehicle?"

The rancher pointed to his left and said, "right there under the snowdrift."

The Sergeant turned his head and followed in the direction that Carlos pointed. He immediately saw the tailgate of a maroon vehicle with *SUBARU* stamped on it, along with an exposed driver's side. The rest of the car was buried in snow, as Carlos had previously described.

Eddie shouted through the howling wind, "nobody would see that vehicle from the road because of all snow covering it."

Carlos nodded and shouted back, "I saw it on my way back from checking our water tank a little up the hill from here."

He pivoted directly into the wind and squinted his eyes. Then, he made out the form of a water tank, just as Carlos described.

Once Carlos exited his pickup, they walked over to the abandoned vehicle and met Tracy and Chief Traynor, who had already begun looking it over. Eddie scraped the snow off the license plate, revealing a white background with distinctive green-colored mountains bordering the top. It meant only one thing: the license plate was from Colorado. The entire plate read: *UH66991.*

Eddie waived at Tracy to come over and take down the plate number, and then she also wrote down the VIN that was visible on top of the dashboard through the windshield.

"What do you think, Chief?" Eddie shouted toward Traynor.

He leaned over to Crandall's ear and said, "I think it is definitely abandoned considering the snow covering it. I also think we need to tow this thing into town so we can pick over it somewhere out of the wind and cold."

"Where do you propose we do that, Chief?"

"We have an empty ambulance stall in the emergency services garage. We could have Steve haul it there, but it is your call, Eddie."

"But Chief, if the driver shows up to reclaim the vehicle and finds it missing, then what?"

Traynor let out a belly laugh. "Eddie, wouldn't the owner just call the cops?"

He nodded to Traynor that the suggestion was correct. At least the proposal placed all of them out of the cold and the biting wind. Then, Eddie motioned for everyone to gather around him, and when they did, he revealed the plan.

"We are going to open the driver's side door, and I am going to move the transmission shifter into NEUTRAL so Steve tow it to town. Chief Traynor said we could use an empty bay in the town ambulance garage to investigate the contents out of the weather. Any questions?"

When he looked around at everyone, every head nodded in agreement. While four of them dug around the vehicle to free it from the snowdrift, Steve Otten repositioned his truck and then extended out enough cable to attach it to the Subaru's frame. As planned, Eddie opened the driver's side door and cautiously reached inside. Being careful not to touch anything else, he grasped only the manual transmission shifter gave a quick tug, which shifted it out of gear. Steve then made short work of lifting the front end of the Subaru off of the ground and secured it behind his truck to tow back to town.

Once the caravan reached the ambulance garage and had rolled the maroon Subaru Brat into the empty stall, the law enforcement officers went to work. Chief Traynor took pictures while Deputy James methodically looked under and behind the driver's seat. At the same time, Eddie Crandall poured over the contents inside the glove box.

They failed to find a wallet belonging to the vehicle's owner, nor did they find a registration card or insurance information in the glove box. Also missing inside the car was anything that indicated a physical struggle, namely spatters of blood. Additionally, the Subaru was devoid of any weapons or any illegal items like drugs.

But Tracy did find a hotel receipt wedged between the seat and the change box under the emergency brake handle. The pickup bed was empty on the interior except for a few stray pieces of grass that the wind must have deposited.

While the Chief and Tracy looked over the Polaroid photos and the paper hotel receipt, Eddie, instead, walked over to the garage office. He then used the phone to do a license and registration check with the County dispatcher. A few minutes later, Eddie returned to the bay. He revealed that the vehicle registration address was: *Maude Cashman, P.O. Box 1978*, Crook, Colorado, 80726.

Eddie shrugged his shoulders and further commented, "wherever, that is?"

Chief Traynor lifted his left eyebrow and said, "well, that hotel receipt is from the Oxbow Motel in Steamboat Springs, Colorado, under the name of one Jim Hawkins. He checked out on October 30th last year."

Eddie shook his head and paced around the empty part of the garage stall for a few minutes to think. Then, he stopped suddenly and turned toward Traynor. "Would you mind if I seal this vehicle up with crime scene tape and lock it up here until I know what to do with it?"

The Chief nodded. "Sure, Eddie, we can do that."

As if an internal alarm went off inside of him, Chief Traynor looked down at his watch and then asked, "Eddie, do you realize that it is nearly 5 o'clock and don't you have a game starting at 5:30?"

He started to panic because he had been so consumed in the case that time slipped away. So, Chief Traynor suggested to Eddie that he run home and change clothes. Then he assured Crandall that he would stay behind with Tracy to finish sealing the vehicle to avoid possible evidence custody issues. Eddie nodded his head in agreement and then quickly exited the garage.

Traynor turned toward the deputy, "don't worry, once we will get this sealed up, I'll give you a lift to your vehicle. Then how about I buy you a pop and a bag of popcorn at the game? Sound like a deal?"

"Deal, but that is not necessary."

Chief Traynor bent over and grabbed a large roll of sticky crime scene tape out of his pack, and when he stood up, he held it out in front of him for Tracy to grasp. Just as her right hand came within an inch of grabbing the roll of tape, he then playfully pulled it away.

She smiled and asked him, "are you messing with me or something?"

The Chief, however, didn't smile. Then he answered, "or something," which left Tracy momentarily confused. He then said, "now that I have your attention, I want to share some advice with you if you want to receive it?"

Tracy's stomach knotted just like it did when she faced up to doing something wrong. She surprised Chief Traynor when she replied, "sure, I am open to your advice."

Traynor relaxed his shoulders and cracked a small smile and then counseled, "Tracy, I can see that you are not accustomed to people being nice to you or trying to help you. Am I wrong?"

She shook her head.

After spotting her nonverbal response, he resumed. "I knew from the moment that I met you that you have the makings of a great cop. I also know that Eddie feels the same because he told me so during our drive this afternoon. Now, you must understand something. You see, Eddie is one of the best human beings I have ever met, save for one, which is another story. Still, if Eddie is acting nice toward you, he is not looking for any reciprocity. Instead, he believes in treating people the same way he wants others to treat him. The fact that he trusts you already after two days of working with him speaks volumes to me."

Traynor extended his hand again that held a roll of crime scene tape, but he didn't pull it back and allowed Tracy to grab it.

"But one last thing, once you get to know people out here, you will understand that we all look out for one another, so don't ever hesitate to ask me for help. Got that?"

Tracy nodded, and she understood very clearly the message that Chief Traynor tried to explain.

For the next few minutes, they placed pieces of tape across both of the doors and the hood as a tamper seal of sorts. While doing so, Tracy thought about her habit of putting up a strong, independent, and capable front to cover up any personal insecurities. She recalled how she hadn't always been that way, even as a teenager. But things in her adult life had hardened her, and her trust in people was one of the first things to go.

Thirty-five minutes later, Tracy, while still in uniform, made her way inside the Midwest High School gym with a Coke in one hand and a bag of freshly popped popcorn in the other. She followed Chief Traynor to his usual seat directly behind the scorekeeper's table where Eddie sat.

The Sergeant had changed out of his uniform and into a pair of Wrangler jeans and a gray long-sleeve Henley shirt with a Sheriff's Department logo on the right breast. He turned and greeted both Tracy and Chief Traynor as they sat down behind him.

Tracy looked around the gym and noted that it was smaller than what she experienced when she lived in Cheyenne as a youth. The gym had bleachers on both sides of the court though each section had only six rows, and the playing surface ended against the stage on the west end. So, she turned her head toward the door that she came in on the east end of the court. However, something on the east wall caught her eye. She spotted a State championship banner for Wrestling in 1978 and another in 1980, plus a championship banner for football in 1979. But there was a sheet covering something else on the wall. Extending downward from the mysterious covering was a thin rope that dropped down the wall to the floor.

Chief Traynor looked to where Tracy fixated her eyes. Then he leaned in close to Tracy's ear. "This is an exciting night for all of us. Under that sheet is the latest banner to commemorate the 1991 State 9-man Football Championship team that we won just a few months ago. We will reveal it to the crowd between the boys' and girls' games, so plan on staying."

Tracy smiled and noted that Traynor had said "we" when describing the win instead of "they" and concluded what everyone had told her:

this place was a community. It seemed strange that this small humble place could exact the essence of quality social interaction. She also recalled hearing politicians pontificating about their notion of community every election season- how sad it was they knew so little.

Another three hours later, in the pitch-black darkness, Tracy drove her Sheriff's Department sedan south along Highway 259 and was just before the entrance ramp to southbound I-25. She let out a long yawn. Tracy felt tired but not exhausted, even though it was a very long day. Her original plans of leaving after the girls' junior varsity and varsity games went out the window. Instead, it seemed that just about everyone in the area was eager to meet her.

She decided to stay until after they revealed the new championship banner. The unveiling was so exciting that Tracy stayed until after the last game. She even joined in with the crowd to chant "O-F-T" whenever the townsfolk did.

What shocked her was when Twila Corbin approached and gave her a gift. It was an oversized maroon t-shirt with large white block letters that read: '*ONCE AN OILER, ALWAYS AN OILER*' on the front and "*OFT*" on the back.

Better yet, she thought, she observed Eddie and Chief Traynor outside of their professional element, and, more importantly, she saw each of the men as ordinary people.

Tracy then remembered that just before she got into her car to leave, Eddie said that he would call Sheriff Doan in the morning to report their progress in the case.

But most important to her, Eddie said, "I will see you on Monday, Tracy."

* * *

9

Saturday, January 4, 1992

Midwest, Wyoming

Eddie waited until mid-morning before he called Sheriff Doan's pager. After dialing the numbers, he heard his call go through, then after the second ring, his call connected, and he listened to an audible three beeps. He punched in his phone number on his newly purchased push-button cordless phone and hung up.

In all respects, Eddie was probably the last resident in all the Salt Creek area that still had a rotary phone. However, the department kept up with the newest technology and issued personal pagers to all department employees. Yet, his pager was still in a box inside the desk.

Ten minutes later, Eddie's desk phone rang, and after he picked up the receiver, he said: "Good morning, this is Sergeant Crandall."

"Yeah, good morning," said a gruff voice that Eddie recognized as Sheriff Doan.

"Good morning Sheriff, I am ready to give you an update on the Gas Plant mystery man case."

"What do you have," Doan replied, even curter.

"We believe that the deceased man's name is Jim Hawkins because that matches the description of a man who checked into the Salt Creek Inn. We also found an abandoned 1980 Subaru Brat parked two and a half miles southwest of Gas Plant along the same creek where the body turned up. However, inside the vehicle, we found a hotel receipt with the same name."

Sheriff Doan interrupted Eddie and asked, "what is this 'we' stuff, aren't you running the investigation?"

"Yes, Sir, I am running the investigation, but I have a partner on the case since you assigned Deputy James out here to me."

Sheriff Doan barked, "don't get sassy with me, Sergeant, I know full well that I sent Miss Tracy out there," and then there was a long pause.

Meanwhile, Eddie reached out with his right hand and grabbed his coffee cup. Then he took a long sip during the conversation's hiatus.

Finally, Doan continued, "did you search his room in Edgerton?"

Momentarily caught off guard with the question, he paused, which forced the Sheriff to repeat, "did you search his room at the Salt Creek Inn?"

"No, we did not. The owner of the Salt Creek Inn said that we need a search warrant if we need to search the hotel room."

"Are you serious?"

"I am afraid so, Sheriff," he explained and waited an interminable twenty seconds before Doan began to speak again.

"Where did that Jim whatever stay according to the hotel receipt?"

"The Oxbow Motel in Steamboat Springs."

"Is there anything else?" the Sheriff asked, clearly annoyed.

"Yes, when we recovered the vehicle, I did a vehicle VIN search and ran the plates, which points us to a woman who lives in Crook, Colorado."

"Where in the world is Crook, Colorado?"

"I don't know, Sheriff?" Eddie said and waited for the Sheriff to reply. Instead, he could hear the distinctive sounds of the Sheriff's breath huff across the receiver.

"Did you recover any fingerprints yet off of the car?"

The question caught Eddie was in the middle of another sip of coffee. After he swallowed, he replied, "not yet, I will dust the car this morning, and I will bring anything I find into town this afternoon to the lab."

Sheriff Doan only grunted a response and then took another long pause in the conversation.

Eddie had finished the last bit of coffee left in his mug when the Sheriff spoke up again, "good, bring those prints in today. But I want you to do something else."

He furrowed his brow. "What's that, Sheriff?"

"On Monday, you and Miss Tracy will drive to Steamboat Springs to find out more about the dead guy. Then, if necessary, go to Crook, wherever that is, to find any connections to the stiff lying in my morgue."

Crandall stood up from his desk with the receiver still planted firmly on his ear and shook his head. Then, he protested, "but Sheriff, I can do all of that with a few phone calls and…." but Sheriff Doan cut him off.

"Sergeant, that is an order, now get off your butt and take Miss Tracy with you. Are we clear?"

Eddie was utterly dumbfounded, and finally, he said, "yes, Sir, I am clear, and I will take Deputy James with me."

"Good! I also want you back to my office by next Thursday at 9:00 a.m. to brief me and the others about what you found."

"Yes, Sir!" he replied, although the line went dead before Doan uttered another reply.

Eddie sank into his desk chair and looked out his window that faced Navy Row. He understood that the Sheriff did not like him, but that had never mattered until now. He felt as if the Sheriff was looking for a reason, any reason that was egregious enough for a cause to relieve him of his duties.

Suddenly he sat up and opened the top left drawer of his desk. He then sorted through several state maps of Wyoming, Montana, Nebraska, and then found Colorado, which he took out. Eddie opened it atop his desktop and quickly found Steamboat Springs. He picked up a pen and a piece of paper and wrote a quick note that the city was in Route County.

Next, Eddie looked on the back of the map for the city and town index section. He traced down the list with his right index finger until the name of *Crook* appeared along with its accompanying map grid coordinates. It amused him that Crook did not have any numbers in parentheses to show its population like other towns and cities. However, when he turned the map over, he found Crook in the northeastern corner of Colorado in Logan County.

With his right hand, Eddie lifted the telephone receiver. He called the county dispatcher to give him the phone numbers to the Route County and Logan County Sheriff's offices. Once receiving them, he hung up with the dispatcher and made the two calls. Eddie hoped his reaching out to his Colorado brethren would increase a spirit of cooperation between departments.

Afterward, he looked at the clock on the wall. Then, finally, he determined that he needed to finish looking over the abandoned Subaru. But, before he left his house, Eddie called Chief Traynor at home and asked him to meet at the ambulance barn to dust the Subaru for fingerprints. When Traynor asked why it was such a priority, Eddie explained that he didn't have much choice because Sheriff Doan ordered him to hurry along with the investigation.

Chief Traynor's only comment was, "watch yourself. I have a feeling in my gut that your boss is up to something, and that is not usually a good thing."

Later that afternoon, Tracy was relaxing on her couch, dressed in her newly acquired Midwest t-shirt along with a pair of comfy sweatpants while watching television. Then, a sudden knock on her door aroused her. She got up from her sofa and walked over to the door and looked through the peephole, and found Eddie standing there in uniform. Tracy was a little embarrassed by her appearance but knew there wasn't enough time to make herself more presentable. So, with a deep breath, she opened her door.

"Hello, Deputy James. I hope I didn't disturb you?"

"Oh, not at all, Sergeant Crandall. I was just thinking about you." Tracy told the truth, for her thoughts had returned to him several times that morning in hopes she proved herself worthy as a deputy and a trainee. If Eddie caught the comment, he did not show it.

Instead, he said, "I have bad news on your day off."

Tracy furrowed her brow and shook her head, indicating that she didn't understand the implication.

He caught the expression and explained further, "Sheriff Doan has ordered us to go to Colorado to track down leads into our mystery man, Jim Hawkins."

Tracy nearly stumbled from the bursting excitement that jolted through her body. Then, when her endorphin rush subsided, she asked, "I don't understand why the Sheriff wants us to travel when all we have to do is pick up the phone?"

"I know, I even said the same thing to him myself, but orders are orders."

She momentarily stood bewildered but then realized her rudeness by not asking Eddie to enter her apartment. "Please, Eddie, why don't you come in and tell me more."

Eddie felt uneasy as he stepped over the door threshold and took a seat in the chair closest to the door.

Tracy sensed it too and broke the ice by asking, "so, did you drive into Casper to share this news when you could have just called me on the phone?"

"Yes, I could have called, but I was in town anyway because this morning, with Chief Traynor's help, we lifted four good fingerprints off of the Subaru. I just dropped them off a few minutes ago at the crime lab for analysis."

"Oh, okay. Though I wish you would have called first because I must look like a mess?"

"Not at all, Tracy. You are just fine."

Without acknowledging the compliment, she asked, "so, when do we leave for Colorado?"

Eddie reached up and scratched the side of his face with his right hand. Then he asked Tracy more than telling her, "I was hoping we could be on the road from here tomorrow at 1 p.m.? If we leave then it should put us in Steamboat Springs by 7 or 8 tomorrow night. I have already scheduled an appointment to meet with a Route County Sheriff's Deputy at 8:00 a.m. Monday morning. But I would pack for a couple of days because we may need to drive across northern Colorado to another town located in the northeastern corner where the Subaru is registered."

Tracy instantly replied, "okay, I will be ready," but then silently regretted that she appeared too eager for the trip. Instead, she was just anxious to do something meaningful. This particular case posed an excellent opportunity for her to do so.

"I'm sorry, where are my manners? Do you want something to drink, or can you stay awhile?" Tracy asked.

"No, I appreciate the offer, but I need to be going. The Denver Broncos play the Houston Oilers in the Divisional round at 4:00 p.m., and I need to get home."

She teased, "oh, you have a date, huh?"

He shook his head and said, "no, it is nothing like that. The head custodian at the school, Reed, always shows up at my place to watch the Broncos whether I invite him over or not. From what Reed tells me, he used to watch games with Tim Savolt as well."

"I see, so is Reed his first name or his last name?"

Eddie shrugged. "I don't know, and I don't think anybody else knows either. Rumor has it that the captions under every one of Reed's pictures in the school yearbooks only lists his name as '*Reed.*' I don't think anyone has dared to ask him about it."

When Eddie finished talking, he stood up abruptly and walked toward the door, and then he stopped and turned around. He looked over to Tracy, who was still sitting on her couch, and said to her, "okay, I will see you tomorrow at 1 o'clock." Then, he turned once more and let himself out of the apartment.

After the door shut behind him, Tracy got up off the couch, walked over to her front window, and peered through the small gap in the sheer curtains. She then watched Eddie walk down to the Blazer, start it up, and pull out of the parking lot toward the street outside of her view. While doing so, Tracy pondered once again that he was not like any of the men from her memory. But, more importantly, she also wondered if he was a guy that she could trust, unlike other men that had treated her poorly and had even humiliated her. But still, she thought, he was different.

Minutes later, Eddie traveled north on Poplar Street toward the interstate highway. While driving, he mused about Tracy, which had already happened to him twice since he had left her apartment. But this time, Eddie could not shake his thoughts from her. He liked Tracy's personality and he also found her physically attractive. But he cautioned himself about acting on his impulses because it could shatter the fragile trust established between the two of them.

When Eddie merged on to I-25, he recalled the conversation with his department buddy after the phone call with Sheriff Doan earlier that morning. The friend called to provide some more background on Tracy, as he requested. Simply put, Eddie wanted to know the reasoning for her transfer to the Salt Creek community. But as his friend spoke, he regarded much of the information as nothing more than office gossip. Instinctively, he knew that only Tracy could fill in the missing pieces. But then again, sometimes office talk held some fragments of the truth within it.

Eddie also knew that if what his friend said was true, it would become his job to do something about it. But, in the meantime, he needed more time for Tracy to feel comfortable enough to speak about the events on her own accord without feeling coerced.

He also told his buddy about Sheriff Doan's order to take Tracy with him to Colorado to track down the particulars on Jim Hawkins. His buddy remarked that it was weird for the Sheriff to make such an order a few phone calls were necessary. However, the friend warned Eddie to watch his back because the whole thing felt like a setup for some reason. Additionally, the friend relayed that Deputies McKinnon and Peck had started calling him *Casper Crandall the Friendly Ghost*. When Eddie failed to connect the apparent entendre, his buddy espoused that it was because of his written report on Jim Hawkins. Hence the deputies focused on the words *ghost lights* written in the witness statements to connect him to the cartoon character.

* * *

10

Sunday, January 5, 1992

Casper, Wyoming

Sergeant Eddie Crandall pulled into an empty slot in the parking lot of Deputy Tracy James' apartment complex. After turning off the ignition and removing the key, he opened the door to his Sheriff's Department Chevrolet Blazer. Once again, the January sky was bright and brilliant blue, but the ever-present wind made it seem even colder. Though it was in the afternoon, the outside temperature had not eclipsed over 20 degrees yet, and with a wind chill that made it feel like it was just five above zero.

When Eddie stepped down to the pavement, his left cowboy boot struck a slick patch of ice that caused him to do the splits. He hung there for a few seconds until he managed to bring his extended left leg back underneath him. Eddie stepped out again but managed to swing both legs out simultaneously on the second attempt. Finally, he slowly stood up and eased his entire body weight upon the slick soles of his boots while maintaining a firm grasp on the door frame of the truck.

Eddie then half-walked and half-ice skated his way across the parking lot. But before he stepped up on the freshly salted sidewalk, a gust of biting cold wind blasted him. The wind sent him sliding backward on the ice with little or no control. Aggravated now, he leaned against the wind and shuffled both feet until reaching the sidewalk once again. As much as he loved living in Wyoming, he detested the wind the same.

With each step on the concrete, the salt crystals left there to melt the ice and snow popped loudly under each boot. When Eddie reached

Tracy's apartment, he rapped softly on the door and patiently waited for her to open it. Almost immediately, Tracy swung open her door and greeted him with a smile.

"Hi there," she said.

"Good morning Deputy, are you ready to go?"

"Yes, just let me grab my coat and my bag."

"Here, let me get your bag for you," He insisted while stepping through the doorway. As his hand grasped the twin handles of the duffle, her fingers met his.

She asserted, "it is okay, I got it, thank you."

Embarrassed by the rejection of his chivalry, he shrugged his shoulders and stepped away. Then he stammered out a reply, "okay, suit yourself, but watch your step in the parking lot because the ice is slick as snot!"

Once outside of the apartment, he observed her close and lock the door. When Tracy turned around to face him, Eddie led the way across the walkway and down the flight of stairs.

"Wow, that was a good game yesterday," Tracy said. Eddie slowed down a half-step and turned and looked back at her with a confused expression on his face. So, she clarified, "the Broncos and Oilers game yesterday."

"Oh, that, yes. Mile High magic strikes again. Never count Elway out until the final seconds tick off. So, I take it that you are a Broncos fan?"

"Well, I am, but then again, I am not. I always liked watching games with my dad though I still root for them even if I don't watch."

"Perhaps you could join Reed and me for the AFC Championship game this next weekend?"

"Okay, you are on, just tell me what I can bring."

"Fine."

After they reached the end of the sidewalk, Eddie waited for Tracy to walk beside him to help her navigate the mini ice flow. She made three steps on the ice sheet when her left foot slid out from underneath. While starting to somersault backward, Tracy tossed her duffle bag in a valiant effort to counterbalance. He had predicted as much and caught her as she fell backward. When Tracy established footing again, she turned and smiled at her boss in appreciation.

Then, without warning, a gust of wind knocked both of them off balance. Eddie fell to the ground first, followed by Tracy, who landed firmly on top of him. With four arms and four legs splayed out on the pavement, Tracy started an infectious giggle that erased Eddie's responding humiliation, and he too chuckled at their plight.

Minutes later, they continued to share their laugh as they loaded up into the Blazer and made their way west on CY Avenue, eventually turning into Highway 220. As they reached the Paradise Valley subdivision on the western outskirts of Casper, Eddie pulled over at the Mini Mart and bought coffees for both of them.

Later, while they continued driving west, Tracy saw something outside the passenger side window that intrigued her.

"Eddie, what is Bessemer Bend?"

"Oh, you saw the sign, did you?"

She turned to him and nodded.

He explained, "it is a place on the Immigrant Trails where they made the crossing over the North Platte River. From there, they headed over to the Sweetwater River just west of here, you will see."

She shook her head. "I have never been out of Casper this way. I mean, I remember riding the team bus from Cheyenne to Riverton one time, but we must have taken a different road west out of Casper?"

He nodded. "Yes, you are correct. The road to Riverton is US Highway 26. This one is Highway 220 that we will follow until we get to US Highway 287 that will take us to Rawlins."

"Oh, I know Rawlins. I remember that bus ride well to Green River, Rock Springs, and Evanston. Of course, that was always a lot of nothing outside the bus windows."

Eddie chuckled and remarked, "many people feel the same way about going across the Great Divide Basin. I've always liked it out here, and maybe it is because it is so lonely."

He then took his right hand off the steering wheel, grabbed the two case file folders sitting on the seat between them, and handed them over to her.

"What is this?"

"Well, if you get bored, you can catch up on your reading."

Tracy picked up the files and looked over at Eddie, who did not return her gaze. Instead, he cracked a slight grin while keeping his eyes focused upon the road in front of them. She set the folders down upon her lap and opened the cover of the one on top. The tab read *Savolt, T.* Inside the front cover, a man's photograph was bound by a paperclip. She took her time to thumb through the material in silence for nearly half an hour. If Eddie wanted to talk about the case, he did not indicate it.

A little while later, Tracy looked over to Eddie and spotted the many freckles on his face, which made him look like he wore a perpetual beach tan in the shadow of the visor.

Eddie sensed her gaze upon him. So, he asked, "do you have a question?"

"I do, this guy, umm, how do you say his name?"

"Phonetically, his last name is *SAY-VAULT*. So what is your question?"

"Did you know him?"

"I did, but only for about a year. We also played basketball together in the adult basketball league."

"What was he like? I mean, was Tim a good guy?"

Eddie shrugged and was thrown off-balance by the question as nobody outside the community had ever cared to ask. Finally, after a long pause, he replied, "yes, he was a good and decent guy. I mean, he was someone I liked to hang around with if that is what you are asking?"

"How far did you get along in the case, like did you find any evidence of him somewhere else or...." she asked before he cut her off.

"I know in my heart, and so does Chief Traynor, that mercenaries murdered him, but we never found his body. Instead, we recovered Savolt's backpack, complete with bloodstains that matched the teacher. Plus, we found spent military-grade .223 shell casings nearby. We even had the dead body of one of the suspected thugs. Yet, when it was all said and done, the County District Attorney wouldn't go forward in the case until we found Savolt's body."

Tracy furrowed her brow. "What did you mean, 'we?' Are you referring to you and Chief Traynor?"

He tried to change the subject. Instead, Eddie pointed in front of the Blazer and said, "look, Independence Rock is coming into view."

She snapped, "yes, I've seen it before in a book, but what about my question?"

Instead of responding, Eddie rolled his neck to attempt to relieve the tension that started to build up. Then he looked over at Tracy, who sat quietly and patiently for him to respond.

Finally, he said flatly, "Chief and I had some help."

"Who helped you? Sheriff Doan?"

"Are you kidding me? Sheriff Doan only involved himself when he could take credit for something that made him look good!"

The silence in the vehicle became as thick as peanut butter, and the tension within Eddie also started to boil over. He shook his head and took a deep breath.

"Do you remember last week when I told you about Josh Anderson and his friends conducting their investigation?"

"Oh, now I get it now," Tracy replied.

Eddie nodded. "the boys found Savolt's field book, his backpack, and then became hunted by the two mercenaries in a 1978 Ford F-150. You will also read near the end of the file about Bill Crooks. Though his day job is the high school social studies teacher, he is also a BLM law enforcement officer. One fateful day in November 1984, out by the old Electric Plant, three of those boys, including Josh Anderson, were attacked by the mercs. But Crooks was out there too and ended up shooting and killing one of the perps named William Pruitt. His partner, Marvin Stiles, managed to escape and hasn't been seen since."

It wasn't the information that astonished Tracy; instead, it was Eddie talking longer than a sentence or two. But his answer puzzled her about why the report failed to document any mention of the high school boys. She cleared her throat and began to ask that very question when Eddie lifted his hand and cut her off.

"I can see your wheels turning in your head about why there is no mention of the boys in the report."

Tracy nodded and then waved her left hand in a rolling motion that intimated him to continue, which he did.

"Chief Traynor and I decided long ago to keep their names out of the investigation. But, you have to understand something here; the Sheriff did not back an investigation. Instead, he wanted it swept away as quickly as possible. Doan considered it a walk-away from life type of deal."

"But you don't?"

"No. I knew Tim Savolt personally, and he was a dedicated teacher and coach who the kids loved. So no, I will never accept any theory that insinuates he just walked away."

Tracy thought about what Eddie said and turned her head to look out the vehicle's passenger window. It was then that she spotted a massive split in a small mountain made of granite, and it looked to her that the Sweetwater River flowed through it.

"What is that?" she asked while she pointed toward the mountain.

Eddie said flatly, "that is Devil's Gate. It is one of many landmarks along the Oregon Trail, which we have been on since we passed by Independence Rock."

She turned toward him and asked, "again, why is it that you left the boys out of the report?"

Eddie smiled. "I see you are catching on with the interviewing techniques, but yes, Traynor and I made a conscious decision to leave the boys out of the report. At the time, it protected the boys, and it saved the Sheriff's Department some embarrassment."

Tracy glanced back down in the notes and found the report written by the two deputies who conducted the first search. She then flipped to the last entry in the file and read Eddie's official statement, and now she understood why the case meant so much to him. But, she said to herself, "it was his first major case and still unresolved. I hope this case isn't going to turn out the same for me?"

She set the Savolt file aside and picked up the folder on the current case. By then, they had already turned off Highway 220, and now traveled south on US 287. While reading, Tracy occasionally lifted her eyes to look around at the terrain. A few of those times she became briefly mesmerized by the dancing ground blizzards that jumped on the pavement from the west side of the road and collected again on the east side. At one point, she noted an enormous tract of snow fencing that stopped snowdrifts from forming on the pavement. To her, the fences looked similar to the ones outside her hometown in Cheyenne.

The sky was still a crystal-clear blue hue, and the sun brought a welcomed warmth through the vehicle's windshield. But the closer that they got to the city of Rawlins, it seemed the wind blew with more force than before. Eddie noticed it too, and he managed to keep the Chevy Blazer within his lane after each gust of wind. He was quietly thankful that the pavement was clear of ice, or otherwise, they might have ended up in the ditch.

A few minutes later, the sudden drumming of his left leg bouncing up and down caught her attention. "Are you nervous?" she asked. Eddie was slightly confused about Tracy's question, but she added, "your leg. Are you bouncing your leg because you are nervous?"

Eddie stopped bouncing his leg almost immediately. He then thought about how he could delicately discuss why he appeared nervous.

"I am anxious to get to Rawlins because I have to use the restroom; that's all."

"Oh, I thought I was the only one that had to pee, so don't waste any time getting there," she said with a smile.

Just then, the Blazer crowned a hill, and the outskirts of Rawlins came into their full view.

Tracy shouted out, "finally," in anticipation that relief would come soon. When Eddie drove past the first gas station, Tracy sighed. When he drove past the second gas station, she felt like fainting. Finally, the Sergeant pulled over at a truck stop next to Interstate 80.

As soon as he placed the Blazer's transmission in the PARK position, neither said a word to one another. Instead, they both made a beeline for the front door and the restrooms.

Minutes later, Tracy found Eddie by the coffee maker filling another cup.

She asked, "Is that all you drink? I mean, all I see you drink every day is one cup of coffee after another."

Eddie straightened up his posture as he was kind of taken aback by her blunt observation, then he uttered, "no, I like iced tea too. I make sun tea all-year around, not just in the summer."

She nodded. "You know sun tea is not good for you since none of the bacteria in the tea bags get cooked out?"

He pursed his lips and shrugged. "I didn't know that, and I don't care because I've never gotten sick."

Tracy shook her head in disbelief, then asked, "are we going to get gas here?"

"No, we should be good, but if the gas gauge drops close to ¼ of a tank, we can always stop in Baggs or Craig, Colorado, further south."

Tracy shrugged apathetically.

"Speaking of that town, I figured that we could stop at a restaurant that I like there and have some supper. What do you think?" Eddie asked.

"How far is Baggs? I have never heard of it?"

"It is a little over an hour from here, and the reason you haven't heard of it is that you are a city girl," he said teasingly. Then he added, "come on, let's go."

* * *

11

The drive west on I-80 was a familiar sight to Tracy from her high school days on the sports bus. She recalled that once one drove outside the Rawlins city limits, the land became void of nothingness. Yet, after a glance out the window, it seemed to her that nothing had changed over the years. For as far as she could look out of either side of the Blazer, she didn't spot a single tree, just a lot of grass, hills, and sagebrush.

Eddie turned his head. "Don't you just love the Red Desert?"

Tracy remained silent and shook her head, but she did appreciate the effect of the long shadows caused by the sun that steadily sank toward the western horizon.

"Well, I love it. Take a look around. This land is what authentic wild country looks like without the undue influence of man. But, you know, I wish that the East Coast types with all their environmental causes would come to look at a place like this.".

His comment piqued her interest. "You don't strike me as someone sympathetic to the environmental cause?"

"Why are you?"

"No, not exactly. I like nature, but I also like some development too. I mean, we have to live, don't we? So I think that for every tree we cut down for lumber, we should plant back another in its place," she said.

He nodded. "Well, that makes two of us. I think if the environs found themselves out here in this desert, they would find nothing appealing and would probably put up a coffee shop." Eddie shook his head and continued, "but seriously, the Red Desert and many other places in Wyoming to include the stretch between Casper and Buffalo is wild. Out here, untamed land will always win against those unprepared."

Later, while seated across from one another in a booth inside the Battle Mountain Restaurant and Hotel in Baggs, Eddie and Tracy studied menus. The residents who dined there looked over at the uniform-clad dyad repeatedly. Some wondered aloud why Natrona County Sheriff's Officers were in the southernmost stretch of Carbon County. The sets of eyes and even the whispered discussions did not go unnoticed by Eddie as he had experienced this behavior before. Tracy, conversely, seemed unaware of the scene around her.

After a while, Eddie set down his menu on the table and waited quietly for the server to arrive. Finally, Tracy lowered her still open menu down on the table and looked up to Eddie.

"What are you having?"

"I like #4, which is biscuits and gravy with fried potatoes. It is my usual order here."

"Oh, do they serve breakfast all day? I didn't see that?"

Eddie chuckled. "Yes, look at the top of the breakfast page."

"Oh, I see it now."

"Do you see anything you want?"

"Yes, I am going to have huevos rancheros," she said and placed her menu on top of Eddie's. Tracy continued, "back home in Cheyenne, we had this Mexican restaurant on the south side that had fabulous food. Their specialty breakfast specialty was huevos rancheros because of their homemade green chili recipe."

"Are you talking about the place that is just over the Central Avenue viaduct and over one street to the west?"

"Yes, how did you know?"

"A friend of mine from high school went into the Air Force. Then he was stationed at F.E. Warren Air Force Base from 1983-1989, so I used to come down to Cheyenne a few times a year to see him. So, frankly, the reason I picked this very place to eat was because of him, too."

"Really? This place is a long way from Cheyenne. How did he...." her words fell silent when Eddie cut her off.

"We used to come down here to hunt deer just north of Baggs off Wild Cow Creek Road. We also hunted elk east of here at the base of Singer Peak. As usual, after a few days of eating camp food, it was always nice to come to town for a hot meal."

The server interrupted their discussion and asked for their orders. Eddie then asked the server to fill out separate tickets because they had to file independent expense reports. If the inconvenience bothered the server, she did not show it and took down their food orders.

When the server departed the table, Tracy asked, "so, where is your friend now? Overseas?"

Eddie pursed his lips and spoke very dryly, "he died in 1989 in a training accident when an armored security forces vehicle he was in rolled over."

Her once beaming smile suddenly vanished with the news. She tried to empathize with Eddie's sadness but could not. She searched in her mind for the right thing to say, but then she remembered what people had said to her grandmother after her grandfather passed away a few years ago. She had observed that people, while caring, can never offer the right words to abate grief entirely.

Instead, Tracy asked, "what was his name?"

"His name was Rob."

"What was he like?"

Eddie shifted uncomfortably in his seat because nobody ever asked that question before. He reached out and took a sip of water from the glass left by the waitress. It was hard for him to describe Rob, but then something came to mind.

"Rob had a great sense of humor. He was amiable and a little goofy at times," Eddie said as he chuckled. But, he continued, "when Rob laughed out loud, it was one of those silent laughs that didn't make much of a sound. Instead, Rob would stand there smiling at you while his Adam's Apple bounced up and down. It was the goofiest thing."

The waitress interrupted the conversation when she took their orders. When the server left them, Tracy reached her left palm across the table and set it on the top of Eddie's right hand.

She leaned forward very close to his head and whispered a simple, "I am sorry for your loss," and then sat back to her original position.

Eddie did not reply verbally; instead, he gave her a quick nod of his head to acknowledge the sentiment. Instead, he quickly changed the subject by discussing the rest of the trip in front of them that evening. He described that after they left Baggs, they would cross the Colorado/Wyoming border. Then upon reaching Craig, Colorado, they would venture east to find Steamboat Springs at the base of the mountains.

The waitress interrupted them once more when she brought out their food orders, and after a quick pre-meal prayer by Eddie, they ate in silence.

On her last fork full of food, Tracy broke the long stillness when she offered, "I wish I could have met your friend Rob, he sounded like a nice guy. Sadly, I don't know many of them," though she mumbled the last part of her comment.

Eddie stretched a slight smile across his lips and replied, "Thanks, yes, he was a nice guy, and he was one that you should have known."

Soon afterward, Eddie and Tracy paid for their food and stepped out of the restaurant into the pitch-black winter evening. The few streetlights offered a little bit of light to guide their steps back toward their Chevy Blazer. Suddenly, Eddie stopped short just before they reached the front of their unit.

Instead, he pointed to a small bar across the street with a Coors neon sign half-illuminated in its front window. Then the Sergeant told Tracy about the local legend that the infamous Butch Cassidy used to stop at that place decades beyond his reported death in Bolivia along with the Sundance Kid. He further explained that the same legend was also popular in Kaycee, just north of Midwest. That version was attributed to Butch and Sundance's famous hideout, the Hole-in-the-Wall, located west of town.

Once again, they rode together in silence. Soon afterward, the Blazer crossed over the state line and toward the town of Craig. It was so quiet that the only noise inside the cab came from the whistling of a leaking window seal. However, while Eddie drove, Tracy turned on the reading lamp above her seat and looked over their current case file. She mostly looked for a clue connecting the cryptic poem to Steamboat Springs, and she voiced her intention as such.

"So, other than the word Steamboat in the poem, I don't understand where there is another connection here?"

Eddie tilted his head to one side while he processed her question. Then he shrugged. "I don't know either, but maybe the Deputy Sheriff we are scheduled to meet tomorrow morning can shed some light."

His comments dropped off suddenly when the headlights of his rig illuminated the bodies of two cow elk that stood in the middle of the road. With a deaf hand, Eddie gingerly maneuvered the Blazer around the animals. Best of all, he did not panic, for if he had jerked the wheel to one side or even stomped on the brakes, they probably would have ended up off the road and a long way from help.

Afterward, he glanced over to Tracy. The soft glow of the reading light revealed that she still looked panicked from what had just happened.

He assured her, "It is okay, we are safe, but you can help me by keeping watch on your side of the road for deer or elk."

"What do I look for?"

"Just look for the headlight reflecting off their eyes and the movement of their bodies."

They rode in silence into the town of Craig, Colorado, where Eddie stopped and filled up the Blazer's tank with gasoline. The route from Craig to Steamboat Springs was easy enough to find since large road signs pointed to US Highway 40. Tracy again took up her role as a spotter and called out sets of eyeballs along the road to their destination.

After they entered Steamboat Springs, US Highway 40 turned into Lincoln Avenue, which traversed through the heart of the downtown. The small city was fully ablaze with streetlights and fully active with plenty of vacationing skiers. Christmas décor still hung on the trees, complete with lights, which made a striking scene against the fresh powder snowbanks. As they exited the heart of downtown, the road sojourned next to the partially frozen Yampa River.

Finally, Eddie spotted the neon sign for the Bunkhouse Motel, which held their reservations. He turned the Blazer into the parking lot and then avoided a crowd of vacationing skiers who huddled around a roaring campfire next to the parking area. As they exited their department vehicle, it amused them that the revelers instinctively disguised their alcoholic beverages as soon as they spotted the two uniformed officers.

Tracy teased Eddie. "I can't take you anywhere, can I? First, every car refuses to pass us on the road. Then in Baggs, everyone wondered who we were and what we were doing. Now, everyone around the campfire is looking at us like we are a couple of narcs."

He nodded. "It is a part of the job, I guess."

Inside the office, Eddie provided his reservation number to the motel manager, who, in turn, provided keys to rooms 19 and 20 at the end of the building. He then started to protest and pointed out that the two rooms were too close to the fire pit with the loud party. The manager countered that the two of them were lucky enough to get two rooms considering it was the heart of the ski season. Eddie sighed, accepted the room assignments, and handed Tracy the key to room 19, while he kept the key to room 20.

Thirty minutes later, Eddie sat on his bed dressed in a t-shirt and baggy sweatpants and tried desperately to find something or anything worth watching on the television. He then heard a soft knock on his door. When he opened the door, he found Tracy standing there and dressed pretty much the same as him.

"Aren't you going to invite me inside? It is cold out here."

Eddie was dumbfounded because he wanted to keep the appearance of professionalism at all times with Tracy. The thought of inviting her into his room ran juxtaposed to his intentions.

She interrupted his thoughts, "Come on. It is like two degrees out here."

He finally consented. "Okay, come on in," to which she hurried through the doorway. But before closing the door, Eddie spotted a black Ford Bronco that sat almost directly across from his door. The thing that alerted him was that he could hear the low rumble of the Bronco's engine as it idled, and he saw the wisp of exhaust rising from the rear of the unit. But he could not see the driver or a passenger because of the vehicle's dark tinted windows.

After Eddie finally closed the door, he spun around and found Tracy sitting in the chair next to the desk in the room.

She preempted him. "I know you want to maintain the notion of appropriateness, and I do appreciate it, but there is something I want to do."

Eddie flushed with embarrassment and stammered out, "Umm, ah, Tracy, umm, I don't think...."

To which she again cut him off, "it is not what you are thinking. I just want us to go over everything we know about this case before we meet with the Route County Deputy in the morning, that's all."

Awash in a wave of sudden relief, he then walked over to his briefcase and removed the file marked *Jim Hawkins*. Then he placed it on the foot of the bed. Tracy reached over and lifted the folder off of the mattress and opened it. Only then did she look up at him.

She asked, "so who are we meeting with tomorrow?"

"Hold on a second, I have to look it up," and he stood up again and walked over to his uniform jacket and removed his small notepad. He skipped through the pages until he found it and read the name aloud, "Deputy Monica Tombrello and we meet with her at 8 a.m."

He then walked back over and sat down on the bed, where they sat in tranquility while scouring notes within the file.

A few minutes later, Tracy looked up and said, "there isn't much here to go on as far as coming up with questions other than the obvious ones like have you seen this man, and what was he doing here?"

Eddie nodded. "I know. We are operating on pretty thin evidence."

She silently agreed with a head nod of here own, then she picked up the cryptic poem again and looked at it. But, then she asked, "I left my copy of the poem at home, so do you mind if I take this one back to my room to make another copy? Maybe I can also decipher something?"

Eddie shrugged and quipped, "I don't see why not. I mean, everything helps at this point, right?"

She suddenly stood up and moved toward the door, and he followed suit but stopped her before she opened the door. So instead, Eddie slowly opened the door and glanced over to where the Bronco was previously parked, only to find the vehicle had left sometime before. Next, he looked to the right and spotted at least a half-dozen vacationers still huddled around the firepit where they drank and laughed raucously. Only then did he turn around and allow her to exit.

She looked up at him with a quizzical look that pertained to his cautiousness though she did not say anything about it. Instead, she offered only a simple "goodnight."

To which Eddie replied the same, "goodnight."

* * *

12

Monday, January 6, 1992

Steamboat Springs, Colorado

6:30 a.m.

Eddie stood over the coffee maker in his motel room and waited impatiently for his cup of coffee to finish brewing. It was already his second cup of the morning since he woke up at 5 a.m., partially out of habit and also for the fact that he rarely slept well in a motel room.

Instead, he decided to get up and get dressed instead of prolonging his torture of lying awake in bed. Soon after putting on his uniform, he donned his department jacket, walked out to the Chevy Blazer, and scraped the ice off all the windows. It was still dark outside, and the sun would not rise for another hour. However, in the shadow of the mountains, full sunlight might not reach the land until eight or even nine o'clock that morning. Eddie grabbed his cup after it had finished brewing and took a sip. It tasted like bad instant coffee at best, but he accepted it since lousy coffee is better than none at all.

While he took another sip from the Styrofoam cup, Eddie watched the morning news. In the seconds that followed, he found out that US Highway 40 east of Steamboat Springs had closed overnight at Rabbit Ears Pass due to heavy snow and blowing snow conditions. Nevertheless, it was the route that he planned to take if they needed to drive to Crook after all. The weather forecaster came on next and predicted even more mountain snow from the Wyoming border down the front range to the Eisenhower Tunnel on Interstate 70 in the central part of the state.

Eddie finished his coffee and looked over to the clock next to his bed, which read 6:59. So, he stood up, turned off the television, and collected his gear. Then after placing his bag inside the Blazer, Eddie started the engine to warm up the inside of the unit. Only then did he walk over to his partner's room and knock on her window.

Tracy answered the door, and not surprisingly, she was already fully dressed in her uniform.

"I take it you are ready to go?" Tracy asked Eddie.

"Yep, I suggest we go get some breakfast before we take our appointment."

"Good, I am hungry. Can you grab this bag and put it in the back of the Blazer for me?"

He took her bag without a word, and she followed him to the Blazer while carrying a smaller backpack. When Tracy took her place in the passenger seat, Eddie asked her for her room key. He then walked over to the Motel office and checked both of them out of their rooms. When he returned to the vehicle, Eddie held two separate receipts.

"So, where do you want to eat?" he asked.

Tracy hemmed and hawed and then finally eked out, "how about McDonald's? I know we passed by one last night on our way here to the motel."

"Okay, I'm always in the mood for a McMuffin sandwich, plus I like their coffee."

After breakfast, Eddie and Tracy drove over to the Route County Sheriff's Department building located just south of the main highway through town. When Eddie parked the Blazer in a designated VISITOR slot, he and Tracy exited their vehicle. Right away, Crandall noticed the different paint schemes between Route County and Natrona County patrol units. But that was the only difference he noted. Once they walked inside the building, they observed that their uniforms pretty much matched those of their Route County law enforcement cousins.

Eddie then approached the reception desk situated directly in front of the main entrance, where he asked for Deputy Tombrello. The civilian receptionist quickly called the deputy and then reported back to Eddie she would come out shortly. The receptionist also suggested that they take a seat to wait. Within a minute, Deputy Tombrello emerged from the locked double doors to the left of the reception desk, and she made her way directly over to the waiting Natrona County Sheriff representatives.

Tombrello was an attractive woman with jet black hair drawn back into a tight ponytail and had dark chocolate brown eyes. Her meticulously crisp uniform fit snug over her fit body. But, if she intended to impress him, it had not surpassed Eddie's attention.

"Hello, I am Deputy Monica Tombrello, and you must be Sergeant Eddie Crandall?" she said and extended her right hand outward to shake in a greeting.

He took her hand, shook it appropriately, and said, "yes, I am Eddie Crandall, and next to me is Deputy Tracy James."

Tracy thrust her hand out, and Deputy Tombrello warmly shook her's as well. Meanwhile, Tracy sized up her counterpart in one glance from the perfectly shined shoes up to the black scrunchy that held the other deputy's hair.

Then Deputy Tombrello suggested, "why don't you both follow me back to my desk where we can talk about what brings the two of you so far from home?"

Eddie nodded, and they followed as instructed.

Once they walked through the electronically locked double doors, Eddie and Tracy entered a hallway with offices on either side of the hall. Eventually, it opened up into a large room containing at least a dozen desks. Opposite each officer sat two additional chairs for interviewing purposes. When they arrived at Deputy Tombrello's desk, Tracy sat in the right seat, and Eddie occupied the left.

Tombrello broke the ice when she asked, "so, where is Natrona County exactly?"

Eddie replied, "it is in the center of Wyoming, and Casper is the county seat. Though we live and work in a small town called Midwest, which is 40 miles north of that city."

"How big of a department do you have up there?"

"We have a little over 100 sworn employees, but that is to cover a land area of roughly 5,000 square miles plus a large county jail," he explained.

"Wow, that is double what we have here in Route County, both in land size and in employees. So, what is it that I can help you with today?"

Tracy sat forward and quickly explained how they found a mystery man frozen to death outside of Midwest. She revealed the man's alleged name and then disclosed the finding of a hotel receipt with the same name on it located in Steamboat Springs. Deputy Tombrello furiously scribed notes that included the name, Jim Hawkins.

Tombrello paused for a second and searched her memory to see if the name meant anything to her, but it did not. Then, before she could ask another question, Tracy handed her a copy of the cryptic poem the deceased man had also carried.

After she quickly glanced at the sheet, Deputy Tombrello exclaimed, "oh, now it makes sense! So your Jim Hawkins or whomever his real name turns out to be is one of those treasure seekers around here!"

Puzzled by the revelation, Eddie asked, "you mean you know this man?"

The Route County deputy shook her head. "No, not him exactly, but for the last two years, we've had a bunch of treasure hunters scouring the mountains for a hidden treasure. They all swear that this poem directly names our area because of the words *STEAMBOAT* and *BEAR*. Some say the latter refers to Bear Lake 20 miles away."

"Are any of the treasure hunters still in town?" Tracy asked.

Deputy Tombrello shook her head once again. "No, they mostly live in tents throughout the warmer months, but by early November last year, they all returned to wherever they came from originally. Those fools can stay away for all I care because this department had to rescue a couple of men last summer when they fell into an abandoned mine that dated back to the 1860s."

Then Tombrello handed the poem back to Tracy.

"Can we go over to the Oxbow Motel and talk to the owner?" Eddie asked.

"Sure, I don't see why not? Are you parked out front?"

"We are. Just look for the Natrona County Sheriff marked Chevy Blazer."

As they stood up to leave, Deputy Tombrello asked Tracy if she wanted to ride with her, to which she nodded affirmatively. Then the Route County deputy told Eddie that he could follow behind while she led the way.

Minutes later, Deputy Tombrello and Deputy Tracy James pulled around the building and into the visitor parking area. There, they found Eddie waiting patiently with his engine already running. Tombrello then led the way, and Eddie followed in behind as planned. However, as soon as they left the parking lot, Tombrello began to ask Tracy many questions.

"So, how long have you known Sergeant Crandall?"

Tracy grinned. "Less than a week, as I recently transferred to his sector."

"Is he married?"

"Wow, that is direct! Do you have the hots for him or something?"

Tombrello tilted her head to one side. "I think he is cute, and I love his freckles. But, it makes him look a little...what is the word? Exotic!"

Tracy shrugged. "I haven't noticed since he is technically my boss." Although, in reality, she did think he was handsome, even with the freckles.

"Why not? Are you seeing anyone?"

Tracy answered curtly, "no."

While negotiating a turn over a snow-packed intersection, Tombrello briefly paused the discussion. Then, on the other side, she continued, "well, if he is available, then I suppose I am going to have to find a reason to come up there."

Tracy nodded not because she agreed but because she wanted to appear friendly. She then changed the subject when she asked about Steamboat Springs in general. Deputy Tombrello obliged by informing her that the area that made up Steamboat Springs was once a camp of the Ute Tribe. It was their favorite because of the natural hot springs and abundant wildlife, especially in the winter. Tombrello also added that the first white settlers came in the 1860s to mine gold.

As Tombrello pulled into the parking lot of the Oxbow Motel, she provided the last piece of Steamboat Springs history- the County was named after Colorado's first governor, John Route.

With Deputy Tombrello leading the way, the trio entered the office and stepped up to the small registration desk lobby. Immediately, they received a warm "hello" from a diminutively built but fit woman who had jet black hair complete with obvious streaked highlights of gray.

Then the clerk said, "Welcome to the Oxbow. Do you all need a few rooms?"

Tombrello shook her head. "No, we aren't looking to stay, but these Sheriff Deputies behind me want to ask a few questions about a man that turned up in Wyoming."

"Well, good as far as the rooms go because we are full of college kids on Christmas break up here skiing," the woman replied. She then looked directly at Eddie and Tracy and asked, "what do you want to know?"

Crandall stepped forward and introduced himself and his partner. He further explained that they drove down to Steamboat Springs from Midwest, Wyoming, to track down information of a man that stayed at the Oxbow. Then Eddie handed the woman a photograph of the mystery man.

The woman received the picture and immediately replied, "ya, I remember this guy, but I don't remember his name?"

"Does the name Jim Hawkins ring a bell?" he asked.

The woman thought reflectively for a few seconds, and then her eyes suddenly opened wide. Everyone in the room could tell that she recalled something. "I remember him now; he was one of those treasure hunters who always show up here in the spring. When he stayed here last, I remember that he stole two towels from his room when he checked out. So, what about Mr. Jim Hawkins?"

"Jim Hawkins was found dead four days ago outside of Midwest, Wyoming. We found an old receipt inside the man's vehicle from your establishment. We hoped by coming down here that we might uncover an additional clue about his identity and his history."

The woman shook her head. "I am sorry, but I don't know anything about him."

Tracy stepped forward and asked, "do you have a registration log that we can look at that indicates where Jim Hawkins calls home?"

Without remark, the woman got up from her seat at the desk and bent down to retrieve something from under the countertop. The trio could audibly hear something slide off of a shelf outside of their view. When the woman stood up, she placed an old ledger on the desktop.

"Let's have a look, shall we? Umm, what month did the receipt say?"

Tracy looked down at her notes and replied, "he checked out on October 30 of last year."

The woman quickly found the tab for October and went to the last sheet to work backward until she found Hawkins' name. After a few seconds, she announced, "I found it. He checked in here on October 24 and stayed here six days. Then, I remember something else, he told me that he had camped beneath Bear Lake for most of the last fall, but it got too cold to sleep up there in a tent."

Tracy gently asked the woman, "where did he list as his home?"

"Oh, I am sorry, dear, it says here that he is from Crook, Colorado, P.O. Box 1978. But don't ask me if I know where that is because I have no idea," the woman said.

Eddie looked at Tracy, and they both knew what their next move would be. First, he thanked the woman and then gave her his business card if she recalled anything else about Jim Hawkins. Next, in one motion, all three deputies exited the Motel lobby and met around the hood of Eddie's department-issued Blazer.

Eddie looked over to Tracy and said, "well, I guess we've finished our job here, and now we need to get to Logan County."

"Logan County?" Deputy Tombrello asked.

"The registration of the vehicle that we believe Jim Hawkins drove is the same address as the one listed on the motel ledger. It is in the town of Crook, which is in Logan County in the northeastern part of the State."

Tombrello tilted her head slightly to the right and subtly lifted her chin. "I am curious by one thing: why did the two of you drive down here? I mean, I am happy to meet with both of you, but all you had to do was call and talk to me over the phone?"

Eddie's face flushed with embarrassment, but he managed to say, "I asked that very question to my Sheriff, but he ordered us to come here personally."

The deputy then raised a single eyebrow over her left eye. Then, she suggested, "maybe your Sheriff wanted both of you out of town because he has something up his sleeve?"

Eddie and Tracy exchanged glances. Then Tombrello offered, "I know that sounds crazy, but one of our deputies here once ran contrary to his Sheriff in a neighboring county. While that deputy was out of town on vacation, the Sheriff fired him. So, I would watch my back if I were either one of you."

Eddie and Tracy exchanged glances again one more. Finally, they all traded business cards when it was time to depart, and Crandall thanked her assistance.

Tombrello accepted the professional courtesy, but then an idea came to her: "What route do you think you will be taking to get to Logan County?"

Eddie shrugged. "Well, I planned to continue on US 40 East and then take Highway 14 through the mountains to Fort Collins and then through the plains and onto Sterling."

Tombrello shook her head. "No, you will have to find another way because US 40 is closed now at Rabbit Ears Pass, and Highway 14 is closed outside of Walden."

"Well, what do you suggest?" Eddie asked.

"Do you have a map?"

"I do. Let me get it from inside the Blazer."

Eddie quickly retrieved the map and then spread it across the hood of the Blazer. Deputy Tombrello crowded in close to Eddie, so close that he felt uncomfortable. Undeterred, Tombrello traced an alternate route with her manicured fingernail along Route 131 south of Steamboat Springs, placing them on Interstate 70 at Wolcott. From there, Eddie and Tracy could drive into Denver and then take Interstate 76 to Sterling and, ultimately, Crook if they wanted to.

He abruptly stepped back from the hood, which allowed him to gain back some personal space between his body and Tombrello's. Once again, he thanked her for her help.

Once Eddie climbed into his seat, he looked over at Tracy, who sported a sly grin. Then she began to shake her head from side to side. It dumbfounded him why she did so.

Then she broke the ice. "You don't get it, do you?"

"Get what?"

"Deputy Tombrello! She is totally into you, and you are just oblivious. That is what I am getting at."

"She was just nice to me, that's all."

"Come on, Eddie, she told me that she thinks you were cute. But I also saw how your tongue practically dropped out of your mouth when we first met her. Are you going to maintain that you overlooked her clues?"

"I did see them, but I wanted to keep things professional."

Tracy shook her head. "I don't buy it, Eddie. But you must have your reasons for not acting on all these opportunities."

"What opportunities?"

Tracy sighed heavily and said in resignation, "oh, just drop it." Then after a brief pause, she asked, "before we leave town, can we stop, so I use the restroom?"

"Sure, we can do that. I need another coffee refill anyway." Eddie said and was relieved that Tracy had forgone pursuing her line of questioning.

* * *

13

Tuesday, January 7, 1992

Sterling, Colorado

6:45 a.m.

Tracy woke abruptly to the annoying sound of a ringing phone. Momentarily perplexed by her surroundings, she quickly regained her senses and remembered being in a hotel. Tracy then vividly recalled that the trek yesterday afternoon and evening from Steamboat Springs to Sterling was a long and exhausting drive. While the journey started fine with dry roads, the rest of the ride along Interstate 70 was a white-knuckled nightmare of heavy snow coupled with sheets of black ice from Vail to Denver. Further hampering the trip, three separate accidents involving tractor-trailers caused significant delays.

Turning her attention back to the phone, she reached out and grasped the receiver and pulled it close to her ear.

"Hello," she said.

"Tracy, it is Eddie. I am reminding you that we need to leave here at 7:30 to meet up with Deputy Ty Hillman from the Logan County Sheriff's Department at 8:00 for breakfast."

Tracy closed her eyes and was annoyed. "Yes, Eddie. I remember this tidbit of information from our discussion last night."

"Oh, I am sorry, I just wanted to give you a heads up. I will see you in 45 minutes," and then he hung up.

She replaced the phone onto the cradle and carefully swung both legs out of bed and onto the carpeted floor. After she rose, she walked over to the bathroom and looked at herself in the mirror. It reflected the image of her loose-fitting and extra-large t-shirt that she always wore to bed.

While she brushed her teeth, she contemplated taking a shower. But then Tracy remembered when she had tried to do so the night before and found out that her tub only ran cold water. So as she spat toothpaste into the sink basin, she grinned at the thought from the night before when she called over to Eddie's room and asked to use his shower. The thing that made her grin was that he was such a gentleman by saying yes, but he also left his room. Then he proceeded to sit out in the Blazer until she finished her shower.

Tracy looked again at herself in the mirror and asked aloud, "come on, who does that today? Is this guy from another era or what?"

Thirty-five minutes later, Eddie waited patiently inside the Blazer for Tracy to emerge from her room so that they could also check out of the hotel. His back ached from the long drive the day before. He was also tired from lack of sleep since his dreams replayed the six hours of driving through ice and snow from Wolcott to Denver. Furthermore, his mood soured when he watched the weather segment on the news earlier that morning. The meteorologist predicted blizzard conditions across Wyoming and the northern Colorado mountains starting later that afternoon. It would become imperative then to accomplish everything quickly in Crook so they could beat the storm.

Eddie looked at his watch again, which read 7:20, and still no signs of Tracy. He sighed, and he waited. The sunrise had just begun to show itself to the east through broken gray clouds. Earlier, he was pleasantly surprised about the outdoor temperature. When he went out to start the Blazer, the air felt warmer since there wasn't a hint of wind despite the nearby bank displaying 28 degrees on its marquee. Eddie further mused that he could get used to living without the daily biting wind that climatized him every Wyoming winter. Unfortunately, Tracy interrupted his thought when she opened the passenger door and threw her bag into the backseat.

"Ready to go check out?" she asked.

"I have been ready for a while," he grumbled sourly.

Tracy furrowed her brow. "Did I do something wrong? You said 7:30, right?"

However, he recognized the snarkiness in his previous reply and said, "I am sorry, you did nothing wrong. I am tired, and my back hurts. That's all."

"Apology accepted. Now, let's get checked out and get to Crook for breakfast because I am starving."

"No complaints from me. I am hungry too."

After leaving the hotel office, Eddie steered the Blazer onto US Highway 138 and headed northeasterly toward Crook. They rode in silence as they listened to the Denver radio station, KOA 850, which provided weather updates about every 15 minutes or so. To Eddie's delight, the talk show hosts spoke endlessly about the Denver Broncos' stunning come from behind victory over the Houston Oilers the previous Saturday.

Tracy passively listened while she looked out of the passenger window and became engrossed by the endless grove of Cottonwood trees growing along the northern bank of the South Platte River. Meanwhile, Eddie's attention was captivated by the farmland to the north of the highway. He contrasted the differences in agriculture between this part of Colorado and that of central Wyoming. His home state had a lot of dryland farming crops and hayfields along water courses. Still, here along the South Platte River, it seemed that every crop was either irrigated corn, beans, sugar beets, or alfalfa. Nonetheless, it pleasant ride, though, as they approached the town of Iliff, Tracy perched up in her seat.

"Eddie, slow down and turn left onto the main street for a second!" she exclaimed.

He complied but asked, "why?"

Tracy then spotted an old hand-driven water pump in the center of the town. She at the pump and said, "I wanted to see that."

"A pump?"

"Yes, a pump. Did you ever read James Michener's book called *Centennial*?"

"No, but I bet you are going to tell me about it."

She let the comment go and then explained, "I read *Centennial* a few years ago. It was written about life along the banks of the South Platte River from the days of the Arapahoe to the fur trappers to early farmers. It then culminated in modern time, albeit the early 1970s."

"Okay, but what about the pump?" he asked.

"So, I watched a television special once that interviewed Michener about his extensive research in this area of northeastern Colorado. Though he didn't identify the town of Iliff by name, there was a picture of this public hand pump that other commentators attributed to the town. Michener did, however, explain that his idea of the huge Veneford Ranch in his book was loosely based upon the Iliff ranch right here."

Eddie nodded his amusement but then looked down at his wristwatch again. He then lifted his eyes toward her and said, "very interesting, but we have to go."

"Okay, though, I think you need to read the book because you remind me of a character in it."

"Whom would that be?"

"I think you are similar to Jim Lloyd, but you will have to read the book and then tell me what you think."

"Okay, I will get a copy of the book once we get back home."

Eddie turned the Blazer right, drove one block, and turned left to return trekking northeast along US Highway 138. Along the way, the duo spotted hundreds of cattle standing alongside the roadway in empty cornfields and pastures. Interestingly, as each bovine exhaled a breath, spouts of steam funneled through each nose. Additionally, they saw large flocks of ducks and geese that flew in formations over the roadway toward the river.

A few minutes later, he spotted a school sign on the north side of the road, and he nudged Tracy to look at it. The sign read:

CALICHE
Home of the Buffaloes

Eddie grinned and looked at Tracy when he spoke, "I kind of like this place, small school, farmers, ranchers, and a lot of Cottonwood trees. Who could ask for anything more?"

Tracy tilted her head to one side and hadn't fully objected to Eddie's statement. Instead, she offered, "I could use a little more population in Sterling to bring in more shopping choices. However, I wouldn't like paying Colorado state income taxes and having a yearly vehicle safety inspection. But I do find this area of the state appealing in a strange way that I cannot explain."

He smiled and nodded. "Yep, the additional taxes in Colorado would be a limiting factor."

Just outside of Crook, Eddie reached down to find his notebook that listed the directions to where they were to meet Logan County Deputy Sheriff Ty Hillman. When he saw the piece of paper that he searched for, he handed it over to Tracy.

"Could you read off the directions to me, please? Thank you."

After reading his scribbled notes, she giggled. "You are kidding me. Where are we? Mayberry?"

Eddie frowned at the remark. "Seriously, read them off to me quickly. The edge of town is less than a quarter of a mile away."

Tracy shrugged and instructed Eddie without hiding her flippant attitude. "Okay, as you come into town, look for the gas station on your right, followed by the town park and water tower. The café is across from the park and two doors left of the Post Office."

Eddie gave her a thumbs up with his right hand. He then verbally called out each landmark. "There is the gas station, the town park, and that has to be the café with the Logan County Sheriff's Department unit sitting out front."

Tracy laughed. "You have some mad navigating skills there, Eddie. Good job!"

If he received her last comment, his face did not show it. Instead, he turned the Blazer into one of the many unoccupied parking spaces along the park side of the road. Tracy bounded out of the passenger door and waited at the rear of the unit. Meanwhile, Eddie took his time getting out since he grabbed both a file folder and a notebook before exiting.

Before crossing the Street, he looked easterly beyond the Post Office and the grain elevator. He also saw a hint of houses that began at the bend in the road. Then Eddie scanned to the west to see only two other vehicles parked at the curb outside a bar. One car was a rusted-out Toyota Corolla with white paint. The other one was a black Ford Bronco. He then looked back at Tracy and motioned for her to follow him across the street to the front door of the café.

The establishment was a quaint and cozy diner with a long counter complete with swivel top seats and high-top wooden booths on the other side. Deputy Ty Hillman was easy to spot as he rose from the second booth and immediately approached Eddie and Tracy.

Deputy Hillman shot out his right hand and greeted them, "you must be Sergeant Crandall, I am Ty Hillman, but you can call me just Ty."

Eddie accepted Ty's hand, shook it, and responded, "thanks, Ty, and you can call me Eddie. And the deputy to my right is Tracy James."

"Hello," Tracy said, and she extended out her right hand and waited for Ty to take it. She took a mental note of his 6-foot-tall and muscular frame, complete with blond hair and blue eyes.

Ty dropped Eddie's hand and shook Tracy's hand, and said, "ma'am."

Tracy gripped Ty's hand a little tighter and coached, "you can drop the ma'am stuff. I am Tracy. Secondly, when you grab a woman's hand, especially a female law officer's hand, don't be afraid you will break it. Shake my hand as you mean it."

The deputy felt a little embarrassed and showed it too when a rose-colored hue climbed up his neck and cheeks like he was a human thermometer. He gave her hand a fuller squeeze and then released it. His eyes flashed between both of them and he asked, "are you guys hungry? Why don't we take a seat?"

Eddie nodded and walked forward toward the booth though he stopped short of it and allowed Tracy to slide in first. Then he sat down next to her. Next, he wedged his notebook and the case file between his and Tracy's thighs.

Immediately afterward, the lone waitress in the café arrived at the table and carried three brown ceramic coffee mugs and a carafe of coffee and began pouring one for each of them. Eddie quickly took a sip and found the taste most appealing; however, Tracy asked the waitress for some cream. When the waitress spun on her heels to obtain retrieve some, Eddie looked across the table at his counterpart.

But what caught his attention was located just above Ty's head. The wood contained hundreds of initials left there by scores of people over the years. It seemed that the booth could tell many stories about those who once occupied the same space.

Ty spotted Eddie's gaze was attending to something above his head, and he instantly knew what had captivated his counterpart. Ty shifted in his seat and looked above him. Then turned his body back toward his guests.

"I see that you notice the initials and names carved all over, huh?" Ty questioned, and then he continued, "I carved mine in the booth behind me," he said with a chuckle.

"I have. This place reminds me of a café back home minus these booths. Though there is something to be said about a small-town café, don't you think, Ty?" Eddie mused.

"So, where did you folks say you were from again, Casper, was it?"

Tracy guffawed! "Hardly! Our assignment is in a small town 40 miles north of Casper called Midwest. It is a little bit bigger than here though we share the same distinguishable water tower."

Ty smiled and then asked, "What kind of football do you play up there? Caliche switched from 11-man to 8-man not too long ago. We have never won the state championship, but we've been in the title game once. Our girls' basketball team, though, has won three state titles."

Eddie set his coffee cup down on the table. Then he answered, "we played 9-man last year for the first time and won the state title. But, before that, we played 11-man exclusively. But in total, we've won two state championships and boast three other title game appearances."

"I have never heard of 9-man football. So why not switch to 8-man or even 6-man?" Ty asked.

Eddie shrugged. "I don't know. Wyoming just does things a little different, I guess."

After a short pause, Eddie said, "I like the look of it here based on my first impression. It reminds me a lot of being back at home."

Ty smiled and offered, "welcome to Crook then. I grew up 10 miles from here to the northeast near Jumbo Reservoir. I graduated high school in the class of '77 from Caliche High School, which you probably passed by on the way here."

Eddie nodded, and Ty continued, "Crook used to have a high school until '74 when Crook and Iliff merged into one school. After that, the elementary schools followed suit in the early '80s. Then after completing two years at Northeastern Junior College, I got hired by the department. I have served this area ever since."

Tracy smiled and nudged Eddie. "Ya, there is a lot of that going around. Eddie here has been in Midwest since he started the department back in '83."

"What about you, Tracy? Where do you hail from?" Ty asked.

She smiled. "I guess you would call me a city girl since I grew up in Cheyenne, but the small-town scene is starting to rub off on me."

Ty smiled in response, which faded quickly when the waitress arrived back at the table and handed a small tin cream dispenser to Tracy for her coffee. But before she left the table, the trio gave the waitress their breakfast orders.

"So what case are you working on that brings you here of all places?" Ty asked.

"Do you know a guy named Jim Hawkins?" Eddie asked.

"No, the name isn't familiar. Do you have a photograph for me to look at?"

Tracy quickly dug out the photograph and handed it over to Ty.

His expression immediately changed, and then he guffawed aloud and said, "that guy is Dan Pruitt!"

Eddie and Tracy exchanged confused glances with one another, and then she interjected, "okay, Jim Hawkins- Dan Pruitt, whatever, can you tell us about him?"

"I know more about him than I know of the man personally. But Dan grew up around Ovid, which is another small town just northeast of here. His aunt used to live here, though."

"Is his aunt Maude Cashman?" she asked.

"Yes, how did you know her name?" Ty inquired with a stunned look on his face.

Eddie took a deep breath and explained, "Jim Hawkins or Dan Pruitt was found dead just outside Midwest. It was apparent to us that he froze to death. We also found his car, an old Subaru Brat, which, when we ran the VIN, Maude Cashman's name showed up. So we drove down here to speak to her about the connection."

Ty dropped his head and looked down at his lap and then reached out with his right hand and lifted his coffee cup. But just before the cup reached his lip, he said, "that would make sense to me. Dan has leeched off of Maude for years." He took another sip of coffee and continued, "I hate to break it to you, but Maude died a few days ago from a heart attack. She was only 69 years old."

Eddie was both astonished and dumbfounded by the news. He looked over to Tracy, and her facial expression matched how he felt inside- a literal dead-end case.

Ty observed Eddie and Tracy as he sipped his coffee. Then he offered, "how about we go over to the Cashman place and look around to see if there are any links as to why Maude's nephew ended up in Midwest."

"Isn't that unlawful entry? I mean, don't we need a warrant?" Tracy probed.

"You are right, ma'am, um, I mean, Tracy. But her place is being watched over by Doug Campbell, who has lived with Maude for the last five years. So if he allows us in, then we are fully covered, right?"

Eddie interrupted, "I appreciate the gesture, Ty. It does seem legal if a responsible agent allows us access."

"Exactly, so how about I ride with both of you, and I will direct you where to go after breakfast," the deputy proposed.

"Why not drive and let us follow you?" Tracy queried.

With a perfect deadpan response, Ty looked directly at Tracy and said, "I don't want you both to get lost in this big town," and then he gave her a quick wink.

* * *

14

As the trio climbed into the Blazer, Eddie gently set down a large Styrofoam cup of coffee from the café on the dashboard. Tracy begrudgingly hopped up into the backseat and allowed Ty to sit in the passenger seat. After backing out of the parking slot, Ty motioned for Eddie to drive east on Highway 138. Then, at the third gravel-covered Street on the left (6th Street), Ty gestured to turn left. After they crossed the intersection of 6th Street and 3rd Avenue, Ty pointed out, "do you see the second house on the left?"

Eddie nodded, and Ty continued, "one of my favorite teachers and coaches used to live in that house with his family."

"What happened to them?" Tracy asked.

"Well, since you two are from Wyoming, it made me think of Coach. He moved to Cheyenne in the summer of '78 to work at another high school up there. He coached me in football and made me a State wrestling champion too. Sometimes I wonder about what happened to his oldest son, who used to be at every football and wrestling practice carrying his dad's clipboard? He was a nice kid and always cheered us on. Anyway, the house we seek is on the next corner. From the looks of the car in the driveway, Doug Campbell is home."

Eddie pulled into the gravel driveway of a small house with gray-colored asbestos shingle siding. Circling the entire lot were also at least a dozen Russian Olive trees. Above the door hung a wooden sign engraved with the name *Cashman*. Eddie then stopped his rig next to a sky blue 1965 Chevrolet El Camino.

For whatever reason, while Eddie waited for both Ty and Tracy to exit the Blazer, he glanced down to the license plate attached to the front of the El Camino, and it read: *UG0367*.

"*UG*," he questioned himself silently, and then he thought, "*where have I seen that before?*" Then, after a second's pause, his memory hit him like a thunderclap. Eddie felt his blood drain out of his torso and into his feet, and he felt a slight faint coming on.

"Are you okay buddy, you look like you are going to be sick?" Ty asked.

Eddie shook his head. "I'm fine," and then, "let's go."

Doug Campbell soon answered the door, and Ty Hillman explained why they were there and asked if they could enter the house to look around. Campbell was a gruff older man, and at the mention of Dan Pruitt's name, he shook his head and expelled an incoherent sound. He did, though, willingly allow the deputies to enter the house.

Campbell then pointed to the bedroom in the rear of the tiny house and said, "Dan's room is back there, but keep it down. I am watching the end of the morning news show."

Ty offered, "no problem, Mr. Campbell, we will keep it down."

They opened the bedroom door, and presumably, it looked just as Pruitt had left it. Inside was a jumbled mess of dirty laundry on the floor and an unmade bed. Against the wall between the edge of the headboard and a filthy closet sat a small desk. Papers, maps, and pictures adorned the wall above the desktop as well.

Eddie walked over and spotted something: an identical copy of the cryptic poem like the one in the file. The map next to it displayed Colorado, Utah, and Wyoming. Still, curiously, both *Steamboat Springs* and *Midwest* had bright red circles drawn around both town names. However, in the space next to Midwest, he saw "Bill" written in the same ink.

Next, he looked to the right of the map and examined four photos thumbtacked to the wall. One of them displayed Pruitt with four mallard ducks from a hunt, the following picture showed Pruitt at a lake, and the bottom two were of Pruitt with whom he assumed were a couple of his friends.

Ty stepped over to join Eddie, and he pointed to the top photo and said, "ya, Crook is one of the best spots in the West to hunt ducks, and even the mascot of old Crook High School was the Mallards."

Ty continued to the next photo and offered that the scene was Jumbo Reservoir.

Then of the third and fourth photos, Ty remarked, "that is Pruitt with his brother Billy, the dark-haired one, and one of their best friends, Marvin, the blond one."

Eddie looked closer, and he noticed the one named Billy had a narrow face, but both of the men in the picture with Pruitt had short-cropped hair. Suddenly, he had a lingering thought that the two other men looked familiar.

Tracy broke up his thoughts when she tapped him on the shoulder. Eddie turned to her, and she asked, "are we about done here? I am starting to get a little skeeved by this filth."

He understood and instructed her to take a few Polaroid shots of the desk and the wall containing the map, poem, and photos. However, as Eddie turned, he knocked against a box that sat on the floor under a discarded hooded sweatshirt. As he bent over to inspect the shoebox, Ty began to talk about the photos again.

"Ya, those three boys were a handful, let me tell you. They raised a lot of hell around here, and they were known for taking all kinds of wildlife without a license too, but nobody caught them in the act. Ya, it was a good thing Billy and Marvin went into the Army together. Special forces are what I heard."

Eddie looked back down the box and saw a stack of letters from Dan's buddies. He quickly shuffled through the envelopes and examined each of the post markings. He stopped at the very last envelope postmarked *Midwest, Wyoming*. Then it hit Eddie, Billy was William

Pruitt, and Marvin was Marvin Stiles. The same men with suspicious connections to Tim Savolt's disappearance in 1984.

Eddie abruptly stood up, and again, the blood drained from his head. He motioned for Ty and gave him the box of letters and instructed him to inquire with Mr. Campbell if he could have them. He then excused himself and walked out the front door, and leaned against the Blazer.

A few minutes later, both Tracy and Ty emerged from the house while the latter carried the box of letters, which he then promptly set on top of the hood. Then he stared at Eddie.

"What was that all about, partner? I would say it was breakfast, but what could go wrong with pancakes and bacon?

Eddie looked up to Ty. "Did Billy Pruitt and Marvin Stiles have a 1978 Ford F150?"

Ty reached up and adjusted his cowboy hat and scratched his head, and shrugged his shoulders. "I don't know, but why is that important?"

Eddie explained that when he saw the license plate with the letters *UG*, it had sparked a memory of the Savolt case since the Ford Pruitt and Stiles drove bore the same two letters. He then reached into the box of letters, pulled out the one postmarked Midwest, and quickly read aloud the one-page letter that told Dan Pruitt that they were in Wyoming doing a job. Billy also wrote that they planned to come home for a visit when they finished their work. Then Eddie carefully folded the letter and placed it back into the envelope, and set it on top of other letters inside the box.

"Savolt, huh? We have a prominent family of the same name here. I wonder if they are related?" Ty asked.

"I don't know, maybe? As far as I know, Tim Savolt had no other relatives, according to the file."

Tracy interrupted and asked, "Ty, I am confused, are Dan and Billy cousins?"

The deputy turned toward Tracy and answered, "no, not cousins; they were brothers. Billy was the oldest one, and Dan was the youngest."

"Why didn't Dan go into the military like his brother and buddy?" Eddie asked.

Ty reached up with his left hand and adjusted his hat. "Well, for one thing, Dan had a pretty long criminal record and even spent a year in prison, so I doubt that the Army would take him. As for his brother Billy, he was lucky enough to have all of his records expunged once he turned 18 years old."

Then the deputy's face flashed as if he remembered something and blurted out, "Was you there when Billy Pruitt got himself killed? We all heard about it, though very few around here were surprised if that was what you were thinking. From what I have heard, those two boys hired themselves out as mercenaries." Ty paused long enough to shrug his shoulder, then he offered, "they are just bad dudes, sorry."

Eddie answered, "no, I wasn't there when Billy Pruitt died, but I was on the scene afterward. He died while attempting to murder three high school boys, but a BLM law enforcement officer was on the scene and shot Billy. I was also involved in the four-day search looking for Stiles, but we never found him."

Ty nodded. "Yep, I wish you would have found him because I am sure he is going to show up somewhere else and probably hire himself out to kill someone else for the right price. He's the meanest one too."

Eddie nodded and feared the same reality.

* * *

15

It was noon before Eddie and Tracy left the town of Crook and their newfound friend in Deputy Ty Hillman. However, after leaving Maude Cashman's house, Ty guided Eddie and Tracy through another part of the small town. He called out other highlights like the site of the two former school buildings long ago toppled and a movie theatre that now served as the maintenance shop for a trucking company. Soon, afterward, Eddie pulled up in front of the café where Deputy Hillman left his truck. Ty then suggested they go back inside the café and order some lunch to eat on their drive back to Wyoming.

However, the once beautiful Colorado winter morning had turned into a typical January day. It was complete with heavy gray clouds that looked as if they could dump their load of snow at any time. While Eddie was still at the café and waited for their hamburgers to cook, he paid attention to the weather forecaster in Sterling. The latter noted the rapidly changing weather conditions from Cheyenne up to Casper.

Ty then suggested that they backtrack up US 138 to the west side of Iliff and take Highway 113 north to Sidney, Nebraska, where they could get onto Interstate 80 to Cheyenne.

Lastly, Deputy Hillman offered to guide them on a duck hunt the next year if they would return to northeastern Colorado. Likewise, Eddie returned the gesture by offering to take Ty antelope hunting around Midwest if he wished to do so.

As Eddie and Tracy drove away, it seemed hard to wrap his mind around the information they found out about their mystery man, Dan

Pruitt. He expressed his opinions and questions to Tracy, who sat quietly and ate from a sack of greasy but delicious French fries.

Furthermore, he feared that maybe Pruitt was in the Midwest to snoop around for a treasure and look for the person who killed his brother, Billy. Tracy shrugged, which he took as she did not know the answers.

When they passed the sign for Caliche High School once again, Tracy wadded up her hamburger wrapper and thoroughly wiped her hands clean with a half-dozen paper napkins. "I have to admit it, that was one of the best burgers I have ever eaten. Did you like yours?"

Eddie turned his head quickly, met Tracy's eyes, and then turned his attention to the road before him. "Yes, I liked mine too, but I was thinking about Deputy Hillman and giving us the grand tour of Crook."

"So, what about it?" she asked.

"Oh, nothing. I realize now that I did the same thing to you last week on your first day in Midwest."

"Are you apologizing or something? If you are, then don't. I kind of like seeing people being proud of where they live. I mean, when I first came to Casper, the only thing the other deputies told me was where I could find the mall and which bar off-duty cops and deputies met for a beer. Honestly, I still don't know much about Casper, but I do know a lot about both Midwest and Crook."

Eddie nodded. "Thank you. I appreciate the compliment."

After turning onto Highway 113 toward Sidney, Nebraska, the Blazer climbed out of the South Platte River Valley. From Eddie's vantage in the rearview mirror, the river valley looked impressive. However, once the river dropped out of sight, a single snowflake appeared. Then it hit and slowly melted on the windshield of the Blazer. Then another snowflake, then another, and within minutes, a light but steady snow started to cover the ground and the road.

Instead of following the highway back to Sidney, Eddie opted to take the interstate bypass that placed them onto westbound I-80 even quicker. With each passing mile, however, the snowfall increased. As she did the day before, when they traversed the mountain snow, Tracy remained quiet and allowed Eddie to concentrate on his driving. By the time they arrived at the eastern exit to Kimball, Nebraska, the right-hand lane had looked like a two-track pasture road. In contrast, two inches of fresh snow covered the left lane.

"You have got to be kidding me!" exclaimed Eddie as he also pounded the steering wheel with the palm of his hand.

Tracy startled out of a quick catnap at Eddie's bark and looked up and saw the thing that irritated him so.

"I-80 is closed? What are we going to do now?"

"Well, I don't know exactly, but since we have to exit, we can pull over and get some gas, and maybe I can ask a local if there is another way we can go."

When they exited the interstate, they turned off the exit ramp onto US 71. They then proceeded north and down the hill into the center of Kimball. Next, they turned into the service station at the lone traffic light and found an empty fuel pump to top off their gas tank. Tracy immediately exited the vehicle and made her way inside to use the restroom. At the same time, Eddie stayed behind and had begun fueling.

A Kimball policeman pulled up to the pump across from Eddie and stepped out as if by coincidence.

"Good afternoon, officer," Eddie greeted.

"Good afternoon, umm, you are a Sheriff's deputy, right?" the officer replied.

Eddie approached him and said, "yes, I am Sergeant Eddie Crandall from Natrona County, Wyoming. I am desperately trying to get back home today."

"Well, Sergeant, good luck with that. I-80 is closed, which you probably found out already. But you should also know that snow has socked Cheyenne, and both I-80 and I-25 are closed. So your best bet is to continue following Highway 71 here north up to Scottsbluff and hope that US 26 is open that will take you across the Wyoming border to Torrington."

"Thanks, officer, but what are the weather forecasters saying?"

The police officer shrugged. "I don't know. They keep changing their minds and their predictions. At first, they said that western Nebraska would only see a dusting of snow, and now they are predicting 7-8 inches by this evening."

Eddie didn't like the news that he just heard, but it was the hand that he was dealt and would just have to adapt. Suddenly, the handle attached to the pump nozzle "clicked," informing him that his tank was full. He replaced the pump handle in its holder, re-installed the gas cap, and went inside to pay the clerk.

As he approached the counter, Tracy came up to him and handed him a fresh tall cup of coffee. Eddie took the cup and said, "thanks."

Tracy responded, "don't mention it," and then asked him, "so what are we going to do now? Wait it out here?"

Eddie shook his head and relayed the information he had just received from the police officer about the road closures in and out of Cheyenne. He then told her they would drive north to Scottsbluff and pray that US Highway 26 was still open to Torrington.

As they headed north of Kimball, the duo only encountered light snow that danced across the highway in tiny tendrils. However, the topography changed once again as they saw miles of resting wheat fields on both sides of the road. The only thing that diverted Tracy's attention was a curious 8-foot-high steel fence that enclosed a square area.

"What do you think that is over there? Tracy asked while pointing out her passenger window.

Eddie glanced at it and replied, "that is a missile site."

"Are you sure? It doesn't look like anyone is there?" she quizzed.

"Yes, I am sure. One time, my buddy Rob pointed out the missile sites next to I-25 north of Cheyenne. He told me that each site is unmanned, and well below ground sat an Intercontinental Ballistic Missile. The ones in Wyoming are Peacekeeper missiles, and these in Nebraska are Minuteman III missiles."

After a brief pause, he continued, "But you should know Tracy, you grew up in Cheyenne. Didn't you ever go all the way down Pershing Boulevard to the front gate to F.E. Warren Air Force Base on the west end of town?"

Tracy's eyes opened wide. "Oh, those rockets at the front gate were not rockets after all. Those were missiles on display! Now that I think about it, Grand Forks Air Force Base had one too at the front gate."

"Yep. The destructive power of those things is unreal, and my buddy Rob used to say that F.E. Warren was the most powerful base in the world in terms of firepower."

Sixteen miles north of Kimball, the visibility decreased down to a quarter of a mile down as sheets of wind-driven snow blasted the Blazer from the northwest. Even worse, the temperature had dropped as well. It was only 3 p.m., but the storm had completely blocked out the sun that cast dark shadows across the land. Eddie switched on his headlights, but it seemed like they were not working. He repeatedly toggled the headlight switch with his left hand, but it didn't make a difference.

"Why are you slowing down, Eddie?"

"I am going to pull over at the crossroads at the top of this hill, and we can get out and clear off the headlights and taillights because I want to see the road and be seen by others coming up behind us."

They then exited their vehicle once at a time, which they did so for a reason. If they had opened both doors simultaneously, then all the contents inside the cab would have blown into the nearby wheat fields. But, once outside the vehicle, they rejoined again at the front bumper. There, they cleaned a thin layer of snow and ice off the headlights. But, as Tracy stood back up, she looked across the dirt road and spied something curious to her.

It was a white picketed sign that held the faded names of *Nelson, Snyder, James, and Carlson.* Next to each family name was a tiny number. She looked back at the name *James* and wondered if she had any distant relatives in this area?

"Eddie, what kind of sign is that?" she shouted through the wind.

He turned and walked up close to her to keep from yelling. Then he said, "that sign tells you who lives on this road, and the numbers indicate how many miles away from here that the farm lies. I used to see signs like these down in Kansas when I visited my grandparents in the summer."

Before he returned to the driver's side of the Blazer, Eddie bent down to wipe off the front license plate, and suddenly another idea struck him. He stood up and quickly slid behind the wheel and looked over at Tracy, who had already climbed inside.

Tracy saw that he was thinking about something from Eddie's expression, so she asked, "what's up?"

He motioned toward the backseat and then asked her, "could you get that poem out of the case file because I think I have discovered a clue."

As Tracy reached for the file, she teased him, "I hope you aren't turning into one of those treasure hunters."

"Come on, Tracy, I am serious."

"Yes, yes, you are always serious, Eddie. Hang on while I find it." She grabbed the file and set it in her lap, and began looking for the piece of paper. Then she replied, "found it. Now, what do you want to know?"

"Skip down to the line that mentions the word Steamboat and read that line out loud for me."

"Sure, it goes like this: *EVER STEAMBOAT STANDS IN FROZEN POSE,*" she said, but Eddie had cut her off.

"Steamboat stands in frozen pose! That's it! It has to be it!" he exclaimed.

"What's it?"

He turned quickly toward her and said, "follow me."

Eddie quickly stepped back out into the snow and wind and stopped at the front of the Blazer. Tracy begrudgingly abided by request and slowly opened her door. Then, she said, "okay, what do you want to show me?"

Eddie smiled and squatted down and pointed at the bucking horse symbol on their license plate. He squinted due to the wind as he looked back up to her and said, "the name of the horse that is also the Wyoming symbol is *STEAMBOAT*, and as you can see, he is standing in a frozen pose."

Tracy nodded. Yes, I see that. But can we talk about this inside the Blazer? It is freezing out here."

The drive north toward Scottsbluff became more treacherous with each passing mile as the snow continued to fall, and the wind had increased in strength. They had stopped talking about the poem as they entered the steep accent up Stage Hill that took them over the top of the Wildcat Hills to the south side of Scottsbluff. The climb turned out to be easy, but the descent was treacherous at best. Twice the Blazer started to skid, and both times Eddie successfully made minor corrections with the steering wheel that straightened out the vehicle.

After the highway opened up into the bottomland, Eddie then asked Tracy to find a local radio station to get a road report. She complied and found several signals but settled on AM 960 KNEB. Within minutes of tuning into the station, the commentator mentioned that US 26 was closed westbound at the Wyoming border and cautioned all travelers to seek shelter to wait out the storm.

They followed the Highway 71 bypass around the west side of Scottsbluff instead of going through downtown Gering on the south side of the North Platte River. Eddie then turned right onto 27th Avenue because it looked as good of a place as any to find a hotel for the night. Tracy immediately spotted a candidate called the Oregon Trail Motor Lodge and suggested Eddie give it a try.

Later, after checking into their rooms, they once again loaded into the Blazer with hopes of finding a grocery store where they could buy some food. Tracy had suggested it because she was a little sick of restaurant cuisine and also openly opined that she had put on at least five pounds on the trip. Though Eddie mentally disagreed with her assessment about her appearance, he, too, craved something different.

Soon, they returned to their hotel, and each carried a small paper bag. At the store, Tracy purchased a premade salad along with a banana. Conversely, Eddie bought a deli sandwich and a small container of coleslaw. Finally, they each said goodnight and entered adjacent rooms from one another.

Once inside his room, Eddie turned on the television to stay abreast of the weather. Then, he sat down in the chair next to a dinette table to eat his dinner. Unfortunately, he didn't have the luxury of a remote-controlled television, which forced him to get up to change the stations manually. Still, at least, it was cable tv. While taking a bite of the sandwich, he looked around his room. Generally, it looked perpetually stuck in the 1970s based on the décor.

Later that night, Eddie awoke to several thoughts that raced through his head. First, he rolled over and turned on the small lamp on the nightstand next to the bed. Eddie then swung both legs out of bed, walked over the case file marked *Jim Hawkins*, picked up a pen, drew a single line through the name, and wrote the words *Dan Pruitt* in its place. He then took the file and his notebook over to the bed, where he set both of them down on the floral-patterned bedspread.

He then withdrew a copy of the poem and began to decipher a few more items, and he quickly wrote down a few ideas in his notebook. Finally, he briefly thought about waking up Tracy to talk to her about his intimations. But he opted to wait until morning to speak to her. So, Eddie placed the file and his notebook aside and once again turned on the television.

The news channel out of Denver aired nonstop coverage of the storm that blanketed most of Wyoming, western Nebraska, and northeastern Colorado, including the Denver metropolitan area. As a result, Eddie has only one glimmer of hope of getting back to Casper and then onto Midwest: he would have to hope that the storm would subside before sunup. And only then would the snowplows begin clearing the roads.

Eddie knew that he would have to call Sheriff Doan in the morning to give him a progress report, and oh how he dreaded the prospect of talking to the man, period.

* * *

16

Wednesday, January 8, 1992

Scottsbluff, Nebraska

The rumbling sound of snowplows rolling down 27th Avenue startled Eddie awake. He looked over to the clock radio next to the bed, and it indicated 7:45 a.m., and he rolled back over again and stared at the ceiling. Then, his mind initiated an inventory of tasks to do that day. At the top of the list included calling Sheriff Doan and ended with the daunting task of driving from Scottsbluff to Midwest over snow and ice-covered roads.

But first, Eddie decided to get up out of bed and go to the bathroom, where he brushed his teeth, shaved his face, and finished by putting on his customary uniform. Then, since the room did not come with a coffee maker, he instead put on his coat to walk over to the office for a complimentary cup.

When he closed his room door behind him, he turned and approached the adjacent door just a few feet to his right and gently rapped on the panel. He heard nothing but silence. He rapped on the door again, but this time a little harder, yet still no answer. Confused, Eddie turned and looked at the department Blazer. It was parked in the same position that he left it in the night before. *"Perhaps she is in the shower?"* he thought to himself and resolved to try again after he found a cup of coffee.

While Eddie walked down an icy sidewalk toward the office, he spotted a speeding snowplow that threw a cascade of snow off the road. But as his eyes shifted back to the parking lot, he marveled at the 6 inches of undisturbed snow. But Eddie also noted the morning air was frigid too. It was so cold that his breath caused a large cloud of condensation that seemed to obscure his view of the path. Additionally, an icy breeze stung his face and ears when he rounded the corner to enter the motel office.

Eddie quickly entered the office and made sure the door had shut behind him. Then he stamped his feet on the doormat to remove any snow that clung to his cowboy boots.

"Good morning," rang out in a familiar voice.

He turned to his right and found Tracy sitting at a small table next to the front window that soaked up the fragile morning sunlight that filtered into the room.

"There you are, and good morning to you too. I knocked on your door just a few minutes ago, and I figured I would find a cup of coffee and then try you later."

"So, what is on the docket today, Eddie? Getting home, I hope?"

"Yes, getting home is a priority, but first, I have to call Sheriff Doan with an update on the case."

"You mean cases, don't you?"

His eyebrows pinched together as he struggled to connect what she had implied and indicated. So he asked, "cases? What are you inferring?"

Tracy sat up straight and was a little energized by the fact that she, for the first time, was taking the lead in something.

"Yes, cases. We know that Jim Hawkins is Dan Pruitt from Crook, Colorado, and he was searching for treasure in both Steamboat Springs and outside of Midwest. We also revealed some new information into the Savolt case by linking William Pruitt and Marvin Stiles to Crook, Colorado as well."

Her observation made him stop and think. Finally, after a long pause, he turned and made his way across the motel lobby. There the deputy found a stainless steel 30-cup coffee maker on a small table. He lifted a paper cup from the stacked sleeve and then filled it. Then Eddie slowly turned and looked around the room.

The lobby was empty except for the desk clerk and one other hotel guest who seemed engrossed in a newspaper spread out on the table. The only quirk that Eddie noticed was the man had a large camera case with him, and it too sat on top of the table. Only after he satiated his thirst with a sip of coffee did he return to Tracy's table.

"You put all these facts together very well, Tracy. Good job. But for the life of me, I don't know how knowing these facts now justified the expenses of sending two Sheriff deputies across three states. Again, we could have handled this with a few phone calls." Then he blew a pin-pointed breath over the top of his cup to cool his coffee.

Tracy shrugged. "I don't know, but it has been fun ...."

Eddie cut her off mid-sentence and cautioned, "yes, I have enjoyed the road trip too, but we had best keep that sort of comment to our-selves. If the other deputies in the department hear anything of us hav-ing any fun, there will be hell to pay for both of us."

Tracy shrugged again and indicated that she understood when she said, "I got it. My lips are sealed."

"Good. I am going to go back to my room to prepare for my phone call with the Sheriff. Do you want to help?"

Tracy immediately rose out of her seat. "Sure, lead the way."

"Okay, but first, let me ask the desk clerk something," and he turned and walked five steps over the desk. "Excuse me, Sir, but do you know if US 26 is clear over the Wyoming line?"

The clerk looked up at Eddie from his seat and replied, "yes, I saw it on the news this morning. US 26 is open to Guernsey but is closed there to I-25. Is that where you are heading this morning?"

Both Eddie and Tracy nodded affirmatively, and the clerk continued, "well, good luck then. I hope you make it where you need to safely."

Eddie expressed a simple "thank you," and they left the lobby.

Instead of walking the square framed sidewalk back to their rooms on the far side of the motel, they decided to cut over the snow-covered parking lot. Tracy made five steps and slipped on a hidden sheet of ice under the snow. Eddie immediately extended out his right arm and grabbed her around the shoulders. She regained her balance by placing her right hand against the side of a black Ford Bronco parked next to them.

"What is it with you and ice? he asked.

Tracy laughed and snapped back a quick reply, "I know, I keep you on your toes, don't I?"

Unamused by her comment, Eddie balanced Tracy over the snow and ice to the far side of the parking lot.

His room was tidy, to her surprise. For one thing, his bed and looked like he had found it the night before. The other thing Tracy noted was that Eddie's travel bag was already packed and ready to go at any moment. She quietly felt ashamed that her room looked like a train wreck compared to his though she adroitly hid her embarrassment. Then she took a seat next to the small table near the window. Meanwhile, Eddie gathered up his notebook and the case file and brought them over to the table and sat them down, and took a seat himself.

Eddie shook his head. "We have some pretty thin facts here...."

She cut him off. "Eddie, the case on Jim Hawkins or Dan Pruitt is still open. First, the man came to Midwest to search for a treasure, and he froze to death. Second, he used a false identity for whatever reason, and he has no living relatives. Third, it appears that the man also went to Midwest seeking to avenge his brother's death. I would stick to those facts with Sheriff Doan and nothing more and nothing less."

Eddie indicated that he understood her with a quick nod. Then, he spun around and grabbed the telephone off the nightstand, and set it on the small table between them. Next, he reached into the right-hand back pocket of his jeans and removed his wallet. Then he opened it and pulled out a long-distance calling card.

The call connected after a series of number entries, and the Sheriff's office assistant soon answered it.

"Hi Sherry, this is Sergeant Crandall. Is the Sheriff available?"

"Oh, hi Eddie, let me check. Is it okay that I place you on hold?"

"That is fine, thanks."

Sheriff Doan picked up his line from inside his office after making Eddie sit on hold for five minutes. It irked him a little that the long wait had burned up precious minutes on his personal pre-paid phone card. However, after exchanging salutations, Eddie immediately relayed the facts that he and Tracy had found out in the case. Sheriff Doan seemed satisfied with their work as he usually criticized his findings.

Doan's only negative retort was the added travel expense of staying an extra night in Scottsbluff, Nebraska. Eddie argued that he didn't have a choice since all the roads into Wyoming were closed due to the storm. The explanation fell on deaf ears as the Sheriff again complained about the cost. The phone call ended with Doan explicitly and repeatedly insisting that Eddie and Tracy be present for a department-wide meeting at 9:00 a.m. the next day. But, before he could acknowledge the request, the Sheriff abruptly hung up.

Meanwhile, Tracy sat by quietly while she listened to the conversation. From her vantage point, it disgusted her to hear the Sheriff's smug voice that offered nary support nor appreciation for their efforts. She wondered internally why she still believed that she could succeed in the department even though the Sheriff would never let that happen.

The contortions of Tracy's face amused Eddie as he watched her move from a scowl to a pout and then to a blank, emotionless stare. At the same time, she rolled something over in her mind.

"What are you thinking?"

She shrugged. "Nothing that you want to hear because you will remind me of being loyal to our leader."

Eddie raised his eyebrows and silently agreed with her on that point but changed the subject quickly when he offered, "how about we go get some breakfast and then hit the road? We still have a drive ahead of us."

She remarked curly, "sure," and then rose out of her seat and left his room to collect her belongings.

* * *

ighway 26 west of Scottsbluff was open but was also slick in spots
as they proceeded through the Nebraska towns of Mitchell and
Morrill and all of the way to Torrington. Once in Wyoming, there was a
discernible increase in snow, mainly evidenced by the large drifts. Meanwhile, the slow drive allowed Eddie and Tracy to share thoughts about
deciphering the code within the cryptic poem found in Dan Pruitt's
possession. Additionally, Eddie relayed his ideas from the previous night
that the following lines from the poem now made sense to him:

DISAPPEARING TREES GIVE WAY TO GRASS
WELL DOWN THE COURSE OF PILGRIM'S PASS

He reasoned that the course of pilgrim's pass was, in fact, the Oregon
Trail. When Tracy didn't seem to follow his intimation, Eddie further
explained that the Oregon Trail began on the western bank of the Mis-
souri River. It was also the location where the midwestern forest gave
way to endless grasslands.

She listened patiently and did not disrupt him, nor did she question
his hypothesis. When he completed his thoughts, she agreed because it
just made sense. Tracy then pulled out the poem again and told Eddie
that she would figure out the first two lines while he drove.

Once again, they rode in silence as they had at many other points
during their now four-day journey. The only times Tracy made a sound
was when she looked up from the paper in her hand and spotted another Volkswagen Beatle, and punched Eddie in the arm and shouted,

"punch bug!" After each incident, he shook his head and wondered aloud about the many Volkswagens out on the road.

Just east of Fort Laramie, Eddie jolted Tracy's attention away from the poem when he abruptly tapped on the brakes of the Blazer. After lifting her eyes off the paper and onto the road, she watched in horror as an oncoming tractor-trailer began jackknifing a half of a mile ahead of them. Then, instinctively, she placed her hands on the dashboard to brace herself. However, Eddie expertly brought the Blazer to a stop.

As fate would have it, the tractor-trailer slid off the south side of the road without hitting another vehicle. Immediately, Eddie turned his emergency light bar with a switch mounted just below their radio and moved his rig into the oncoming lane. Once there, he parked the Blazer across the road to stop traffic.

Eddie quickly unbuckled his seat belt and exited the Blazer to check on the truck driver. Simultaneously, Tracy grabbed the microphone off its cradle and turned the radio on and selected the statewide mutual aid channel, and broadcasted her position with a complete description of the scene. Additionally, she requested an ambulance for the truck driver.

A highway patrolman responded first on the radio and said she was on US 85 north of the town Lingle and was en route. Then a Goshen County Sheriff's Deputy reported that he could arrive on the scene within 5 minutes. Assured that help would soon arrive, Tracy put on her department coat and hat and stepped out to direct traffic around the accident scene.

When Eddie walked over the edge of the road toward the ditch drifted deep with snow, he noted that the truck had pushed through a barbed-wire fence. The cab of the semi was also against the end of a sizeable pivoting irrigation walker. Upon opening the driver's side door, he saw a broken windshield to the flat-faced Kenworth cab-over tractor.

But, worse, a piece of the damaged irrigation sprinkler had impaled the driver through the shoulder that pinned him to the seat.

The man was conscious and answered Eddie's questions. He then walked around the tractor's front and climbed into the passenger seat to view the wound closer. There was blood everywhere on the chair, and it dripped onto the floor mat between the two tractor seats.

Eddie reached behind the seat and half-pulled and half-ripped a discarded t-shirt that he then used to apply pressure to the wounds to abate further blood loss. Meanwhile, he incessantly talked to the man to thwart him from passing out due to blood loss and shock. Eddie knew that if help didn't arrive soon that the driver could lose his arm at the very least, and at the worst, the man could lose his life.

Just then, the wind picked up and blew a huge gust that blasted snow across the surface of the ground before the tractor. However, in doing so, the force of the wind rocked the truck enough for the impaling piece of metal to sink further through the man's shoulder. The driver shrieked in pain and started to lose consciousness, but Eddie slapped him on the cheek with his open right hand.

Then Eddie shouted, "come on, stay with me, buddy. Help is on the way. Stay with me."

He continued the routine until long after hearing the sirens of other responders arriving on the scene. Eddie stayed at his post until a paramedic relieved him and requested that he exit the tractor.

Outside the semi, Eddie reached down and scooped up a couple of handfuls of snow and scrubbed the driver's blood off of his hands. Then, he walked up to the road and over the back of his unit, where he opened the back tailgate and found a clean rag to wipe his hands.

"Good work, Sergeant," called out an unfamiliar voice behind him. When Eddie turned his head, he was surprised that the voice belonged to the Goshen County Sheriff Dwayne Keller, who also responded to the scene.

Eddie looked down at his right hand again and verified it was clean, and then reached out and shook the Sheriff's hand. He replied, "thank you, Sheriff, but no thanks needed. My partner and I were just doing our job."

The Sheriff smiled and let go of Eddie's grip. "Well, lucky for that driver that you were Johnny on the spot here. You probably saved his life, you know?"

Eddie nodded in reply but remained notably silent.

"So, what brings you and your partner down here from Natrona County? Did you transfer a prisoner down to the Torrington prison?"

He reached up with his left hand and slowly adjusted his hat. He then looked up and answered the Sheriff.

"No, Sir, we were running down some leads on a case we are working on that started in Steamboat Springs. Then we went over to Logan County, Colorado. But then the storm forced us to spend the night in Scottsbluff. So today, we were just trying to get home when all of this happened in front of us."

"I see...so, Casper is home for you?" the Sheriff asked.

"No, Sir, well for Tracy it is, but I live out in Midwest. Have you ever heard of it?"

"Are you kidding? I know Midwest. I played football for Guernsey from 1982 to 1985, and we played the Oilers once at home and twice in Midwest. Does it still smell like rotten eggs on the outside of town?"

"It does on some days but not all the time like it did a few years ago. So, I saw you play then, both in '83 and in '85. The Salt Creek community was my first and only assignment that began in the summer of 1983."

"It is a small world, isn't it, Sergeant?"

"Yep, it is, Sheriff." Then after a short pause, he asked, "can I ask you a question?"

"Sure."

"How did you get to become Sheriff so quickly? I mean, don't take offense, but you are younger than me, and you have already achieved something I can only dream of at this point in my career?"

Sheriff Keller shifted his gaze momentarily toward the tractor-trailer in the ditch and then glanced back at Eddie.

He cleared his throat and said, "for one thing, I was fortunate to keep my nose clean in my early years. Secondly, when the State of Wyoming DCI did a sting operation on my department, both the presiding Sheriff and Undersheriff were implicated in accepting bribes a few years back. I am sure you heard about it. So, I figured, what the heck? And I put my name on the ballot, and I won by the skin of my teeth. So, that is how it all came to pass."

"I appreciate your humble nature, Sheriff. I surely do."

Then Tracy walked up to Eddie, and he introduced her to Sheriff Keller. The Sheriff then informed them that they were free to go, and the good news was that US 26 was snow-free to I-25. However, as they turned to get into their vehicle, Sheriff Keller stopped them.

"I just want you both to know that I am going to write a letter of commendation for each of you. I know your boss, Sheriff Doan, all too well, and I also know that he treats most of his employees like dirt. And oh, before I forget, here is my business card for both of you. If either of you gets tired of Natrona County, give me a call. You can always find a place on my staff."

Eddie let the snide comment about his boss go without retort, but he thanked Sheriff for the kind gesture.

The anticipated drive to Casper that started off as a half-day prospect had further delayed the duo because of the accident. Further impeding their travel were the sloppy road conditions throughout the remainder of the drive along US 26. Providentially for Eddie and Tracy, I-25 was clear of snow, and, more importantly, it was dry.

Soon after they merged onto the interstate, Tracy had resumed her task of deciphering the poem. Then, just outside of the city of Douglas, she exclaimed, "ah-ha!"

"What did you find?"

"I got it, well, I think I do. Let me read you this line: *MUTTS FALL EASILY INOT INIQUITY*. It doesn't have anything to do with a dog; rather, mutt is another name for a fool."

"Okay, but what about the rest of the line?"

"I was just getting to that, *iniquity* is generally another term for evil or sin, but it can also mean an error. So, if I got the translation right, the line means that 'fools fall easy into error.'"

"Okay," he said abruptly, and hoped she would continue.

She did. "The next line: *INKLINGS ADHERENCE BECOMES NECESSARY* means that 'following clues is a must.' So, what do you think?"

"I think you did well, though I am not as well read as you are, and I don't think I have enough smarts to help you with interpreting most of the poem."

"Stop it, Eddie! You are too smart enough; you just need to trust your instincts. So, please, I need you to think about is this: *SURMOUNT THE FLOW AT GHOSTLY PROSE* and tell me what you think it means."

"Fine," he replied curtly and focused his attention back on to the road.

The two of them continued to ride in silence even after they entered the Casper city limits. Finally, Eddie took the Poplar Street exit and followed the road south up and over the railroad overpass. He then slowed the Blazer to a complete stop at the stoplight at the intersection with US 26 as it exited Casper to the west. After the light turned green, Eddie proceeded across the highway, over the North Platte River, and next to the hulk of the Amoco Oil refinery. Then he noticed a sign for Fort Caspar at 13th Street, and something jolted him as if struck by lightning.

Eddie asked aloud, "What does *SURMOUNT* mean?"

Tracy shrugged. "Without a thesaurus, I believe it means to overcome."

Suddenly, his face drained of all color like something shocked him.

Tracy quizzed, "what? It looks like you have seen a ghost."

Eddie cracked a small smile. "Exactly."

She failed to understand his implication and shook her head in response. But, before asking for clarification, Eddie provided it.

"As we drove back into town, I began dreading tomorrow's meeting with the Sheriff and all of his suck-ups that have nicknamed me Casper the Ghost. But, when I saw the sign for Fort Caspar, it dawned on me that Fort Caspar was once a place to cross over the North Platte on the Oregon Trail. Next to the bridge that takes you over to the town of Mills is an old sign marking both the fort and the river crossing. I bet that *SURMOUNT THE FLOW AT GHOSTLY PROSE* means 'overcome the river at ghostly writing.' At least, that is what I am thinking."

Tracy thought for a few seconds and replied, "yes. Yes, it does. See, I told you that you have some smarts. I knew the definition of prose too but couldn't connect it until now."

He gave a quick shrug and said it was purely a guess. But, unfortunately, before Eddie could talk further on the subject, Tracy's apartment building came into view. So, instead, he pulled into the parking lot and stopped alongside the sidewalk, saving Tracy from walking across the ice. But, after looking at the ice, Eddie surmised that it looked even thicker than it had days before.

As she opened her door, Tracy thanked Eddie for his safe driving throughout the trip, and the compliment made him blush. However, he was thankful that it was dark enough outside that she couldn't see him. They both exchanged a quick "see ya," and just like that, their adventure together was over.

Twenty-five minutes later, Eddie took the offramp from I-25 at the exit for Wyoming Highway 259. He noted that the night sky overhead was cloud-free. For the first time in days, Eddie could identify stars and constellations. By the time he neared the end of the offramp at the Yield sign, he had spotted the Big Dipper and mused over its Latin name: *Ursa Major*. Suddenly, Eddie pressed the brake pedal and skidded to a stop. He spoke aloud to himself, "Big Bear." Then another thought jolted him.

THE OMNIPRESENT BEAR POINTS THE WAY!

* * *

Thursday, January 9, 1992

On the outskirts of Gas Plant

In the pre-dawn light, Eddie stood on the high bank of Castle Creek while looking over to the exact location where the boys found Dan Pruitt's body. Even though the sun would not rise for another hour, it was light enough to see, and Eddie made out the topography well enough.

It had been one week since the discovery of the body, though to him, it felt like it had been a month. Maybe it was all the driving or all of the snow that made it seem so long, but it did not feel like it had only been seven days.

The air was freezing that morning, and according to Eddie's thermometer outside of his kitchen window, it was only 11 degrees. Fortunately, the snowstorm that blanketed Nebraska, Colorado, and southeastern Wyoming had only left two inches of powder snow in the Salt Creek community.

Still, Eddie could not pinpoint why he felt obligated to drive out to the site of Dan Pruitt's death that morning. Though, as soon as he finished his daily Bible reading earlier, he felt inclined to go. Eddie reasoned that visiting this spot was God's way of showing him the results of living a life only for one's selfish desires, like Pruitt.

"Good morning, Sergeant Crandall," said a small voice behind Eddie that interrupted his thoughts.

He turned slightly and spotted young Wesley Corbin, who stood only a few feet away. Instead of replying to the boy, Eddie bent over, grabbed Wesley's coat's zipper, and pulled it up to the top to close it entirely.

"There you go. I wouldn't want you to catch a cold. But, my, you are up early. What are you doing out here? Don't you have school this morning?" Eddie asked.

"I do, but I saw you drive by my house a while ago, so I thought I would come to check things out," the boy stated.

"Have you been coming out here a lot, Wesley?"

"Only a couple of times with my buddy, Stu."

"So, what did you find?"

Wesley looked back at the deputy with a confused look. So, Eddie repeated his question, "what did the two of you find?"

The boy shifted his eyes down to Castle Creek, then looked toward Midwest in the distance. Then he turned his head toward the Rimrocks that loomed before him. He looked everywhere but directly at Eddie for fear that he would be in trouble.

"It is okay, son. You are a lot like me in that we both like finding answers. So, again, what did you find?"

Wesley shifted his feet, and after 30 seconds of silence, he finally reached into the pocket of his coat and produced a man's wallet. He lifted his hand and placed it on Eddie's outstretched palm.

He took the wallet and said, "thank you, Wesley. Where exactly did you find it?"

The boy pointed southwest along Castle Creek and then said, "Stu and I walked from here to that pump jack over there, and we found that wallet and a set of car keys."

Suddenly, he stood erect in reaction to Wesley's story. Eddie dropped his gaze onto the thin nylon wallet in his hand. He pulled on the wallet flap with his other hand and slowly peeled back the Velcro strip that fastened it together. Inside the fold were $17 in mixed bills, a driver's license, and an ATM card.

Eddie looked back at Wesley. "Where are the car keys now?"

The boy grimaced. "Stu has them."

He took a deep breath and let out a massive column of condensed breath in the cold air. Eddie instinctively knew that the boys didn't do anything technically wrong. However, he also knew that if he went over to Stu's house, it would cause two sets of parents to come down on the boys. So, when Eddie lifted his head, an idea struck him.

"Wesley, when you talk to Stu in a little bit, ask him to fetch the keys from his room and then take them to school with you."

"But what are we supposed to do with them at school, Sergeant?"

"As soon as you get off of the bus, I want you to walk over to the high school wing and give those keys to Mr. Crooks. He will hold them for me."

"Why do you want me to give them to Mr. Crooks?"

"Don't worry about that, Wesley, just do what I ask, please."

The boy gave a quick shrug and mentioned that he had to get back to the house to get ready for school. Eddie remained still while watching the boy walk away and make a new trail in the snow. Finally, however, a glance at his watch revealed that he, too, needed to leave. So he climbed into his department Blazer and slowly drove across the open field and then onto Ash Street.

Eddie went west until arriving at the last house on the right. He then pulled his Blazer onto the paved parking pad, exited his rig, and walked up the short sidewalk. The soles of his boots made a squeaking sound with each step on the snow. But, of course, that particular phenomenon only occurred when the outside temperature was frigid.

At the top of the steps, Eddie rapped on the front door and waited for an answer. Lois Crooks opened the door and said, "good morning, Eddie. Please come in, will you? It is freezing out there."

He said, "thank you," and removed his hat when he crossed the door threshold into the living room, and he stamped his feet on the floormat.

Bill Crooks walked into the living room, and he carried two cups of coffee, and without a word, he handed one of them to Eddie.

After they each sat down, Bill asked, "what were you doing this morning over by Castle Creek?"

Eddie shrugged. "I don't know, just thinking, I guess."

"So, you have been gone four days. Where are you at with the case?"

He gave Bill the details on what they had found in Colorado. Then, he spoke about their hypothesis that Dan Pruitt had come to the Midwest to look for treasure and possibly seek revenge for his brother's death.

Bill let out a gruff, "well, it is a good thing Pruitt didn't live long enough to carry out his retribution, don't you agree?"

Eddie nodded and then handed Bill the wallet. He then explained that Wesley and Stewart found it along Castle Creek.

Bill looked at it and asked, "what do you want me to do with this?'

"I want you to open it. Then tell me if there is anything peculiar inside it?"

Crooks abruptly opened the wallet, which made a loud zip sound as the Velcro flap let loose. He examined the bill holder flap and counted the money, then pulled out a Colorado driver's license with Dan Pruitt's name on it. Strangely, a white paper business card fell into Bill's lap in the process. He picked up the paper, which read: *Sheriff John Doan*. The business card also listed his office address and phone number on the front side. Conversely, the reverse side had another local phone number written in blue ink.

Bill looked up and stared at Eddie, but before he could speak, Crandall pre-empted him, "I am asking myself the same question: why does Dan Pruitt have Sheriff Doan's card in his wallet? Am I right?"

Crooks nodded and then replaced the driver's license and the business card precisely as he found it and closed up the wallet. "So, tell me, Eddie, what do you want to do?"

Without hesitation, he responded, "I want you to hang onto that wallet and the set of keys that Wesley will bring by your classroom in a little while. I am officially transferring evidence to you since the area where the boys found the articles fall squarely on BLM land, which is your jurisdiction.

Bill nodded. "But now answer my question, what are you going to do about Sheriff Doan since he is involved somehow now?"

Again, Eddie did not hesitate. "I will let him know about someone finding Pruitt's wallet and that it is in BLM custody. Then I will play the waiting game, you know, just like when we question a suspect? I will wait to see what he does next. I am certain his actions will determine why he is involved."

Bill grimaced. "Thanks a lot. Now the Sheriff will be barking at me to hand over evidence. But you know something? The wheels of the government turn slowly, and the federal government moves at a snail's pace. I think I can stave off Doan for a week or so."

Eddie smiled and patted Bill on the back and said, "I know it moves slow. I am banking on it."

Both men sat quietly together as they finished their cups of coffee. Then Eddie stood up, handed Bill his empty cup, and bid him farewell.

While en route back to Midwest, Eddie glanced down to his wristwatch, which indicated 7:10 and still 20 minutes from sunrise. He knew that he had to leave for Casper to make his mandatory Sheriff's Department meeting by 8:00 that morning by the latest. Eddie abruptly changed his mind, and, instead, turned onto Lewis Street rather than returning home.

He then drove the length of the town and passed the school on his right, and he traversed the cattle guard that demarked the town limits. Finally, he progressed on Highway 387 to Edgerton. Then he came to a stop outside of the Edgerton branch of the Natrona County Library.

From the street, Eddie spied Katrina Alvarez's dark Blue Nissan 4 X 4 pickup parked behind the building. The lights were also on inside the lobby. So, he got out of the Blazer and walked up to the large glass door and rapped on it with enough force to make noise but not enough power to break the brittle glass from the cold. Then Eddie watched as

Katrina looked up from behind the checkout desk, quickly rose out of her seat, and approached the door.

Katrina opened it an inch or two and said, "I am not open until eight. Can you wait until then, Eddie?"

"I am sorry for any inconvenience, Katrina, but I have to leave for Casper in a few minutes. I wanted to see if my materials have arrived."

Katrina took a deep breath and let out a long sigh, and said, "okay, come on in."

"Thank you, I sincerely appreciate it."

"I know you do Eddie, that is why I am doing you this favor."

Once inside the building, he approached the checkout counter while Katrina went into the back room and returned with a stack of papers. She then placed the materials on the desktop.

After adjusting her glasses she said, "so, here is what we found on micro phish slides at the main library. All of these pieces of paper are from magazine articles about Arthur G. Daniels."

Eddie furrowed his brow. "Have you read over them? I mean, is there anything interesting in there?"

She smiled. "Tons of stuff, Eddie!"

Next, Katrina proceeded to inform him all about Arthur Daniels' career with the Standard Oil Company. Ironically, it was the same company that owned most of the oil rights around Salt Creek after buying out Midwest Oil years ago. It also appeared that Arthur had a great mind. His genius led to the discovery and the large-scale production of polyethylene terephthalate. Before Eddie could ask a question, Katrina explained further that the chemical name was more commonly known as polyester fiber. She also informed him that Arthur had lived in Hammond, Indiana, until he died.

Eddie nodded but then opined, "that still doesn't account for why he wrote the poem."

Katrina also nodded in agreement. "Well, we still do not have all the information in yet. The librarian I spoke to in Casper informed me that she would need some extra time to print out the rest of the stuff she found."

"When will that be?"

The librarian shrugged. "Perhaps by Monday or Tuesday, so check in with me then, but next time, do it after I open."

Eddie grinned back at her sheepishly, and he picked up the stack of printouts and left the library.

* * *

19

Sheriff's Department Headquarters

Casper, Wyoming

An hour and 15 minutes after leaving the library in Edgerton, Eddie arrived in a large briefing room equipped with four rows of tables and fifty folding chairs. He was the second person to enter since he despised being late to anything. Incredibly, the other early arrival was none other than his trainee.

Tracy's face lit up when Eddie approached, and she patted the table next to her that meant she had saved him a seat. First, however, Eddie walked over to a side table and refilled his travel mug with coffee from the 30-cup maker. Next, he looked over the rest of the table, saw nothing but donuts, and decided to pass.

Eddie took his seat next to Tracy and said, "good morning."

Tracy beamed and repeated, "good morning." Then she shifted in her seat and asked him, "so, what are your plans this weekend, Saturday specifically?"

He thought for a second. Then he answered, "well, tomorrow I have to operate the clock for the junior high basketball games. But I don't have any plans on Saturday since both the boys' and girls' high school teams are on the road. So, what are you thinking?"

"I was hoping that you could help me move? I called Liz Duggan last night, and she said she would rent me one of the small houses she owns in Midwest."

"How did you get her number?"

Tracy smiled, "That is a funny story. I called the café in Edgerton and told the person who answered the phone who I was and asked for Liz's phone number. I just have to say, wow, are you small-town folks are trusting souls!"

"What street is the house located on?"

"It is two blocks from you on Watson Street. But my only snag is getting out of my current lease. I talked to my landlord, and she said that I could break my rental agreement without penalty. But I need to provide an official statement from a person of authority in the department to authenticate my reassignment out of Casper."

Eddie shrugged. "We could ask the Undersheriff to sign something today. He is a reasonable man and wouldn't hesitate to help."

"Okay, great, I will talk to him right after the meeting. So, can you help me move? I don't have a ton of stuff, just my bed, a couch, a television, and a bunch of boxes. So, how about it, will you help me?"

Eddie knew that he would struggle to say "no," so he didn't. "Yes, I can help you. But how about I find a trailer that we could use to get everything in one trip."

"Oh, that would be awesome, thank you!" In her excitement, she started to reach out to give him a quick hug, and then she caught herself because they were in uniform and on duty.

As if flood gates of a dam opened up, scores of uniformed Deputies filed into the room, and they quickly took up seats near and around them.

It seemed to everyone present that Sheriff Doan waited until 9:05 before entering the briefing room to create a dramatic entrance. He walked with laser focus to the podium and promptly greeted everyone. First, Doan spoke of the department's performance markers, like the number of investigations completed, the number of traffic citations, and prison control efforts. Then the Sheriff discussed the department's budget and announced some new changes.

Next, he pointed directly at Tracy and instructed her to turn in the department sedan. He further explained that she could ride around with Eddie in "that one-horse town," which raised a cacophony of laughs and jeers. Finally, one deputy quipped from the back of the room that "Casper doesn't need a vehicle; he is a ghost that can float across the ground." Worse yet, Sheriff Doan even joined in on the laughter. Only then did he raise his hands to quiet the room.

"I have another policy change to announce. From now on, I want all of you to keep things professional between male and female deputies. What I mean is, I am not against intra-department dating. However, I don't want to see nor hear about anyone playing handsy or footsy with anyone else while in uniform and on duty. If I do, you will find yourself out of a job!"

The comment hit Tracy hard since she was one of only three female deputies.

The Sheriff continued, "I am also pleased to announce that the mystery man case in Midwest is officially closed. We searched his hotel room two days ago and found his stuff, including the man's notebook and his plans to look around treasure hunting. Additionally, Sergeant Crandall and Deputy James found his home in Colorado. As to cause of death, the Coroner believes the guy froze to death."

When the Sheriff paused, he noticed that several the deputies looked at one another at his mention of the word "treasure."

Then he continued, "now, I don't want anyone to go around talking about some treasure cached around here. If that happens, I am sure a bunch of wackos will show up looking for it. So, again keep it to yourselves."

Eddie raised his hand and waited for the Sheriff to acknowledge him. When the Sheriff finally called upon him, Eddie stood and announced, "Sheriff, the man's name was Dan Pruitt. If that name sounds familiar to some of you in this room, it is because he is the brother of William, aka Billy Pruitt." Eddie stopped and looked around the room and then continued, "William Pruitt was the man who was shot and killed in the act of attempted murder of three high school boys from Midwest a few years back."

The Sheriff interrupted Eddie and asked, "is there a point to this, Sergeant?"

"Yes, Sir. The point is that Dan Pruitt's wallet was found a few days ago, which is in the custody of the local BLM law enforcement officer."

Sheriff Doan tried to interrupt him, but Eddie continued undeterred. "We have determined the mystery man's identity and how he died. However, we have no idea if he had any outside guidance to know about looking around Midwest for some treasure in the first place?"

Eddie had witnessed Doan get angry before, though the Sheriff's face looked like a teapot at a full boil this time.

Doan exploded in a shout, "I said the case is closed, and that is the final verdict. Do I make myself clear?"

Eddie nodded his head and quietly sat down. He thought to himself, "the trap is set. Now we will see if something takes the bait."

The meeting ended with each Deputy being placed with a partner to divide and process serve a large stack of court summons in civil cases. Eddie walked over and took the files set aside for him. While scanning over the top two envelopes, he noticed each had addresses in Bar Nunn. However, when Eddie looked down at the remaining envelope addressed for Edgerton, he exclaimed, "you have got to be kidding!"

"What is it, Eddie...I mean, Sergeant?" Tracy asked.

He shook his head and said, "I will tell you about it later when we go get your car. But for now, give me your travel receipts, and I will file travel vouchers for both of us. Then you get the Undersheriff to sign that letter that you need."

"Okay, are you parked out back along the last row like you always do?"

"Yes, I will see you there when you get done. Now go before you miss the Undersheriff."

A minute later, Eddie walked out of the briefing room and down a long hall that contained multiple doorways to individual offices. He stopped briefly at the accountant's office and filed for trip reimbursement. Then Eddie turned left and intended to go down the hall to the stairwell. Instead, as he passed by Sheriff Doan's office, a big pawlike hand grabbed his left bicep and stopped him in his tracks. The Sheriff squeezed his arm and pulled him closer.

"You are on thin ice with me, Eddie. Don't screw up, or you can pack your bags. That includes challenging me over whether or not I decide to open or close a case, got it!" the Sheriff hissed into his left ear.

Eddie violently jerked his arm away from him and said, "I got it, Sheriff." He then warned Doan, "don't you ever grab me like that again because things will go from professional to personal really quick."

Sheriff Doan chuckled. "You don't honestly think you could ever take me, do you?"

Eddie stared directly into the Sheriff's eyes. Then, finally, he coldly replied, "no, I don't think I can. Rather, I know that I would take you!"

With that, Eddie stormed off to the stairwell and quickly descended the two flights of stairs. Then, he exited out the back door, which opened directly into the parking lot.

When he arrived at the back row of vehicles, Eddie found his buddy from internal affairs, Adam Riley, standing next to his department pickup. Ironically, Riley was conveniently parked beside Eddie's Blazer.

Adam asked, "do you want to talk about anything, Eddie? The Sheriff seems like he has got it out for you."

Eddie shrugged. "No, I don't want to talk about it. It is a personal thing and nothing for internal affairs at this point."

Adam nodded. "I just don't see how you can keep so reserved around that guy, though. It is like you have some secret power or something?"

Eddie shrugged again. "That is easy. I have my faith. A passage in Hebrews reminds me that if I do not live in peace with those around me and do not work at living a holy life, then I am unworthy of seeing my Lord in heaven. The difficult thing for me is determining when to seek peace and when to fight off the wolves like King David."

"True, and I am glad you have enormous discipline, but how is your arm?"

"You saw that?"

Adam winked at Eddie, "of course, I did. Didn't anyone tell you; Internal Affairs sees all." Then Adam climbed into his pickup and sped off.

* * *

20

Later in the afternoon, after Tracy had turned in her department sedan, Eddie drove to her apartment so she could pick up her car. While there, Tracy also carried the document validating her transfer out of Casper over to the apartment complex office. After the landlord accepted it, Tracy assured that she would move out on Saturday and that her roommate would then assume the lease.

Thirty minutes afterward, Eddie and Tracy served two separate court summons in Bar Nunn and were soon on the road back to Midwest. While driving up Highway 259 and Tracy following in her car, Eddie thought profoundly about the poem. While rounding a bend in the road, a well-known ranch that sat under a prominent landmark in the area came into view. Then an intimation hit him, and he stepped on the brakes and pulled over off the road. Tracy pulled up behind the Blazer and stepped out to see what was wrong.

He appeared giddy as he greeted her, who looked at him disconcertedly. So she asked, "are you okay?"

"Yes, I am fine. Do you remember any of the lines from the poem? Like the one about twenty ninth's bane?"

"Why, Eddie? You heard the Sheriff; the case is closed. What difference does the poem make now?"

He looked at her sternly. "It matters to me. I don't like loose ends, and that poem has everything to do with why Dan Pruitt ended up here."

Tracy nodded and lifted one finger in the air that intimated for Eddie to wait. Then she dug out a folded piece of notebook paper from her back pocket. Next, she quickly scanned down the note and read the line aloud: *"YONDER IS THE ROCK OF TWENTY NINE'S BANE."*

Eddie smiled and pointed to the landmark and said, "that is the rock of *twenty-nine's bane*, Teapot Rock."

She followed his finger and spotted the eroded sandstone outcropping. He then further explained, "the Teapot Dome oil scandal all but ended the presidency of our twenty-ninth President Warren G. Harding. That rock, right there, became infamously attached to the failed presidency in newspapers across the country."

Tracy realized what Eddie had just figured out. But, before she could remark about it, Eddie continued, "Yep, the *OMNIPRESENT BEAR* refers to the constellation Ursa Major. You may know it by the common name, the Big Dipper."

A few minutes later, at the crest of the *40-mile* hill, Eddie pulled over again, and Tracy followed. This time, Eddie walked back to Tracy's car and implored her to get out, which she did.

He asked her to recite the line about an oasis. She once again dug out the poem and read aloud: "*OASIS APPEARS AT THE END OF THE WANE.*"

Eddie nodded and said, "wane can mean to go downhill, correct? Well, if you look downhill, what do you see alongside the road?"

Tracy held her left hand over her eyes and squinted to look more closely at the valley in front of them. "I see the Castle Rock Bar on one side of the road and a large tree on the other side."

"Correct. But a house and a gas station used to exist across from the bar. So now, I want you to look again and think about what used to be on that site."

Tracy ducked her head. When she lifted it and looked again with fresh eyes, she exclaimed, "an *oasis*! It must have looked like an oasis from up here."

"Correct again," he said.

Moments later, Eddie pulled up into his driveway and allowed Tracy to park her car in front of his home. She quickly joined Eddie in the Blazer, and they pulled away to accomplish their last process service task.

"So, where are we going?" Tracy asked.

Eddie did not reply; instead, he handed the manila envelope over to her. She looked down at the address label on it.

"Roger Sands, do you know him?"

Eddie sighed, "yes, and I know this court summons is probably from his ex-wife. Roger is a good guy, but he married the wrong woman who ran around on him, and she got custody of their two kids in the divorce. So for the last four years, every time Roger gets a raise or a promotion, the ex-wife sues for more child support. It is just sickening for me to have to serve him these frivolous suits."

Tracy argued, "I wouldn't call it frivolous; child support is for their kids, it is necessary."

Eddie exited Highway 387 to the right and onto a short bypass road that would take them to Center Street. Then he jerked the wheel and came to a stop at a pump jack location a few yards off of the road.

He looked over at Tracy and said, "yes, child support is a necessity. But Roger pays an enormous amount already. The fact is, Roger makes about $50,000 a year, and he currently pays out over $24,000, so you do the math. Roger lives like a pauper while his ex-wife has a fine house, a new car, and a new sugar daddy of a husband in Casper that makes sure she doesn't have to work."

"Why doesn't he get a better lawyer then?"

"Tracy, he can't afford one, and his ex-wife knows it. So she sues, and Roger settles because he wants to see his girls. It is an endless game, and meanwhile, the guy gets put through the wringer."

"I see your point," Tracy said curtly.

Roger was not pleased to receive the latest summons, but he withheld venting his frustration upon the deputies. Instead, he already knew it was their job.

After Roger closed the door, they walked over to the idling Blazer parked across the driveway to Roger's trailer. Suddenly, a memory sparked in Eddie's mind.

After they both climbed into the Blazer, Eddie made a U-turn and drove east on Center Street. Then he turned right onto South East Street and stopped on the earthen bridge spanning an enormous gully.

"Tracy, why does water flow down that draw?" he asked while pointing down a massive, deep ravine.

"Umm, gravity, I guess, umm, wherever there is no resistance?" she guessed.

"Correct. Chief Traynor once told me that people are just like water, meaning both follow the path of least resistance. So, when you think about guys like Roger over there, think about how water flows down this draw. Sometimes all a man has left is just go with the flow."

"But, isn't that how some people get caught up in illegal activity by just going with the flow?"

"Yes, that is true. But in Roger's case, he has given up, just like many other people around this area who have faced incredible difficulties." Then after a pause, Eddie continued, "I want you to think about your hometown, Cheyenne. You don't see obvious hardships, do you? I bet you didn't even know your neighbors either?"

Tracy shook her head. "No, I can't recall who lived next door, but what is your point?"

"The point is this: the main difference between a true community and what city folk dream about is rather simple. You see, in the Salt Creek community, we celebrate our successes and deal with our hardships alongside one another. But, again, I bet you didn't see much of that in the city? So think about all of that for a second."

Tracy looked out of her window and thought, *that is a good lesson.*

* * *

21

Friday, January 10, 1992

9:00 a.m.

The tires crunched over gravel while Eddie pulled his department Blazer into his carport. Though still considered early morning by most people's standard, it seemed, to him at least, as if he had worked a full day. He woke that morning a little after 1:30 a.m. when the county dispatcher called his phone. She had asked him to assist a state highway patrolman on Highway 387 near the county line east of Edgerton. But, unfortunately, the only information that the dispatcher relayed to him was that there was a vehicle accident.

Eddie recounted that he had arrived on the scene at 1:52, and he logged the time in his notebook. He then turned on his wig-wag lights and exited his vehicle. Eddie met the patrolman who walked up the embankment to brief him on the situation. What he saw that morning, he would suffer flashbacks for years to come.

When Eddie walked over the highway's crown and down the steep slope, he saw a flatbed trailer on its side. He found the truck's cargo of drilling pipe strewn across the ground like a pile of giant pick-up sticks. Conversely, the detached tractor rested upside down, and it came to rest at an acute angle to the trailer. However, underneath a large pipe pile was the flattened outline of a black car, a 1988 Dodge Daytona. Inside it revealed a grizzly scene. Crushed under the trailer's weight and cargo was a family of three that included a young girl still strapped in a car seat. However, the truck driver suffered a more gruesome death in being impaled on a metal fence post. Everyone involved in the accident was dead.

Eddie assisted the patrolman, who adroitly choreographed the actions of investigating and clearing the accident scene. Next, the patrolman summoned a volunteer ambulance crew from Midwest and another team of paramedics and firetruck from the town of Wright over 30 minutes away. The paramedics diligently worked to free the bodies of the family from the wreckage of their car. Then it took two rescuers to lift the driver's body off of the fence post.

While the rescue crews did their jobs, Eddie and the patrolman photographed every inch of the accident scene. It wasn't until daylight that the duo could make an initial determination of what happened.

It was readily apparent that the truck driver had attempted to pass the Dodge Daytona when it hit a patch of black ice, which caused his unit to jackknife. In doing so, the rig captured the car within its grasp. Then, as the truck slid off the pavement, the trailer tipped onto the Dodge, then the fifth wheel linchpin broke, and the tractor flipped over at least twice. It was hard for Eddie or the patrolman to determine whether or not the trailer crushed the car and killed its occupants or if the load itself flattened the vehicle. A full trailer of 72 30-foot sections of 4-inch drilling pipe exceeds 44000 pounds for someone who does not know the sheer weight of oil field equipment. It did not take a mathematician to determine that the car that weighed only 2,800 pounds could not withstand such a force.

Once the paramedics removed the deceased, it took another three hours and three tow trucks to remove the vehicles from the side of the highway. Meanwhile, two other patrolmen had arrived and directed traffic around the scene. When Eddie finished debriefing with the highway patrol supervisor, who arrived on the scene at 7:30, it was 8:21 a.m. when Eddie climbed back into his department Blazer and drove home.

At 8:40, Tracy called him on the radio to determine his whereabouts. It took Eddie as second to figure out how she had accomplished that without a department-issued vehicle. Then he remembered that after turning in her car, the department issued her a brand-new mobile radio instead. It was the type that clipped to her belt and had a long-corded microphone attached to her shoulder.

He told her that he had an early morning call. However, he did not want to talk about the details openly over the radio channel.

"Wow, you look awful!" Tracy exclaimed when Eddie shuffled through the door.

Instead of greeting her back, Eddie walked over to his recliner and sat down. He did so while still wearing his coat and his cowboy hat. Tracy was at a loss as to what to do. She instinctively knew that Eddie had either witnessed something tragic or was physically and mentally exhausted, or both. Instead of prying him for information, Tracy went to the kitchen, poured Eddie a fresh and hot cup of coffee, and then handed it to him. Then she took a seat on the couch and patiently waited for Eddie to say something.

For nearly 30 minutes, Eddie sat in silence and made small sips of his coffee until the cup was empty. Only then did he utter a sound toward Tracy.

"I just saw the most horrific accident scene in my life."

"Can you describe it to me? Maybe it would be good for you to get it off of your chest?" she asked. But it wasn't her abilities she relied upon; instead, she remembered the trauma witness calming technique taught at the academy.

Eddie stood up, took off his coat and hat, and hung them both on the coat rack next to the front door. He then proceeded into the kitchen, refilled his coffee cup, returned to his chair, and sat down again.

"Tracy, it is hard to describe the scene. Imagine a tractor-trailer breaking apart from one another and then the whole trailer laden with drilling pipe crushing a family in a passenger car."

The pit in Tracy's stomach tightened. Then she asked, "what happened to the truck driver?"

Eddie took a deep breath and then tipped his mug for another sip of coffee before he continued.

"The driver wasn't wearing his seat belt though it is hard to imagine him surviving even if he did. Anyway, the impact threw the driver through the windshield, and he landed with such force that when his body hit a metal fence post, it impaled him. I mean, seriously, it looked like a spiked body out of medieval European painting or something."

Tracy sat back against the rear cushion of the couch, and she was astonished to hear the details about Eddie's ordeal that morning. She instinctively knew that Eddie needed to talk about it, and she did not know where to turn, so she asked him about it.

"Eddie, is there somebody I can call and have them talk to you? Like, I don't know, maybe somebody from the Sheriff's Department or something?"

Eddie scoffed at the idea, "you mean like Sheriff Doan? He would tell me, 'suck it up, buttercup,' which I should do anyway. But thank you for asking."

"Seriously, I think you should talk to someone you trust so that you can process what you saw. They taught us in the Air Force before we deployed to Desert Storm to deal with trauma right away so that it didn't set within the depths of the brain and become haunting memories. Maybe I could call Chief Traynor?"

"I'm fine, really."

Tracy thought for a second or two and then blurted out, "how about I call Walt Merino? I remember you telling me during our trip that you missed your adult Bible study with him. How about Walt? Do you trust him?"

Eddie mulled over what Tracy had said. While he had many friends in the area, he was closest to Bill Crooks, Chief Traynor, Tracy, and Walt Merino. Walt was instrumental in Eddie's Christian spiritual transformational journey. Furthermore, Walt mentored Eddie on the Bible and served as an accountability partner.

"Okay," Eddie said finally and then added, "you may call Walt. You'll find his phone number in the Rolodex on my desk."

Tracy got up from the couch, went into their shared office, and found Walt Merino's phone number.

Tracy shouted out from the office, "Eddie, I keep forgetting. Do I dial the whole seven-digit number or just the last four?"

"Just the last four," Eddie said from the other room. He mused that he didn't know exactly when the phone company planned to do so, but soon Salt Creek area residents would need to dial 437 first before the four other digits.

Walt Merino took time out of work from the oilfield service company he worked for as a welder, and he arrived at Eddie's home at noon. Tracy had kept herself busy all morning by going through Eddie's file cabinet. It was more than busywork since they needed to comply with the new Sheriff's Department file storage plan. When Walt arrived, she grabbed the keys to the department Blazer. Then she told Eddie that she would do some traffic patrols around Edgerton and south of Midwest on Highway 259. As she lifted her coat off of the coat rack next to the door, Walt caught Tracy's attention.

"If I am not here when you get back, I will see you tomorrow, okay," he said.

Tracy shook her head because she was unsure of what Walter referenced. "What's happening tomorrow?"

Walt smiled. "You are moving, of course, and I have some others from church who will be helping to move you in one trip."

"What? Why would you do that? You barely know me?"

Walt nodded his head in agreement and replied, "true, none of us from the church know you very well. However, when Eddie asked to borrow my trailer, I insisted that we welcome you to the area proper by helping you move. That is what neighbors are for, right?" he asked and winked his left eye at her.

Still astonished, Tracy said, "I'm not sure what to say, other than thank you!"

"A thank you is all that is needed, and I will see you tomorrow bright and early."

After Tracy had backed the Blazer out of the driveway, she negotiated a few quick turns that put her eastbound on Lewis Street toward the junction of Highways 387 and 259. She grinned at the thought that she had assimilated the local dialect that labeled the intersection as just "the junction."

Soon, Tracy passed through Edgerton, and instead of parking outside the eastern town limit to set up a radar checkpoint, she opted to drive out to the accident scene. It was not hard to find since she saw the long and wide remnant tire marks of a tractor-trailer skidding out of control on the pavement. Then, she spotted a massive patch of churned-up ground on the north side and down the slope from the highway. The scene reminded her of a child's picture book of Paul Bunyan dragging his gigantic ax and an enormous furrow behind him.

Tracy shook her head and said to herself aloud, "that had to be horrific to come upon."

An hour later, Tracy sat in the Blazer across from the Castle Rock Bar. She called it traffic patrol duty, but instead, she passively listened to KTWO AM radio out of Casper. The biggest story revolved around President George Bush at a summit in Japan. But it wasn't the politics that made the news; instead, it was the formal dinner. President Bush had vomited a few nights ago into the lap of Japan's Prime Minister Miyazawa and then had fainted. Pundits were speculating whether or not President Bush harbored a severe illness.

Tracy had earlier placed the radar gun on top of the dashboard for looks mostly but had not actively checked anyone's speed. What captivated her was that she sat in the area that she and Eddie determined as the *"Oasis,"* as indicated in the treasure map poem. She looked at the following few lines of the poem though she could not make out any land-marks. One of the things that confused her was the nautical terms the author used to describe where to go. Then the thought occurred to her that when they return to the library, she would check out a book on sailing for beginners to help them decipher the clues. The library also reminded her that she needed to finish reading the novel *Friday Night Lights* since it was due in ten days.

Tracy looked around the treeless countryside west of Highway 259, and she thought about all the changes in her life over the last eight days. First, she received a training assignment with Eddie. Then it turned into a permanent move, followed by a three-state road trip, and now she was moving to Midwest.

"Ugg," Tracy said aloud about the thought of finishing up her kitchen for the move.

The night before, she had astonishingly managed to pack up every-thing but one clean uniform and one fresh set of civilian clothes. The rest of the apartment, minus her roommate's belongings and her items in the kitchen, were already boxed.

Tracy returned to Eddie's home precisely at 4:30 p.m., and once in-side, she handed Eddie the keys to the Blazer. However, Walt Merino had already left.

"Hey, Eddie, what have you been up to?"

"I have been familiarizing myself with the new file plan, and thank you, by the way, for doing that without my asking."

"So, do you feel better?"

Eddie shrugged his shoulders and replied, "a little bit, but I was okay before Walt got here. I just needed a moment to compartmentalize everything in my head."

"Do you do that a lot?"

"Do what?"

"Compartmentalize, that is what I mean?"

Eddie nodded his head and offered, "I do, and I guess I always have. I see it this way: there is a time to worry and a time for work, which means they must exist separate from one another. So, if something troubles me, I put it out of my head until I have an opportunity to deal with it."

Tracy tilted her head to the right side. "Ya, I wish it were that simple for me. I end up dealing with personal things at the same time as I am working. I wish my mind weren't wired for multitasking because it is exhausting." Tracy lifted her head and met Eddie's eyes with her own. "Ya, I wish I could be a guy for like, a day or so, just to escape the millions of neurons all firing at once inside my head."

A hiatus of conversation ensued. Then Tracy asked Eddie, "so, are you still volunteering at the school for tonight's junior high basketball games?"

"I don't see why I shouldn't, so, yes, I will be there," he stated pragmatically.

Tracy had her doubts, but she replied, "okay, you know you best."

She turned to grab her gloves off of the counter, and when she did, she looked at Eddie. "I'll see you tomorrow morning at 8 o'clock, and again, I so appreciate your help and for arranging others to assist too!"

"Don't mention it. That is what friends are for, right?"

As she made what she hoped was her final drive home to Casper after work, Tracy mulled over Eddie's word "friends." It occurred to her that, for the first time in her life, she felt at ease. She further contemplated her relationship with Eddie. It was, in all respects, professional, though she sensed in him a foundation for friendship too.

Then the clue hit her: she had never visualized a platonic relationship with a man. The very word platonic made her smile as Tracy never knew a man that could operate around a woman without primordial urges consuming him.

She recalled an infamous exchange between the fictional characters Harry and Sally in the film *When Harry Met Sally*. It was the scene where they each expressed their personal views on a platonic friendship between and man and a woman.

Whatever it was with Eddie, she liked feeling safe with him, and she knew that working with him would help her career in the long run.

* * *

Saturday, January 11, 1992

Casper, Wyoming

8:00 a.m.

The next morning, Eddie Crandall arrived at Tracy's apartment complex as planned. During the short commute, Walter Merino and his wife, Missy, followed Eddie while towing a sizeable closed trailer behind their 1987 Ford F250. But, to Eddie's surprise, when he stepped out of his pickup, Sam and Teri Barrowman and their junior high school-aged sons, Brad and Danny, had already arrived. They were waiting for Eddie and the Merinos to join them on the sidewalk.

Eddie guardedly stepped out of his truck and expected a slick ice sheet underfoot. Instead of ice, he found the ice had turned into a soft slush. For the previous two days, it was not as cold as it had been. The temperature rise came from the Chinook winds. Each January, Wyoming received a brief pattern of mild daytime temperatures in the high 30s or low 40s due to a southerly flow of warm air. However, the warmups were always a ruse, and winter usually came back with even more fury after each warming trend.

"Good morning, Eddie," Sam said.

"Hey Sam, Teri, boys, thank you for coming. Tracy will surely appreciate your help and especially on such short notice."

Sam remained silent but acknowledged Eddie's commendation with a nod of his head.

Eddie led the way up the stairs to the second floor, and when his entourage arrived at Tracy's apartment, he rapped on the door. Tracy swung the door open, and Eddie introduced the moving crew members she hadn't met yet.

Tracy smiled. "Thank you all for coming to help, and I hope I didn't inconvenience you?"

Walt Merino waved off her comment with his hand. "No, not at all Tracy, as I told you yesterday, it is the neighborly thing to do. Besides, you are now one of us. OFT."

"Well, thank you again, all of you so much. I have some freshly made donuts from Daybreaker Bakery, plus coffee and juice if you are hungry. So, please help yourself," she offered.

The boys, Brad and Danny, were the first to dive into the donuts, which initiated the rest of the crowd to indulge themselves. Eddie went last in line and found a delectable apple fritter, his favorite, still available for his taking.

While her boys ate, Teri Barrowman walked around the apartment with a coffee cup in hand. She quickly took an inventory of the task. She counted 20 neatly stacked boxes in the living room and a queen-sized mattress, box springs, and rails leaning against the wall in the hallway.

"Tracy, how in the world did you pack all of your things in what, two evenings? Don't you ever sleep, honey?" Teri remarked.

"I already had some boxes stashed away in my storage area on the compound, but really, it didn't take long. I just put my mind to it, and, poof, I finished it."

Teri joked, "maybe I should have you come over and help me put away all of our Christmas decorations that we have been putting off."

Tracy smiled again and asked, "really, your decorations are still up?"

In an exasperated expression, Teri looked at Tracy and replied, "yes, my husband, Sam, does not like to take the decorations down until after the Denver Broncos are out of the playoffs. It is his lone superstition." Her revelation brought out cheers and jeers from the other adults in the room, save for Sam, who looked embarrassed.

Eddie chimed in and said, "that is okay, Sam. It has brought us good luck so far. After our Broncos win tomorrow, it will be after the Super Bowl before the decorations come down."

As they ate, Tracy told everyone that her roommate was not home and asked them to stay away from the bedroom on the left. When they all had finished their breakfast snack, the men, women, and boys made short work of hauling the boxes and other belongings. It took less than an hour to load the trailer and tie down the contents to keep them from shifting during transport. Finally, all that remained was a living room chair, the roommate's bedroom, and a few odds and ends in the kitchen.

The four-car caravan departed Casper and drove straight to Tracy's new home on Watson Street. Walt then expertly backed his trailer up to Tracy's new house in such a way that the trailer door dropped directly onto the wooden porch. Afterward, with every hand working together, the trailer unloaded nearly twice as fast as they loaded it.

When the container was empty, Walt pulled off to take it home, where he stored it. Meanwhile, the folks that were left had started helping Tracy unpack boxes and set up her house.

At noon, Eddie came back from the café in Edgerton with a few sacks full of hamburgers and French fries, plus he had a medium-sized cooler full of pop. To Wyomingites, soda pop is called either pop or Coke. Sometimes people will order a Coke in a diner, and the waitress will ask, "what kind."

Soon after lunch, the cable television installer arrived and quickly turned on Tracy's service, followed immediately by a US West technician to establish the phone. By 2 p.m., they finished. Tracy was left with a bit of cleaning and making some small personalized touches around the house.

The first to leave was the Barrowman family and then the Merinos. Before leaving, everyone invited Tracy to join them at the church for Sunday service. However, Tracy deferred to another time. It was a decent gesture, she thought. Still, she was apprehensive about church since she wasn't sure where she stood on Jesus, spirituality, or religion. Eddie was the last to leave and would not go until Tracy insisted that there wasn't anything left for him to do.

Minutes later, Eddie arrived home. He knew that he had a couple of daylight hours remaining in the day. So, he called both Chief Traynor and Bill Crooks to see if they were interested in meeting up with him at the shooting range over by Edgerton. Both men jumped at the chance to get out of the house, and they arranged to meet up at 2:45.

"*KABOOM*," thundered Bill Crooks' .308 scoped bolt action rifle. What few people knew was that before Crooks started teaching high school civics and social studies, he was a special forces operator. While in the service, the teacher became intimately attuned to the .308 caliber and used it exclusively as his weapon of choice as a sniper.

"*BANG-BANG-BANG-BANG*," clapped out of Eddie's new personal Ruger P90 .45ACP handgun. Meanwhile, Chief Traynor sat on a picnic bench with a spotting scope and called out hits and misses for Crooks, albeit he never said the word, "miss."

While they reloaded their weapons, Chief Traynor asked Eddie, "so, I hear that it was a pretty ugly scene out there on Highway 387 yesterday morning. The ambulance crew in town told me that you were the second person on the scene. How are you handling all that?"

Eddie removed the empty magazine from his pistol and placed both on the table with the gun's barrel pointed down-range.

"I'm fine, Chief."

"Are you sure, Eddie? Something like that could take down the strongest of men," Crooks counseled.

Eddie looked up at Crooks, amused and slightly inspired, and asked him, "even you?"

Crooks shook his head and quickly retorted, "well, not me per se, but for most people, yes."

Chief Traynor broke out into a belly laugh at Crooks' comment, and soon, all three men shared a hearty chuckle.

"Seriously," Traynor inserted into the brief silence following the laughter, "how did you sleep last night, Eddie? Did you have any wild dreams?"

Eddie shook his head. "No, nothing like that. I slept fine. But what does bother me is what if I had to take Tracy James out there with me. How do you think she would have handled it?"

Crooks set his rifle down on the table with the bolt fully retracted, and like Eddie, the barrel also pointed down-range. But, once he sat down next to Traynor, he opined, "I think you are looking at this the wrong way, Eddie."

"How is that?"

Crooks rubbed his two-inch-long beard on his chin. "First, Tracy will have her time to respond to an accident scene soon enough. Secondly, I think she has more sand than you give her credit for, Eddie."

"I don't know, Crooks, you should have seen her reaction when we walked up on Dan Pruitt. I mean, she puked her guts out."

"Eddie, you forget that she is a veteran, well, sort of, I mean she was in the Air Force after all," Crooks stated and waited for Traynor to stop chuckling at his Air Force remark. "But, seriously, she served during the Persian Gulf War, and she did see some action. I think she is a pretty tough cookie."

Chief Traynor chimed in, "ya, it sounds like you are a little protective of her, kind of like, well, I don't know...."

Traynor's words dropped off, but the other two men, Eddie in particular, were fully aware of the Chief's implication.

Bill Crooks got up from his seat on the picnic table and pointed back to the table for Eddie to take his place to sit down. The deputy complied. Then Crooks moved back to his original seat and then leaned across the table at Eddie.

"What is going on between you and Sheriff Doan? I hear that he's been pushing you pretty hard lately?"

"Who told you that?"

Crooks shrugged his shoulders. "Nobody special, just a little birdy like I said."

"I don't know, fellas; I can't figure the Sheriff out. I mean, I know he is a glory hound and hates everything in the county outside of Casper. He has always been a little weird with me, but now he is doing the same thing to Tracy."

"You are right about glory hound; didn't you hear the Sheriff's press conference today?" Chief Traynor asked Eddie.

Eddie was flummoxed. "No, I didn't hear about it. I helped Tracy move from Casper to Midwest today. What did he say?"

Chief Traynor recalled that Sheriff Doan announced that he had closed the case on Dan Pruitt and stated the man froze to death outside Midwest. He also explained that his team of Deputies determined that the mystery man arrived in the Midwest-Edgerton community to look for a hidden treasure. Plus, Doan announced that Pruitt wanted to avenge his brother's death in the 1984 incident near the old electric plant.

Crooks leaned forward again and said, "it is not a coincidence, Eddie, that he didn't mention you or Tracy by name."

"It doesn't mean anything to me who gets credit, guys. I am just doing my job," Eddie explained.

The trio sat in silence for a minute or two. The warming trend had continued throughout the day, and a slight warm breeze brushed the men's faces.

"Eddie, this is purely supposition here, but hear me out. I think that something, something bad, happened between Tracy and one of Sheriff Doan's henchmen," Chief Traynor proposed.

The deputy shook his head. "Now you are talking crazy, Chief."

Crooks gave Eddie a stern look. "I think you need to hear this out." Then he motioned for Chief Traynor to continue.

"Thanks, Bill. Now, Eddie, the Sheriff has never liked you because you are motivated by doing a good job. You are not a glory hound like him, and you certainly play it straight. But, unfortunately, Sheriff Doan's lackeys don't. In fact, those goons of his harass women at their favorite bar in Casper, *The Pumpjack*, and the Sheriff looks the other way. Maybe they harassed Tracy in the same way. Perhaps that is why Doan transferred her out here?"

Eddie thought back to what his buddy Adam Riley told him last week about an intra-departmental rumor afoot involving Tracy. But Eddie resisted such negative thoughts.

"Come on, Chief. Tracy came out here to train under me, that is all."

Crooks shook his head. "Eddie, you were sent out here too because your arrow is too straight for the Sheriff's liking. He sent you out here in hopes that you would get frustrated and quit the department. It's the same thing with Tracy. Just think about it. Maybe the Sheriff knew that his only option to silence her secret for good was to encourage her to quit by being sent out here."

"Well, good luck with that. I think she likes it out here."

The men shared another quick laugh though Crooks asked one more pertinent question. "Eddie, has Tracy shared with you anything about her time in the department in Casper?"

"Nope."

"I suppose you won't know anything until she tells you, huh?"

"Yep."

Suddenly, Chief Traynor broke up the discussion and said, "Come on, guys, let's get back to shooting. The sun will set within the hour."

Eddie picked up his handgun and continued to point it down-range. He took another pre-loaded magazine out of the holder on his belt and inserted it into the gun. Then he released the slide, which emitted an audible "ca-chin" sound. He quickly shot another seven-round grouping in a target 25 yards away.

* * *

23

Pastor Roberts stood before his Midwest congregation and announced that he was truncating the church service due to the AFC Championship Game slated to kick off at 10:30 a.m. Mountain Standard Time. Surprisingly to Eddie, the congregation met the Pastor's announcement with applause.

Eddie called out, "Pastor Roberts, do you think God is a Denver Broncos fan?"

Although Eddie received some curious looks from others inside the sanctuary, Pastor Roberts seemed unfazed by the question.

Instead, the Pastor replied, "of course, Eddie, God is a Broncos fan. After all, God made the skies blue and the sunsets orange!"

The joke referred to Denver's orange and blue team colors. But once the laughter subsided, the service began.

Eddie arrived home from church at 10:15 a.m., and he knew that at any second, Reed, the head custodian at the school, would show up to watch the game. So, he quickly changed out of his Sunday clothes and into a pair of Wrangler jeans, a t-shirt, and a hooded blue sweatshirt with the word *"BRONCOS,"* spelled out in sizeable orange-colored block letters. When exiting his bedroom, Eddie heard a knock at his door. While expecting Reed, he was slightly shocked when he opened the door and saw his partner, Tracy James, standing at the door, holding a paper sack.

"Good morning, Tracy."

"Hi, I was hoping to watch the game with you, if you don't mind?"

He welcomed her into his home without hesitation, and then he asked, "what is in the sack?"

"I brought some tortilla chips, Picante sauce, and some Velveeta cheese to make some nachos."

He nodded in approval and replied, "well, you know where the kitchen is. Make yourself at home."

"Thanks, I wasn't sure what to bring. I mean, I didn't know if I should bring beer over or not since I haven't seen or even heard of you drinking."

"What you brought is fine because Reed will be here shortly, and he always brings a twelve-pack of Coors Light. The only time I have a beer or two is while I watch the Broncos play."

Then Eddie held the paper bag for Tracy as she took off her coat and hung it up on the coat rack. To his surprise, Tracy wore an orange long-sleeved t-shirt complete with the Denver Broncos bucking horse logo.

As if on cue, the front door opened, and Reed stepped into the living room unannounced. He immediately walked over to the refrigerator, placed a 12-pack of Coors Light on the bottom shelf, and took three bottles out. Reed had still not uttered a word or a sound though he handed a bottle to Tracy, who stood next to him in the kitchen, and then he carried two bottles out to the living room.

Reed then picked up the remote control, turned on the television, and tuned into the local NBC broadcasting station to listen to the pregame show. The announcers repeatedly discussed that the game would feature a battle between two of the league's top quarterbacks in John Elway and Jim Kelly.

At kickoff, Tracy set down a bowl of nacho cheese sauce and the bag of chips on the coffee table and took up a seat next to Reed on the couch. The first half was an excellent game for those fans that like defensive battles. Both teams slugged it out, and Denver forced Buffalo to punt five times. Conversely, Denver crossed the mid-field stripe five times and missed three field goals. As a result, the halftime score remained knotted at 0-0.

The second half saw more of the same until one of the Denver safeties intercepted a Jim Kelly pass. On the next play, a defensive lineman tipped Elway's pass, and a Buffalo defender caught the ball and scored a touchdown. Buffalo then added a field goal later. But, late in the fourth quarter, Elway left the game with a severe thigh injury, and backup quarterback Gary Kubiak entered the game with the Broncos trailing 10-0. Kubiak drove his team down the field, they scored a touchdown, and then the Broncos recovered the ensuing onside kick. Next, Kubiak completed a pass to a Broncos running back in field goal range, but he fumbled the ball. Buffalo won 10-7, and, for Broncos fans, the season was over.

Throughout the game, Eddie and Tracy chatted back and forth and made comments about the game. The only utterance out of Reed was an occasional grunt, "*stupid refs*," when he thought a penalty should have gone in the Broncos' favor. Instead of going home, Eddie's guests stayed to watch the NFC Championship game too.

Eddie switched seats with Reed, and he only passively watched the later game. Instead, he and Tracy two discussed all their observations and assumptions regarding the mysterious treasure poem left behind by Dan Pruitt. Unfortunately, though, by halftime of the NFC game, neither one could be certain that the Salt Creek area was where the treasure rested. Tracy set her personal copy of the ode on the table, and Eddie placed a map on top of it. Then, he got up from the couch to put a couple of frozen pizzas into the oven.

Meanwhile, when Reed returned from the bathroom, he reached down to the coffee table to retrieve his beer bottle off of a coaster. Then he spotted something. Reed reached out with his left hand and gently slid the poem out from under the map. He then sat back down in the recliner.

Eddie and Tracy looked at each other and wondered what Reed was doing. Then Reed picked up a pen off of the coffee table. He made multiple jots on the paper and then handed it over to Eddie, who took it from him.

Reed spoke for the first time. "Look at my marks and then read the first letters vertically, and that is your answer."

Tracy slid in closer to Eddie on the couch, and they spied Reed's marks together. The update read:

MUTTS FALL EASILY INTO INIQUITY
INKLINGS ADHERENCE BECOMES NECESSARY
DISAPPEARING TREES GIVE WAY TO GRASS
WELL DOWN THE COURSE OF PILGRIM'S PASS
EVER STEAMBOAT STANDS IN FROZEN POSE
SURMOUNT THE FLOW AT GHOSTLY PROSE
THE OMNIPRESENT BEAR POINTS THE WAY
WINCHING THE TACK TO YOUR SURVEY
YONDER IS THE ROCK OF TWENTY NINE'S BANE
OASIS APPEARS AT THE END OF THE WANE
MANAGE PORT TILL POINTING THE CRAFT
INTERSECT THE LIP NOT SLOWED BY DRAUGHT
NEIGHBORLY TEA STEEPS INTO BRINE
GUAGE A CRYPT ALONG THE SPINE
UNDER WHOM ENTERS SHOULD KNOW THE COST
SEARCHING COMES EASY ON VIPER'S HISS FROST

Eddie read aloud the first letters of each line, "M-I-D-W-E-S-T-W-Y-O-M-I-N-G-U-S."

"Midwest-Wyoming-US? Wow, the treasure is here!" Tracy exclaimed.

Eddie nodded and then turned toward Reed and asked him, "how did you figure this out? We have spent hours to get where we were at with it?"

Reed took a sip from his beer and then wiped his lip with the back of his left hand. "Maybe it takes a simple mind, like mine, to decipher a simple clue. Unfortunately, the two of you overthink things. I heard you guys talk back and forth about the meaning of individual words and got nowhere. But what started my thinking about it was the very first line, "*MUTTS FALL EASILY INTO INIQUITY*." The keyword for me in that line was "*EASILY*," which meant that the clue was obvious."

Eddie had yet shaken off the astonishment from his face, and he looked to his left at Tracy, who also looked surprised. Then, finally, he looked back over to Reed and stated, "thanks, Reed."

"Don't mention it. But, maybe some other time when you two Perry Masons get stuck on another case, you could give me a call, though you will need to supply the beer," Reed teased.

The trio sat back and watched the rest of the NFC Championship game. Washington had led 17-10 over Detroit at halftime, but the Redskins blew out the Lions for a 41-10 win in the second half.

When the game ended, Reed stood up, stretched his back, and walked to the kitchen to throw away his last beer bottle. When he emerged back into the living room, he announced, "well, I had better be getting home."

Tracy looked at Reed. "Are you sure you can drive; I mean, you finished off two-thirds of that 12-pack by yourself?"

Reed smiled. "Don't worry about me, Miss Tracy. I always walk over here for games because I don't want to get sideways with the law around these parts."

Eddie chuckled and asked Reed, "so, I will see you over here in two weeks for the Super Bowl?"

Reed nodded his head. "Sure, I'll be here as long as Tracy makes those nachos again. Those were tasty."

Tracy agreed to do so, and then she too got up and grabbed her coat to leave. At the door, she turned to Eddie and said, "I will see you tomorrow, Sergeant."

Eddie smiled and returned the sentiment with, "not if I see you first, Deputy."

After the door closed, the house suddenly fell quiet, and it gave Eddie a feeling of loneliness. It confused him because he hadn't ever felt that way before following the scores of games that he and Reed had watched together. In the past, Reed simply left, and Eddie had his space back. Eddie criticized his thoughts a folly and went into the kitchen. He then quickly tied up the trash bag and walked it to the front door, and stepped out into the dark.

As soon as Eddie placed the trash bag into the garbage can and replaced its lid, he remembered what his friend in the department said to him about Tracy. So, he hurriedly put a heavy rock on top of the trash can lid and strode quickly back into his house.

He went directly into his office and pulled Tracy's personnel file out of the cabinet's top drawer. He spread the record out on his desk and began his search. What Eddie sought out was hard for him to define; instead, he just had a feeling.

The thing that bothered him was if the rumor about Tracy was true or not. In his mind, Tracy was a solid Deputy and was pleasant to be around. Next, he looked down at the pages and started with Tracy's background information on file. It read:

Date/Place of Birth: October 10, 1968/ Cheyenne, WY
Parents: Clarence James, Ruby Feltner
Education: Graduate, Cheyenne Central High School, 1986
A.A.S., Criminal Justice, Community College of the Air Force, 1990
Wyoming Law Enforcement Academy, Basic Course, 1991
Military Service: Branch: United States Air Force
Service Dates: 1 Jun 87-31 Aug 91

Deployments: Desert Storm
Assignments: Grand Forks AFB, ND/Kunsan AFB, South Korea
Medals: Bronze Star, National Defense Service, AF Good Conduct
Highest Rank Held: Senior Airman
Discharge Type: Honorable

Eddie closed the file and knew that nothing he could glean from the pages would help him resolve his questions about Tracy's past. He already knew that it would take time to find out.

* * *

24

Monday, January 13, 1992

Sergeant Eddie Crandall had risen out of bed before sunrise as usual. After a quick shave, he got dressed. Just like every morning during his time with the Sheriff's Department, Eddie examined himself in his bathroom mirror. He meticulously straightened his uniform shirt to align with the tip of his belt buckle and the zipper of his pants. His friend and mentor, Midwest Police Chief Wyatt Traynor, always referred to the uniform alignment as a "*Gig line,*" which he learned from his days in the Army.

Generally, over a cup of coffee, Eddie would plan out and prioritize the list of tasks that he had to accomplish for any given day. But, today was an oddity; there were no pressing tasks.

Tracy arrived at the front door precisely at 7:30 a.m. Instead of knocking, she simply entered the door, as Eddie previously instructed her to do on duty days. She wiped her boots on the floor mat and hung up her dark green uniform jacket on the coat rack next to the door.

"Good morning, Sergeant. I hope your sleep was restful last night?"

"Oh, I tossed and turned like normal. How did you sleep last night, Deputy?"

Tracy's face beamed and enthusiastically explained, "I had a fabulous sleep!"

"Really, fabulous? I don't think I have ever had a fabulous sleep, ever."

"Yes, really, it was fabulous. It was my second night in my first very own home!"

"Congratulations, Deputy, on your home, but are you ready to go to work?"

"Go to work? I thought maybe we could go get some breakfast this morning, my treat?" she suggested.

Eddie thought about it for a few seconds and then nodded his acceptance of Tracy's breakfast offer.

"Okay, Deputy, I accept your offer. Now, grab your coat," he instructed.

Tracy donned her coat over her arms and then adjusted the waistline to fit comfortably around her Beretta model M9 9mm pistol holstered to her hip. She was proficient with the make and model since she carried a similar piece during her Air Force days. Meanwhile, Eddie left her behind while he walked back to the office and strapped on his weapon belt. Once he secured the weapon, he grabbed a set of keys to the department Blazer off the top of his desk. Then the phone rang.

"Sergeant Crandall," Eddie said into the telephone receiver.

"Eddie, it is Carlos Mondragon," the caller said.

"Hey Carlos, what can I do for you? So this wouldn't be about the men's basketball league and the team assignments?"

"No, Eddie, not exactly, but since you mentioned it, I could use some players that stand over five foot six. But, I mean, come on, your team is nothing but a bunch of trees compared to mine."

"So, if it is not the league, then what can I do for you today?" he asked.

"Ghost lights, Eddie, ghost lights."

"What about them? I am not following you, Carlos?"

"Well, that idiot boss of yours made mention in his press conference of some boys seeing ghost lights the night before that guy turned up frozen like a popsicle. But, this morning, I found a couple of idiots on my east pasture, you know, the one that buts up against BLM land a mile west of Salt Creek?"

Tracy overheard the running conversation from the living room and decided to enter the office to ascertain what issue had arisen. Eddie nodded at her and answered Carlos.

"I do, Carlos, but what happened next?"

"I pulled up next to these clowns, and I asked them what they were doing? They told me they were getting their equipment set up to catch the ghost lights on film later this evening, hopefully. So I asked them who they were, and they said they were paranormal researchers from Denver. So then I asked them if they knew whose property they were standing on, and do you know what they said to me, Eddie?"

"I wouldn't haphazard a guess, so why don't you just tell me."

"These guys told me that they called the Sheriff on Saturday night, and he said that all the area around Midwest was public land. Can you believe that man, Eddie? Boy, I can't wait to vote that guy out come November!"

"What happened to the trespassers, Carlos?"

"I ran them off, but I wrote down their license plate number. So I was hoping you could meet me next to my property along Highway 387, west of town. From there, I will show you where those morons cut my fence so they could drive onto my pasture. Then I want you to take photographs and see to it the Sheriff's Department pays for the damages!"

"Calm down, Carlos, Deputy James, and I will head your way shortly."

"Okay, see you soon," Carlos said, and then the line disconnected.

Eddie placed the telephone receiver back into its cradle on top of the phone, and then he let out a long sigh.

"I overheard the phone call. I will get the Polaroid camera out of the closet," Tracy said.

Then a thought occurred to him, "Tracy, do you have a ready bag? What I mean is, do you have a bag that has emergency supplies like a blanket, candles, and the like?"

She was confused by the question. "No, I don't have anything like that. Why do you ask?"

He explained, "during wintertime, I always take a ready bag with me when I go out into the countryside."

She lifted both of her hand's waist high and asserted, "but Eddie, Carlos' ranch is just a few miles up the road. I mean, we could walk back here or hitch a ride if something happens."

"Maybe I am overly cautious, but I also know that the land in Wyoming will kill the person that isn't prepared. So, are you ready to go?"

"Yes, Sir!" Tracy reported and jokingly saluted Eddie from the position of attention.

Outside his house, Eddie started up the department Blazer to warm it up, and then he walked over to his backyard shed. He grabbed a small spool of barbed wire, fencing pliers, a fence stretcher, and a large cloth equipment bag and carried them to the rear of the vehicle.

"What do you need all of that stuff for?" Tracy asked.

Eddie turned his head to look at her and explained, "I need this stuff to fix Carlos' fence, and the bag is extra emergency supplies. Now, help me load this stuff into the back."

"Why do you have an extra roll of barbed wire? I mean, who stores stuff like that unless they have a horse?"

He smiled and then explained, "You will see, come hunting season, we get a lot of cut fences out here because out-of-state hunters have no problem cutting wires. They do so that they can drive up on game animals, whether private or public property. So I save the County a lot of time and resources by mending fences myself."

West of Midwest on Highway 387, Carlos was spotted easily since his pickup sported a sizeable Rafter M emblem on both doors. Carlos stepped out of his truck and greeted Eddie and Tracy, and then showed them the damage done by the interlopers. But, unfortunately, the rancher's attitude had not cooled off as much as Eddie hoped for, and he was still on an endless rant about Sheriff Doan.

"Why do you stick up for him, Eddie? You are a reasonable man?"

"Who?"

"That Sheriff of yours, that is who!" Carlos sneered.

Eddie had a problem. For as long as he could remember, he had listened to angry citizens express great displeasure with Sheriff Doan. Eddie had registered at least a hundred complaints about the Sheriff for eight years now, albeit mainly from Chief Wyatt Traynor.

The friction between the Salt Creek community and Sheriff Doan was well-known. First, the Sheriff never attended any official functions in the area but always had a ready excuse and a proxy to take his place. Second, the community reacted to the Sheriff's inattention each election cycle for not one yard, nor any pasture billboard had a sign that read: "Re-elect Sheriff Doan." Instead, Doan's political opponent always did well in the community.

Despite his feeling belonging to the community, Eddie still had a job to do, and always, without fail, he maintained the company line and quietly defended Sheriff Doan.

"Carlos, I have taken down your complaint, and I will address it with the Sheriff. In the meantime, you can provide Deputy James the license plate number and the description of the vehicle driven by the guys from Denver. From there, we will track them down and cite them with trespassing. Are we cool?

"Okay, but what about my fence? I think the Sheriff should pay someone to fix it; it was his fault after all," Carlos demanded.

Eddie took a deep breath and replied, "I have all the tools in the back of my unit to fix your fence for you because I agree that you shouldn't have to do it yourself. So now, you have two choices. Either supervise my patchwork or go back to tending to your horses. It is your choice either way."

Carlos stammered for a moment and then replied, "Thank you, Eddie. I appreciate you taking the flak intended for the Sheriff." Then he added, "no, I won't hang around to watch. I trust you will repair the fence right."

Eddie nodded and watched as the rancher walked over to Tracy to provide her with the license plate number and vehicle description. Meanwhile, he gathered his fencing supplies, lugged them over to the apparent void, and set them on the ground. When Eddie turned around, Carlos climbed into his pickup and drove off. He then waited for Tracy to join his side.

"Tracy, please take some pictures of the cut fence, one from each angle, and the last one will be me holding the end of the wire to show obvious cut marks."

She nodded and quickly snapped off the three photos and then took the prints back to the Blazer and laid them on the passenger seat protected from the wind. He then made short work of his patch job, and within minutes, the three strands of wire were up and taunt.

As he put his supplies away, he noticed that the typical winter pattern had replaced the micro-warmup they had experienced over the weekend. The temperature had declined back into the normal 20-degree range, and the wind blew again, but a bite.

While Eddie waited for the Blazer to warm up again, he took his gloves off and rubbed his hands together to warm them up through friction.

"It is getting cold once again," he stated the obvious to Tracy.

"I know. I was getting used to our early Spring.".

He nodded. "When we get back to the office, how about you take those photos inside and place them in an evidence bag and properly label it. While you do that, I will put my fencing supplies away, and then we can get our late breakfast or early lunch. What do you say?"

"Deal."

Later at the café, Eddie and Tracy stared upon empty plates. Finally, with their appetites satiated, Tracy paid for the meals, and they soon drove back to the office. The first task was to gather up enough stuff to constitute a ready bag for Tracy. While she didn't believe it was a necessity, she helped him collect all the necessary items. She even went back to her place and selected a pair of old jeans, warm socks, and an old sweatshirt to top her new emergency kit.

But, then, a firm knock on the front door interrupted the duo, and when Eddie opened the door, Chief Traynor stood at his doorstep.

"Eddie, we have a problem," the Chief stated.

"What, where, and how many," Eddie joked but saw no humor in the Chief's eyes.

"That idiot Sheriff of yours spoke about a treasure being up here, and now we've got morons running around here with pickaxes and shovels trying to find hidden loot. I've got two guys handcuffed in the back of my unit that I caught trying to dig up the 50-yard line on the football field. I am in the process of transporting them to jail in Casper."

"Wow, Chief, I'm sorry for that, I...." Eddie tried to reply, but Chief Traynor interrupted him.

"Don't apologize for your boss when it is his mess. But I need your help. While I was booking these two in my office, I got a phone call from a truck driver at the junction who said that two guys were digging a hole in the pitcher's mound on Moses Field. I would handle it myself, but I am out of room in my vehicle. Besides, Moses Field is outside of the town's limits and is technically your responsibility."

"No problem, we are on it," and then he turned to Tracy and instructed, "grab your stuff. We've got to go."

Tracy quickly grabbed her belongings and met Eddie near the Blazer, and climbed into the passenger seat.

Just as the Blazer rolled over the cattle guard at the end of Lewis Street and crossed over the intersection, they spotted a small Mazda pickup in the baseball field's parking lot. Correspondingly, Eddie turned the Blazer down the entrance road.

In November of 1925, Moses Field became famous when Casper and Midwest played a football game. But it was not an ordinary contest. Instead, it went into history as the nation's first high school football game played under the lights. While most people assumed that Oiler Field was the historical site, this grassless, flat, and barren patch of earth was the correct location.

Eddie parked directly behind the Mazda and pulled up to within an inch of hitting bumpers. He then looked over and winked at Tracy and pre-empted her burgeoning question, "I like to do this just in case something happens, and one of those guys tries to flee."

Tracy nodded that she was not only heard but fully understood.

The officers slowly stepped out of their vehicle and walked toward the field. Eddie approached the men from the entrance next to the third-base dugout. Meanwhile, Tracy walked over to the gate along the first-base side. Both deputies had their weapons drawn and pointed down in front of them.

Eddie barked out loudly. "Freeze, gentlemen! Now drop your tools, place your hands above your heads, and take two steps slowly backward."

The men complied with his command and waited for him to approach. Meanwhile, Tracy slowly and cautiously walked up behind the men and still had her weapon at the ready.

The taller of the two men asked, "what are we doing wrong, officer?"

"I will ask the questions, fellas, now, what are you doing?" Eddie asked.

The shorter man made a sudden move to run off, but Tracy anticipated the move, holstered her weapon, stepped in his path, and tripped him. When the man hit the ground, Tracy came down on top of him and pinned him to the infield. With the diversion, Eddie stepped forward too and wrestled the taller man down to the ground.

"I will ask you guys once more, what are you doing?" Eddie asked.

The shorter man whined, "we are looking for treasure."

Tracy pushed her knee a little bit harder into the smaller man's back and asked, "what treasure are you talking about?"

"It is the Daniels treasure, you know, from the poem?"

Eddie spoke up, "well, fellas, this park is not public domain. Therefore, unless one of you produces written permission from the Field Operations Officer at MERP, then we are placing you both under arrest."

The taller man under Eddie questioned, "what's a *MERP?*"

Eddie grinned and then replied, "ya, that is what I thought. MERP stands for Midwest-Edgerton Resource Production, and that company owns this park. So, are those other men on the football field friends of yours too?"

Under Tracy, the smaller man asked, "who, Frank?" which summoned a direct rebuke from the taller man, "shut up, man."

"I see, so you are all sharing the same brain. Well, just so you guys know, Frank and the other guy have been arrested and are heading to Casper as we speak," Eddie said.

Eddie looked up at Tracy and ordered, "cuff your suspect, and then we will read both of these guys their rights."

While the men stood outside the department Blazer under the watchful eye of Tracy, Eddie called the county dispatcher. He requested the county contracted tow truck operator to pick up the Mazda pickup and tow it to the impound lot when she acknowledged. In a sense, it seemed a little over the top to haul the men into Casper for booking on a misdemeanor criminal trespass. But, since the interlopers also dug a three-foot deep hole, they also faced a charge of defacing the property, which was a felony. Eddie also knew that the men would bond out of jail quickly enough and then return to Casper for their trial if it ever got that far.

* * *

25

The ride into the city of Casper was quiet as the two men chose to exercise their right to remain silent. Because the department Blazer wasn't equipped with metal grating that separated the front seat from the back, Tracy had to sit an angle to watch every movement of the suspects while Eddie drove.

After they arrived in Casper, Tracy and Eddie booked the interlopers quickly. They found it interesting that each man had a history of trespassing with shovels in Steamboat Springs, Colorado, too. Oddly enough, the men also had a misdemeanor trespass on their records in South Pass City in western Wyoming.

Soon afterward, the booking Sergeant handed the deputies their sets of handcuffs, and they exited the building for the parking lot. There they saw Chief Traynor in a heated discussion with the Undersheriff, Steve Witten. When Chief Traynor spotted Eddie and Tracy's approach, he offered a nod of his head. "Hey, Sergeant, hey Deputy."

"What's going on here, Chief?" Eddie asked.

"I was just explaining to the Undersheriff that the bone-headed Sheriff caused us a lot of grief as a result of his ill worded and ill-begotten press conference. So that is what I am doing!"

The Undersheriff looked to Eddie and asked, "the Chief said, 'us,' what happened to you today?"

Eddie explained that he and Tracy had just arrested a couple of guys for digging up Moses Field. He further told Witten that one of the perps said that Sheriff Doan's press conference provided a clue where to look for treasure. He also informed the Undersheriff of his morning on the Mondragon Ranch, where two guys had cut a Rafter M fence to capture the folklore of the ghost lights on film.

However, Eddie stopped talking when two of Sheriff's Doan's lackeys, Deputies McKinnon, and Peck strolled down the sidewalk and into the parking lot. When the deputies passed by Tracy, the men smiled and tipped their hats in her direction. Unfortunately, though, Tracy's withdrawn reaction to the men did not escape the Undersheriff's attention. Then, as McKinnon and Peck When looked up to the men standing next to Tracy, they said in unison, "Sir," to the Undersheriff. But, when they looked at Eddie. , one of them said under his breath, "Casper," but they could not hide their snickers.

Undeterred, Eddie barked out to both of them. "Come back here, Deputies." Then, when they stood before Eddie, he continued, "I am a Sergeant, and when you address me, it had better be, only, Sergeant. Is that clear?"

McKinnon and Peck looked directly at Eddie and said in unison, "yes, Sergeant."

The men continued about their way. Finally, however, one of them said audibly enough for everyone to hear, "now that was just unfriendly," as yet another reference to the insult of *Casper the Friendly Ghost*.

Eddie cast his gaze back upon the Undersheriff and said, "do you see what I mean? I get denigrated every time I am in town with the *Casper Ghost* stuff because Sheriff Doan does little to stop it."

Then in a moment of clarity, he was confident that his talk with the Undersheriff would soon be reported back to Sheriff Doan.

Eddie resumed speaking when the Deputies were out of earshot. "Like I was saying, Sir, those men who trespassed onto the Mondragon Ranch told the owner that Sheriff Doan told them it was okay, and I quote, 'it is all public land out there' end quote."

He took a moment to catch his thoughts and continued. "Sir, I have never complained before, and I always do my job, and I hope you receive my words seriously. Frankly, I can't believe I am telling you all this. Still, for some reason, the Sheriff has it in for the residents in Midwest, Edgerton, and toward Deputy James and me. There is a long history of derogatory remarks to my friend, Chief Traynor, here. Those are good folks out there in Midwest. I think a county public servant, like a Sheriff, should recognize them once in a while. I mean, residents in Casper virtually ignore everything outside of the 82601 zip code, just like Sheriff Doan. All I am asking is that you see things from our point of view and look into them for us, Sir."

The Undersheriff nodded and reached out and patted Eddie on the shoulder and said, "don't worry, I have your back." Oddly though, he continued with a furtive warning, "hang in there though, it may seem to get worse, but I promise you that it will get better."

After his closing remarks, the Undersheriff excused himself and walked away toward his office building.

"I bet that felt good, didn't it, Eddie? Yes, sir, I bet it felt good to get that off your chest, and you did it right, too, by complaining to the next person in your chain of command," Traynor surmised.

A glimmer of a thought passed through Eddie's head, and he turned toward Traynor.

"You had this planned, didn't you? I mean, you knew I would walk out here and join into your gripe session, didn't you?"

Chief Traynor lifted both hands to his waistline with both palms exposed upward in a "what can I do" sort of fashion. Then he explained further, "Eddie, when I saw the Undersheriff walking out of the parking lot, I saw an opportunity. Yes, I knew you would emerge sooner or later. Yet, I took the opportunity to express my misgivings, though your additions became the icing on the cake."

Tracy's quiet reserve did not go unnoticed, neither did her fidgetiness ever since Deputies McKinnon and Peck showed up unexpectedly. Though she stood next to Eddie and Chief Traynor, her mind was somewhere else entirely.

"Tracy, are you alright?" Eddie asked.

"Huh? What?"

"I asked you if you were alright. You seem out of sorts."

"Oh, I am fine. I just can't stand McKinnon and Peck. I have had a run-in with them in the past, but I am okay."

Chief Traynor chuckled suddenly and somewhat inappropriately. Eddie leaned over and whispered in Chief Traynor's ear, "that was a little insensitive to laugh at Tracy."

Chief Traynor snapped his head straight, and he instantly blushed. "I am sorry, Tracy; I wasn't chuckling at you."

"What were you then?" Tracy asked dryly.

"Oh, I was just thinking what tomorrow is going to bring. I mean, what is going to get dug up next? I just hope that if any more idiots show up that they hit a hot water line and get scalded a little, that will teach them."

Eddie looked over to Tracy and motioned for her to follow him back to the Blazer.

"I will see you tomorrow, Chief," Eddie offered.

"You bet, Eddie, I have a hunch that you can count on that too."

The drive north out of Casper was sullen and quiet. Eddie secretly anguished over his entire conversation with Undersheriff Steve Witten. He felt that he had placed a proverbial foot in his mouth. However, Eddie knew that registering his complaint was correct since gripes always go up the chain of command and never down. If needed, Eddie could call on dozens of people in the Salt Creek community who could vouch for his aversion to voicing disrespectful remarks toward the Sheriff.

Tracy sensed Eddie's internal fear as if she could smell it oozing out of his pores.

"Whatcha thinking, Sergeant?"

Eddie heard her request but didn't know what to say. So instead, he passed off his usual "nothing" and hoped that Tracy would drop her inquiry.

Undeterred, Tracy resumed to pick at Eddie's mental scab and stated, "if you are worried about registering a complaint with the Undersheriff, then don't. It was the right thing to do?"

"What do you mean 'the right thing to do?' What was right should have been me keeping my mouth shut and just taking it like I always do."

"Eddie, you went to your next in command just like the manual spells out. But I wish I had gone to my Sergeant first before I...." Tracy's words trailed off because she didn't want to reveal a painful personal saga.

"What do you mean by 'I wish I had?' What are you not telling me, Tracy?"

Tracy stoically walled Eddie off and refused to say anymore and looked away through her passenger side window and watched as Teapot Rock rose from the valley floor.

Eddie vented an audibly frustrated sigh. "Tracy, you and I need to have that talk that you have avoided ever since your transfer to work with me. If you want me to trust you, then start by trusting me with whatever you are hiding."

She glared at him and said, "ditto."

The singular word cut deep into Eddie's psyche, and he knew that he too was guilty of not always revealing his private thoughts. It reminded him about the Bible verse in the book of Matthew about abstaining from looking at the speck of sawdust in a friend's eye when a log is stuck on his own.

Sufficiently humbled, her replied to her with a curt, "touché," and continued to drive in silence for the rest of the trip up Highway 259 to Midwest.

Once in town, Eddie turned right off of Lewis Street and then left onto Watson Street. A few houses from the end of the street at Fitzhugh Road, he pulled onto the parking pad and came to a stop behind Tracy's car. Still oddly silent, she opened the passenger door of the department Blazer and started to exit but changed her mind and shut the door.

Instead, she turned toward him, and his eyes met hers. He could see that her eyes were moist and could sprout tears at any second. When Tracy opened her mouth to speak, Eddie hissed out, "Shh," while simultaneously placing his right index finger on his lips.

"Please, don't say anything now, Tracy. I don't want to bring up whatever you have been storing away inside until you are ready, do you understand?"

"But, Eddie, I want to talk about it, at least, I think I do?"

He nodded but added, "before you do tell me, I want you to instruct me on what you want me to do with the information. Do you want me just to listen, or do you want me to do something with whatever you have to say?"

"Maybe both, but I don't know for sure?"

Eddie nodded again. "Well, when you are sure, please let me know. I am here for you, not just as your boss, but I consider you as my friend."

At his utterance of the word "friend," her head jerked up, and she looked at him once again. Eddie noted that her expression had softened a little too.

Finally, Tracy asked, "really? You think I am a friend?"

He smiled. "Yes, we are friends. Hasn't it occurred to you that we have been partners for what, ten days now, and you know more about me than people that have known me for years?"

Tracy tilted her head to one side and opined, "sure, I have thought about that too. The best thing that could have happened to us was that four-day trip where we got in a year's worth of conversations and getting to know one another."

"I agree, so since you are my friend, let me know when you want to have a serious talk, and I will help you or just listen. It is your choice."

Tracy nodded that she understood and then excused herself to step out of the Blazer. But, before she shut the door, she asked him, "who is that sitting in the intersection of Watson and Fitzhugh?"

Eddie looked up and through his windshield and made out what seemed to him as a black Ford Bronco.

He looked back at her and said, "don't call attention to the vehicle-just close the door like normal and enter your house. I am going to follow the Ford to see where it goes, okay?"

Tracy nodded and shut the passenger door as instructed. Next, he placed the Blazer's transmission into DRIVE and pulled off the parking pad. Immediately, the Bronco pulled off and proceeded north on Fitzhugh. Seconds later, Eddie stopped at the stop sign, and as he turned right and looked north up the street, the mysterious black Ford Bronco was gone. Eddie then pressed the accelerator pedal down and sped a short block and turned right onto Peake Street. He had anticipated that he would see the Bronco driving eastbound, but again, nothing.

Unexpectedly, Eddie turned at the first road on his left, C Street, went past his home and turned onto Navy Row to double south on Fitzhugh. He then thought that the Bronco might have turned down the alley between Watson and Peake Streets. However, there wasn't a Bronco or any other car when he stopped mid-block and looked east down the gravel alley.

Undeterred, he continued south to Lewis Street and proceeded east. From his vantage point, it looked like a vehicle had just turned right onto Highway 259 toward Casper. Eddie pressed the switch to turn on his red and blue wig-wag lights, and he raced the rest of the way down Lewis Street and over the cattle guard. When he looked south on Highway 259, he did not see the mysterious Bronco nor any taillights.

In resignation, Eddie turned off the wig-wag lights and made a U-turn back onto Lewis Street and headed for home.

A minute later, while turning onto Navy Row from the east, a thought hit him. Suddenly, he slammed on the brakes and skidded the Blazer to a stop.

It occurred to him now that he had spotted a black Ford Bronco repeatedly over the last week or so, but he silently asked himself, *"why? Is it following me, or am I just paranoid?*

* * *

26

Tuesday, January 14, 1992

After getting dressed and pouring himself a cup of coffee, Eddie walked across his living room and into his work office. He first spotted the time on the wall clock, which read: 7:00 a.m., and then looked at his desktop calendar. Eddie quickly scanned the block for the day and did not see any appointment reminders written down.

He set his piping hot mug on his desk, rolled out the desk's matching antique oak chair, and sat down. He then picked up his cup again and looked out the office window that overlooked Navy Row. Eddie mused how it used to be when teachers occupied every house along the north side of the street, but now, two out of the seven homes sat empty.

The sound of the front door opening snapped Eddie out of his reminiscing thoughts, and he called out, "I'm in the office, Tracy. Go ahead and get yourself a cup of coffee. Oh, by the way, did you think about our discussion last night?"

He heard a brief snicker from behind him, followed by a gruff male voice that said, "thanks, Eddie, but I don't think I can be as pretty as Deputy James," followed by more laughter.

Eddie instantly recognized the voice as Chief Traynor's, and he refused to turn his head around to hide the hot blush of embarrassment on his cheeks. Traynor walked into the kitchen, opened the kitchen cabinet above the coffee maker, and selected a mug. He expertly poured himself a full cup and then carried it to Eddie's office.

Once he sat down, Traynor asked, "so you thought I was Tracy, huh? Boy, I wonder what happened to the good old days when I would show up unannounced and drink your coffee because I am too lazy to make my own at my office. Tsk-tsk, where has the time gone?"

"I am sorry, Chief. I guess I have gotten used to Tracy showing up first thing in the morning."

Traynor chuckled and slapped his hand down on Tracy's desk.

"So, tell me, Eddie, why were you speeding down my streets last night? I got a call from Mrs. Tillman on Lewis Street, who said you were going 60 miles an hour with your lights flashing. Any truth to that?"

Eddie nodded his head and then unfolded the exact details of his actions the night before. He also told Chief Traynor about his remembrance of seeing a black Ford Bronco at least four times during his trip to Colorado. "Am I getting overly anxious about this?"

Traynor took a long sip of coffee and then wiped his mouth with the back of his hand before he set the mug back down again.

He looked at Eddie and said, "umm, both yes and no. Yes, you may be connecting too many dots. And, no, because history reminds me that none of us initially thought that the 1978 dark green Ford F150 in the Savolt case meant anything too. If I were you, I would be very cautious, but that is just my opinion. So, what else is on your mind, Eddie?"

Eddie furrowed his brow and replied inquisitively, "what makes you think that I have something else on my mind?"

Traynor's lips spread wide into a grin that exposed his teeth. "I ask because you are my friend, and I can read you like a book." He continued, "is it what you said to the Undersheriff?"

Eddie's eyes darted up to Traynor's face at the mention of the conversation from the day before. He nodded his head. "Yes, now that you bring it up, it has been on my mind. What I don't like is fearing that somehow I will get fired for it."

Eddie's remark caused Chief Traynor to blow coffee out of his nose. "Dang it! See what you made me do. Do you have a paper towel or something to wipe off Tracy's desk?

"Here you go," Eddie said and handed Chief Traynor a roll of paper towels that he kept by his desk for such emergencies. While Traynor wiped up his mess, he assured Eddie that nothing in his sentiments could become construed as a terminating offense. At worse, Traynor surmised, Eddie could get suspended, though.

"Suspended? That is just as bad! How am I going to pay my bills? What am I going to do all day with nothing to do? What then, Chief?"

Traynor shook his head. "calm down. We don't know what the Undersheriff or that dime-store cowboy boss of yours will do, but if you haven't received word by this Friday, then you are in the clear."

"Why do you say by Friday?"

"It is an old human resources trick to lay off or fire someone on Friday afternoon when there are few people around to complain. Usually, cooler heads prevail over the weekend. The now unemployed man or woman will start looking for a new job. But, again, if you don't get a suspension notice by Friday afternoon, then you are right as rain."

Eddie shrugged his shoulders. "Fine, but can we stop talking about that because you are giving me a headache, Chief."

The front door opened again, and Tracy entered and immediately took off her coat and hung it up.

She called out, "good morning, Sergeant," and promptly gathered a cup of coffee for herself.

When Tracy entered the office, Traynor stood up and relinquished his seat to Tracy since it was her space after all.

"Well, I had better get going, you two. Much crime is awaiting me here in Shangri-La to thwart. I will see you both later," Traynor said, and he left as quickly as he arrived.

Eddie got right to the business of the day, which entailed going over Tracy's training record and signing her off on tasks that she demonstrated mastery. She was proficient in traffic detail, radio usage, court summons process serving, and suspect apprehension. Eddie saw it as another training opportunity when each had signed off the very last task on the list.

The Sergeant commented, "my evaluation of your putting a suspect at a position of disadvantage impressed me; good job. You know, it is a tough decision to make as to how much force to use. In that situation yesterday, when the perp started to run, you reacted properly. Again, just be careful when taking the perp down because a brutality lawsuit will happen when you least expect it."

Tracy tried desperately not to laugh, but she could not contain herself any longer when Eddie finished speaking and let out a rolling belly laugh.

"What is so funny?"

"It is your use of the phrase, 'placed at a disadvantage,' that is what is so funny."

After stifling the urge to giggle, she explained further, "when I was in the Air Force, my technical school used to use the same 'placed at a disadvantage' phrase. Then, when I arrived at my first duty station at Grand Forks Air Force Base in North Dakota, I was assigned to guard the WSA."

"What is WSA?"

"The WSA is an acronym for Weapons Storage Area, as in, where they stored and processed the nuclear warheads for the missiles."

He nodded and then queried, "how is it then that you never saw a missile launch facility like the ones we saw in Nebraska?"

"The reason, Sergeant, is that the WSA was on base, and the launch facilities are off base. So, back to my story. When anyone approached the WSA gate and didn't have entry authorization or an identification card, we 'jacked them up,' which is the same thing as placing a perp at a disadvantage."

Eddie understood and asked Tracy another question, "so, I read your personnel file, and it says that you fought in Desert Storm?"

She nodded, and he asked a follow-on question, "what was that like?"

After thinking for a second or two, she then explained, "I arrived during the buildup of troops, or Operation Desert Shield before we went to war. Anyway, I arrived with a Red Horse unit and provided security for them so they could build a base."

"What is Red Horse?"

"Red Horse is a specialized unit that can build a base anywhere from nothing. Remember the Red Dessert? Well, picture it without any grass or sage, just flat sand everywhere. Then you know what that part of Saudi Arabia resembles. Anyway, a Red Horse unit will bulldoze aircraft runways, put up buildings, plumb showers, and everything while also under enemy fire."

"I understand. The file also said you earned a Bronze Star; do you want to tell me about it?"

Tracy shrugged. She insisted there wasn't much to tell. Tracy then recalled about the night before the U.S. stuck the Iraqi's with *Shock and Awe*. She was at the front gate of that Air Force Base out in the middle of nowhere, when during the night, two massive trucks sped out of the darkness toward their position. Her Lieutenant was on scene and was technically in charge because of being an officer. But when he froze in that critical moment and didn't know what to do, Tracy told the other four troops to take up a firing position and open up on the trucks."

"Did you stop the trucks?"

"Yes, I think we all went through a full clip each, and we hit both truck radiators, and we killed the drivers. We called in extra troops, and when our relief opened the back of the insurgents' trucks, they found both of them filled to the brim with explosives. Nobody over here in stateside ever heard that story due to everything being hushed at the time."

"Wow! You are a hero! No wonder you got a medal for that," he commended.

Tracy looked at Eddie very seriously. "Heroes are the ones that don't make it back. Besides, I didn't need a medal for just doing my duty."

The rest of the day was routine and mundane. It was cold and windy outside, and it pained Eddie and Tracy when they received a call to conduct a welfare check on a male retiree in the area. Mr. Sprenger, who was 92 years old, lived alone in a tiny two-bedroom house in Edgerton. His daughter, Vivian Parkman, who resided in Belle Fouche, South Dakota, hadn't reached her father on the phone for three days.

It turned out that Mr. Sprenger was okay and highly agitated from the interruption from watching the new daytime hit, *The Jerry Springer Show*, on television. Oddly, he expressed his displeasure of Sheriff Doan and even said the words, "he is a coward." Eddie brushed off Mr. Sprenger's sentiments and asked him about the phone. Unfortunately, Mr. Sprenger had forgotten to pay his phone bill, and his service was disconnected.

Later, Eddie and Tracy reported their findings back to Mr. Sprenger's daughter, Vivian, when they returned to the office. Tracy further explained to Vivian that her father would need help re-establishing his phone line.

Fifteen minutes after the phone call, Eddie turned on his desktop radio. They listened in with much enjoyment to Paul Harvey's daily program, *The Rest of the Story*. After the broadcast, Eddie did his best to impersonate Mr. Harvey with his classic *"Good Day"* signoff.

Next, they went out on traffic patrol. The duo later cited two different hotshot oil field supply drivers failing to stop before entering the highway. One infraction occurred off of Highway 387 between Midwest and Edgerton. The other happened again on Highway 387, but north of Midwest at the intersection of Light Plant Road. Immediately afterward, Eddie had turned down Fitzhugh Road to go back to town from the north when Chief Traynor contacted him and Tracy on the radio. Traynor relayed that an oil worker spotted a couple of suspicious-looking people inside the old Midwest Cemetery located just south of Highway 387 and west of town.

On the way to the cemetery, Eddie explained that it interned the bodies of children, babies mostly, but one child was the age of twelve. He further discussed that a few rounds of disease epidemics broke out in the Salt Creek Oil Field communities and camps in the 1920s and 1930s.

Eddie also expressed that a foreboding sense of grief and sorrow overwhelmed him in all his visits to the graveyard. He also opined that the wind seemed to cease and blow only in gentle wisps over the property within the fence that outlined the plot. Tracy felt that Eddie told the story with heavy-handed histrionics; until, that is, they had parked the Blazer, and she walked through the gate and experienced the same phenomena.

The men they looked for had long left before they had arrived, but it didn't take long to find evidence of their presence. As they walked along the western fence, they found a freshly dug hole. The excavation was situated next to a dilapidated outhouse in the northwest corner of the cemetery. Eddie stooped over, moved around the tilling pile from the hole, and prayed that he didn't see a human bone. He was relieved that he hadn't. The duo then continued to scan for other desecration by walking, row by row, until they were satisfied that nothing else had been disturbed.

At the end of their duty day, Eddie said "goodnight" to Tracy at 5:30 p.m. when he stopped at her house when they re-entered the town. He secretly dreaded going home and then finding a message from the Sheriff or the Undersheriff on his answering machine. In fact, Eddie had feared that type of encounter all day, and every time the radio squawked with a transmission, his skin started to crawl.

As soon as he entered his home, Eddie ignored stopping at the coat rack and went straight to his answering machine. It flashed a red light, which meant that he had a message.

With complete trepidation, Eddie pressed the *PLAY* button, and the message began.

"Eddie, this is Katrina over at the library. All the materials you requested, plus some other stuff that I found on my own, are available for you to pick up. Be sure to come during normal business hours this time; thank you."

He let out a sigh of relief and saw a ray of hope for the first time that day.

* * *

27

Wednesday, January 15, 1992

Around mid-morning, Eddie Crandall and Tracy James pulled up and parked their department Blazer outside the Natrona County Library in Edgerton. As soon and they stepped in the front door, Katrina Alvarez stood up from behind the checkout counter and greeted them both.

"Well, hello, you two! I was beginning to wonder when you would stop by to pick up the information you requested," Katrina said.

She spun and walked back behind the counter and picked up a sizeable stack of papers, but one item appeared to be a yearbook. Katrina then handed Eddie the pile, and he felt a little overwhelmed at the enormity of the stack.

Katrina noticed Eddie's trepidation and calmed him when she said, "come on, you look like a fourth-grade boy being handed an essay assignment. It won't take you that long to skim through those pages."

He nodded and replied flatly, "okay."

Then Katrina handed the yearbook to Tracy. "The two of you will be shocked to learn that Arthur G. Daniels is originally from Midwest," she said.

When her revelation didn't resonate with either of them, Katrina took the yearbook back from Tracy. Instead, she turned it over and exposed the cover to a 1926 Midwest High School yearbook. Then she thumbed through pages until she found Arthur Daniels' picture and spun the book around for them to see.

"Interesting, huh? In one of those magazine articles that I printed out for you, there was a mention that he graduated from a Wyoming oil field town in 1926. So, on a hunch, I went over to the museum and found him in that yearbook. So, please be very careful with it," Katrina warned.

Eddie immediately referred to the index pages and found Arthur's name. He then turned to a corresponding page, which portrayed the same football team photograph that hung over the library's door.

"Wow, he played in the first High School football game under the lights. He was right here under our noses the whole time," Eddie said and pointed the photo over the front door.

Katrina nodded and added, "just wait; you will find out a lot about the man when you both get a chance to read everything."

A thought suddenly struck Tracy, and she turned to face the librarian to ask her a question. "Katrina, do you have any books on sailing terminology?"

The librarian bit her lip and let out an audible, "hmmm." She pulled out an index drawer and inspected the quick reference list.

"Safari, Saigon, oh, here it is, sailing. Umm, let's see...I have one book titled *Annapolis Book of Seamanship* by John Rousmaniere," Katrina replied.

"Where is the book located?"

The librarian pointed and said, "go to the far side and look for the label *RECREATION*, which is mid-way down the aisle, and then look on the bottom shelf to your right. That is where we place sports and activities that seem incongruent with living in the middle of Wyoming."

Tracy walked down the *RECREATION* aisle and followed Katrina's explicit instructions. She found the book exactly where Katrina described it. It amused Tracy how incredibly accurate Katrina was. But, then again, if she worked here as a librarian, it was reasonable that she too could find anything quickly. Meanwhile Eddie continued to scan the micro phish printouts of magazine and newspaper articles.

After fetching the book, Tracy moved over the take a seat at one of the desks provided and opened it. Almost immediately, she found something that intrigued her on page 54, which described changing directions or tacking into the wind. The term that captivated her most was "jibbing." She looked at the five preceding pages and the five pages following tacking principles. She found all the sailing terminology that they needed to decipher more of Daniels' treasure poem. With a pen and her pocket notebook, Tracy scribbled down some information. When she finished, she stood up and walked over to Katrina to check out the book.

A few minutes later, Tracy asked Eddie, "I've got everything we need, are you ready to go?"

He looked up from the article that captivated him momentarily. "Yes, I am ready." He then shuffled it to the top of the stack to read later.

Eddie then looked over at Katrina and accolated her for her excellent work.

"Don't mention it, Eddie. So, are the two of you going to look for that supposed treasure? I mean, it is cold out there this time of year, and the wind goes right through you."

He shrugged. "Maybe."

The librarian shook her head. "No, sir, you can have it. I'd rather stay inside until it is warm. Maybe I will come out next…June."

"Thanks again," Tracy said, and they slipped out the front door and quickly climbed into the Blazer.

"Wow, she wasn't kidding! It is getting colder by the minute out there. I think I need to put my gloves on," Tracy said while she dug into her coat pockets.

Eddie was oblivious to his partner's ramblings about the cold since he was so used to it by now. Usually, it took the standing temperature to fall well below zero before he even considered wearing a stocking cap.

As they headed back to Midwest on Highway 387, the radio in the Blazer squawked.

"Sheriff-36, Dispatch."

Eddie lifted the microphone off its cradle on the dashboard and placed it in front of his mouth.

"Go ahead, Dispatch, Sheriff-36."

"Sheriff-36, we have a report of three suspicious men in the vicinity of the old Salt Creek township ruins. The BLM Law Enforcement Officer requests your backup. Please proceed. How copy?"

He turned his head toward Tracy and exclaimed, "That is Bill Crooks!"

"What is he doing out there on a school day?"

Eddie shrugged. "How should I know." Then he turned his attention back to the county dispatcher.

"Dispatch, Sheriff 36, we are en route, over."

Eddie hung up the microphone in the cradle, looked over at Tracy again, and asked, "your ready bag is in the back, right?"

She smiled and teased him back, "yes, Sergeant, my ready bag is in the back right next to yours."

"Excellent," he said curtly.

"Do you know where to find old Salt Creek?"

"I do, but good luck finding it on a map. But I have been out there a couple of times, and from when we turn off the highway, it is a straight shot down a gravel road. We can't miss it because the foundation of the old bank is rather conspicuous."

The duo turned south onto Highway 259 at the junction on the edge of Midwest town limits. They crossed over the Salt Creek and soon passed by the Castle Rock Bar. Four minutes later, Eddie turned right onto a nondescript gravel road that led them west from Highway 259.

Breaking the silence in the cab, Tracy asked, "do you think we are going to run into more of these treasure hunting fools?"

Eddie shook his head. "I wouldn't call them fools, but passionate, now that is the term I would use to describe them. But, yes, to answer your question, I think this is a continuation of yesterday."

"Okay, so tell me, what do you know about the town of Salt Creek?"

The Sergeant explained that Salt Creek was just another town like Midwest, Edgerton, and Lavoye. They had all sprung up in the Salt Creek area to house people that worked in the neighboring oil field. He further explained that the town of Salt Creek was once a gem complete with hotels, banks, and the glorious Liberty Theatre.

He then described the downfall and fallout over the Teapot Dome scandal that implicated some of the capital speculators that heavily invested in the field and the town of Salt Creek. Tracy was most surprised to learn that Salt Creek existed for only five years, from 1926 to 1930. Lastly, he informed her that it was easy to walk around the township. All one had to do was follow the slight indentions in the ground that highlighted many city blocks plus a dozen or so foundations and sidewalks were still visible.

The Deputy adjusted her coat and said, "maybe we can snoop around here later, but when it is much warmer."

Eddie agreed and subsequently pointed in the general direction to the north and remarked, "that Subaru Brat we found of Pruitt's was just over that rise and a little less than a mile from here."

"Maybe Pruitt thought the old town of Salt Creek was where he needed to seek? Did you ever think of that?"

He shrugged. "No."

Something else caught his attention. Instead of Bill Crooks' very conspicuous Willys Jeep pickup, two Sheriff's Department pickups straddled both sides of the road in front of them.

As Eddie slowed down within a hundred yards of the Sheriff's vehicles, he caught sight of the occupants.

"You have got to be kidding me. What do these clowns want?"

Tracy looked up and saw the uniformed men too and eked out a barely audible, "oh no."

Eddie came to a stop in the middle of the road between the two department pickups. Sheriff Doan emerged from his truck to the front and right of the Blazer, while Deputies McKinnon and Peck stepped out of the other truck to the left and rear.

Eddie whispered to Tracy, "follow my lead and don't let them goad you into an argument, do you understand?"

She nodded and started to step out of the Blazer. Meanwhile, Eddie quickly unzipped his coat slightly and reached inside to his shirt, and then exited the vehicle too.

Sheriff Doan watched the duo slowly emerge from the Blazer and he placed his thumbs into his overstretched weapon belt and called out to his approaching deputies.

"Well, if it isn't Howdy Doody and Miss Tracy. Oh, I am sorry, it is Casper the Friendly Sergeant now as the boys like to call you."

"Hello, Sheriff, what can I help you with?" Eddie asked.

"You get right to the point, don't you, Mr. Straight Arrow. Okay, let's do that. As of ten seconds ago, I suspended both of you. With pay for now, but as I progress my investigation, your suspensions will escalate to without pay."

"Based on what, Sheriff?"

"I like your directness Eddie, but it is too bad I can't even use it to my advantage." Doan paused long enough to raise his left hand and entering his index finger upward. "First, lets consider your insubordination for starters."

Eddie shook his head and demanded, "what insubordination?"

The Sheriff walked up to within two feet of Eddie and stared at him eye to eye. "Yes, insubordination! I am sure you felt all justified in your gripe session with Steve Witten. But, you know how it is, if you have a problem with me or how I handle my County, you come to me first, never through the back door. That, Eddie, is insubordination!"

Eddie quickly wiped Sheriff Doan's spittle off of his cheek with the sleeve of his coat. Then he looked up and met Doan's eyes once again. "Since when is insubordinate to bring my concerns to my next supervisor in my chain-of-command? I mean, it is in our manual, after all."

Sheriff Doan fumed, "don't get coy with me, Eddie! I have another charge, which is conduct unbecoming of a duly sworn deputy. How about that? Huh?"

Once again, Eddie shook his head in disbelief. "What are you talking about?"

Doan suddenly cracked a smile wide enough to see a few silver fillings on his teeth. Then he instructed, "follow me."

Eddie and Tracy stepped judiciously forward, and both kept their eyes on Deputies McKinnon and Peck. Until now, the toadies had remained stationary by their pickup. By the time they arrived at the open door of Sheriff Doan's truck, Doan had opened a sleeve of photos and laid them out on the seat.

"What are these, Sheriff?"

"Oh, these are photos of you and Miss Tracy on your little honeymoon trip to Colorado disguised as official travel. That is a fraud, come to think of it."

Next, the Sheriff shuffled through the photos, pulled each one out, and provided comments about the scenes. "So, here is one of the two of you frolicking on the ice together, awe how cute. And here is one of you holding hands in Baggs, and this one had me confused," Doan said and held up the photo.

The photograph depicted the scene in Steamboat Springs, Colorado where Eddie, Tracy, and Deputy Tombrello were looking at a map sprawled out across the hood of the department Blazer.

Doan continued, "do you have so much testosterone leaking out of you, son, that women throw themselves at you? I mean, look at that broad all snuggled on you! But then you allowed it, didn't you? Tsk, Tsk, very unprofessional."

"Sheriff, I can reasonably explain all of those photos. But I will do it before the disciplinary board," Eddie asserted.

The Sheriff shook his head. "Oh, Eddie, you will get your chance, but there is so much more to cover. Now please allow me to show you."

Doan shuffled through the small stack of photos and stopped when he found the next specimen to discuss. "Here we see Miss Tracy coming to your motel room in a towel, and wow, you fill out that towel pretty well, miss, but then again, I already knew that."

"You disgust me, you pig!" snapped Tracy, and she lunged forward, but Eddie caught her by the arm and pulled her back.

"Oh, come now, Tracy, let us be professional here. I have so much more to show you two," Sheriff Doan hissed. Then he said, "here, take these duplicate photos. I am sure you two will want to reminisce about your honeymoon and maybe make a scrapbook."

Tracy snatched the envelope of duplicate photos out of Doan's hand. "Where did those photos come from, Sheriff?"

Sheriff Doan returned his thumbs back into his belt and delighted in his humiliating tactics. "Oh, Miss Tracy. I had someone follow both of you. You see, I knew that when I transferred you out here and based on your history, that the two of you would be playing Tarzan and Jane on the County's dime in no time at all."

Tracy feinted a lunge that caused Sheriff Doan to step back, but once again, Eddie caught her by the arm.

"You disgust me. You know that?" she spat.

Eddie turned to Doan and said, "so, it was all a setup, right, Sheriff? You fraudulently ordered Tracy and me to conduct a wild goose chase of an investigation. Then you hired one of your goons to follow us around in his black Ford Bronco, am I right?"

Doan nodded his appreciation. Then he said, "not only are you direct, but you are very perceptive too, but again, it is too bad I couldn't use your innate talents to my betterment."

Eddie stood unwavering and warned, "Sheriff, when this is through, there is going to be a reckoning."

Doan nodded. "Yes, Eddie, there will be a reckoning, and the two of you will walk away from my County in shame."

The Sheriff postured himself as if he had a brand-new intuition, but it was apparent to Eddie and Tracy that it was all a choreographed plan.

He then proposed, "I can make this all go away really quick, and all I ask is that you both resign. Do that, and all this goes away like a snowflake in the wind. What do you say?"

Eddie sternly looked at Tracy and then back to the Sheriff. He then asked, "what if we refuse, Sheriff? What else can you do to us?"

"What else, Eddie? Oh, I can do a lot more. I can shame you in your church, yes, I can do that, and I can refer more and more of those treasure hunter locusts your way too. Oh, I forgot to add that those two guys that you and Tracy arrested and the two that Chief Traynor arrested, I let them go, charges dismissed."

Crandall asked, "just so that I understand you clearly. You refused to enforce the law. Is that what you are saying?"

"Eddie, Eddie, Eddie," Doan said while shaking his head, "it is called exercising discretion. Those guys didn't do anything that bad around your town. But, I mean, come on, digging a few holes around Midwest would be an improvement."

Eddie struggled internally to quiet the desire to lash out at the Sheriff verbally. On the outside, however, he stood stoically silent in front of his boss.

Finally, Sheriff Doan shook his head and demanded, "Eddie, you are stalling. Are you going to give me your resignation or not?"

Following a long sigh, Eddie reached his right hand to his shirt above the left breast pocket. Then he plucked the badge off of his uniform, and Tracy followed his lead and did the same.

"No, Sheriff, we will not resign. We choose to go to the disciplinary board, and we willingly comply with your suspension with pay order. Here, take our badges, but don't lose them because they will be coming back to us shortly."

Sheriff Doan begrudgingly accepted the badges and then demanded, "I need your guns and my department Blazer too?"

Eddie smiled. "That is a negative, Sheriff. You see, both of our sidearms were personally procured and not issued by the department. So, you are not entitled to them. Also, if you want the Blazer back, your goons can follow us into town and drive it back to Casper. But, of course, that is after we remove our personal effects."

"I could just take the Blazer now and let the two of you walk. That is what I think, Eddie," Doan suggested. Then he sneered, "I will ruin you. Even within your conclave of oil field trash, they will reject both of you after I finish. So, again, I offer you both an opportunity to resign. I will even give you until tomorrow evening to do so."

Eddie calmly shook his head. "Sheriff, you already have our answer, and we will have our day to clear our names."

An immediate pause interjected into the conversation. Then, unhesitantly, Eddie spun on his heels and marched back to the Blazer with Tracy in tow.

* * *

28

After Eddie turned the Blazer around, he looked in the rearview mirror. He spied the Sheriff still standing outside his pickup with his arms folded across his chest. Once they put a little distance between themselves and the Sheriff, Eddie reached into his top pocket, pulled out his micro recorder, and clicked the *Stop/Record* button.

Tracy spotted what he had done and smiled. Then, she asked, "you recorded all that? Is that legal?"

Eddie smiled too and answered, "yes, it is allowable in Wyoming, and I think we can use some if not all of the recording to help our cause before the board.

She nodded but then asked, "I don't know how you can remain so calm. We just lost our jobs."

"Actually, I am beyond mad at this point and struggling to maintain focus. If I succumb to emotion, then I can no longer think our way out of this." He took a deep breath and continued, "no, we didn't lose our jobs, Tracy. We are sort of like on leave though it becomes part of our permanent employment record."

Crandall continued driving east along the gravel road and could now see Highway 259 ahead of him in the distance. Sitting behind the wheel of a car had always been a type of meditation. Driving always allowed other parts of his brain to untie the knots and twists of whatever bothered him. When he turned off the dirt road and back onto the pavement toward Midwest, a thought occurred.

"Tracy," Eddie called and waited until she turned her head toward him. When she did, he continued, "Sheriff Doan overplayed his hand. If he had anything on us, he would have fired us outright, but as it is, he is trying to shame us into quitting."

She squinted and shook her head simultaneously and asked, "what are you talking saying? He is going to ruin us!"

Before he could reply, she exclaimed, "It is all my fault. He hates me!"

He shook his head. "Sheriff Doan does just hate you. Unfortunately, he is an equal opportunist since he hates me, you, and everyone in the Salt Creek community equally."

Tracy rolled her eyes and spoke, "Eddie, this is no time for jokes. He hates me, and he thought by assigning me out here that I would eventually resign. And, I have to be honest, when I first looked around the place, I felt like I wanted to hand in my badge."

He continued to focus his attention on the highway before him. He didn't give any outward indication that he heard what she had to say.

"Eddie, did you hear me?"

"I did. I heard every word. I am thinking, that's all."

"Well, stop that! I wish you would voice your thoughts a little more because your silence makes me nervous."

He nodded and began revealing that he had said a prayer and asked God to see them through this trial.

Tracy shook her head in disbelief. "Eddie, I used to pray all the time for God to show me a sign, and if he did, I would do what He said. But then I grew up. We live the real world, and I have to make my successes and happiness."

Suddenly, his head snapped around and looked at her. "Is that what you think faith is all about?"

"Yes."

He closed his eyes briefly, and when he opened them again, he explained, "I have learned that my faith in God is not to have Him show up and miracle away my fears. Faith is not waiting for a sign nor is faith about going to church on Sundays either. Instead, it is about having a relationship with God daily. Faith is about relying on His strength and not my own. Everything I have, I owe to Him. So, yes, Tracy, my faith overcomes my fear."

She received his message but then retorted, "faith doesn't pay the bills. If I lose my job, what am I going to do? Where am I going to go?"

Eddie nodded his head slightly and further explained, "I have the same fear about paying bills. Though in the long run, I know that God will always provide me what I need."

"Come on, Eddie, that is not reality. I need a little more assurance than just faith."

He turned his head toward his partner once more. Then, complete sincerity, said, "my faith, Tracy, allows me to stop worrying about situations that I cannot control. What I can control is my reaction to those situations. Do you understand?"

"Yes, I guess. I just don't know about the whole Jesus thing. That is all."

"Tracy, Jesus is not a thing. Rather, He is alive today more than ever. Now, you have the right to believe what you want. But, I just know that He inspires me to do more in life."

They rode in silence back into town, culminating with Eddie parking the Blazer in its usual spot in the carport outside his home. Tracy immediately began collecting stuff from the front seat to include the materials from the library and the envelope of pictures. Meanwhile, Eddie had already opened the back lid, grabbed their ready bags and other personal equipment, and slung them into the back of his pickup. He then walked around to the Blazer and asked her to go through everything inside the cab, and if something didn't come from the Sheriff's Department, she was to remove it.

Instead of helping his partner, Eddie went inside his home, walked directly into his office, picked up the telephone receiver off its cradle, and punched in a phone number.

When the call was answered on the other end by his friend in Internal Affairs, he said, "Riley, this is Eddie. Tracy and I just got suspended with pay. Did you know about this?"

Adam Riley briefly paused on the other end, and it sounded to him like Riley had just shut his office door. Then his friend replied, "yes, I expected that would happen following the meeting between the Undersheriff and Sheriff Doan."

In Eddie's mind, his patience started to unravel, and in doing so, his attitude followed suit. Finally, he retorted, "I wish that you could have called me and given me a heads up, at least?"

Riley let out a sigh and parsed his response, "Eddie, listen to me carefully. Unfortunately, I cannot discuss matters from an active investigation."

"Investigation? Are you investigating me? For what, Riley? The person you should be investigating is Sheriff Doan! Did you know that he released those treasure hunting trespassers yesterday?"

Again, Riley repeated, "listen carefully to my words, Eddie. I cannot discuss any matter of any open investigation, whether it is on you or even the Sheriff himself."

Crandall suddenly realized the intimation his friend tried to convey to him, which suddenly changed his outlook.

"Eddie, are you still there?"

"Ya, Riley. I was just thinking about what I am going to do next?"

"Well, why don't you treat this as a well-deserved break. You know, a paid vacation. Just wait for the review board to contact you."

"Thanks, Riley," he said and hung up the phone.

When Eddie walked out of the office, he saw that Tracy had already hauled in everything from the Blazer and was placed on the living room floor. He thanked her for the help, and before he could say another word, a Sheriff's Department pickup truck pulled up in front of his home.

Eddie calmly walked out of the front door, walked up to the passenger side door of the pickup, and handed Deputy Peck the keys to his department Blazer without confrontation or even a word of dialog. Instead, he turned and went back inside his house and shut the door behind him.

Before he could sit down, he heard a knock on the front door. He looked over at Tracy, sitting on the couch, and said, "now, what? I bet those clowns couldn't start the stupid thing."

To his surprise, when he opened the door, Chief Traynor stood at the doorstep. Then he invited the Chief in with a quick wave of his hand.

Wasting no time, Chief Traynor asked, "so, are you fired or suspended?"

"Suspended with pay. But how did you know, Chief?" Eddie asked.

"I had a hunch that Doan would try something desperate like this, and as usual, he didn't disappoint. Besides, I saw Doan's lackeys driving off in your Blazer."

He nodded. "I just got off of the phone with my buddy Adam Riley in Internal Affairs, who said something peculiar."

Suddenly interested, Tracy asked, "what's that?"

"He said this exactly, 'I cannot discuss any matter of any open investigation whether it is on you or even the Sheriff himself.' Doesn't that wording say something to either one of you?"

Traynor bobbed his head and wished aloud, "By God, I hope Doan is under investigation. But, I don't think anyone has the political clout to see it through." Then a thought occurred to Traynor. "Do not look at this suspension as a bad thing, rather look at it as a paid vacation."

"Thanks, Chief. That is the other thing that Riley told me too."

Then, without another word, Traynor let himself out the door.

Finally, Eddie sat down on the couch next to Tracy. She looked up at him and asked, "now what?"

He winked at her. "Well, we can start by changing out of our uniforms and into civilian clothes, then once you get back here, we will have lunch and go through all the stuff we got from the library."

She shook her head. "But, none of this seems to be fazing you one bit. I don't get it. Don't you care?"

"Of course, I care, Tracy. If we give in to despair and lose our hope, then Doan wins in the end. So, instead of sitting around here feeling sorry for ourselves, why don't we tie up a few loose ends in the Pruitt case? We can also try to figure out where that treasure poem leads us. Then, if we find anything or not, at least we can get the word out to prevent more interlopers from crawling around here."

Tracy understood what Eddie said but didn't necessarily agree with him. But then again, she thought that working on something was much better than stewing upon all that happened. After all, it was her same attitude when she was assigned to the Salt Creek area two weeks ago.

Soon afterward, she left his house and walked over to her place to change clothes. While she was gone, Eddie had a strange thought, and he followed up on it. He walked into his office and looked through his notes to find the phone number of Vivian Parkman, Mr. Sprenger's daughter. When he saw the number and dialed it, he waited patiently for Vivian to answer.

"Hello?"

"Vivian, this is Eddie Crandall in Midwest. I spoke to you yesterday about your father."

"Is he okay?" she asked.

Eddie promptly replied, "I am sure he is fine, Vivian. The reason I called is that your father said the oddest thing to me yesterday: He referred to my boss, Sheriff Doan, as a 'coward.' Do you know the reason for that?"

He could hear Vivian's respirations increase rapidly, and then she asked, "is your boss, John Robert Doan?"

"Yes, ma'am, I believe that is his full name."

He then waited for Vivian to respond, and started to think that call had dropped, but he could still hear her breathing on the other end of the line. "Ma'am, are you still there?

"I am, but I don't know if I can trust you?"

Instead of an immediate answer, he offered an alternative, "well, ma'am, I understand if you can't trust me. So, how about I give you the number to a friend of mine, the Midwest Chief of Police, Wyatt Traynor, and maybe you can tell him the story."

"Oh, I remember Wyatt. He was such a nice boy! So, you say he is your friend?"

Eddie smiled and replied, "yes, ma'am. He is my friend and a great mentor of mine."

Vivian paused but then said, "okay, I will tell you the story. But please promise me that my story won't get out into the newspapers or anything like that?"

"I promise, ma'am. No news outlets."

"Okay, it all started about 30 years ago...."

* * *

29

It was 11:55 a.m., as indicated by the wall clock in Eddie's living room, when Tracy returned. As usual, she did not knock on the door and walked directly through the entry, and hung up her coat. Eddie saw that Tracy wore a pair of Levi's jeans and a brown University of Wyoming pullover hoodie. She also wore an old pair of tan-colored combat boots, which Eddie assumed were holdovers from her Air Force days.

She looked over at him and asked, "you haven't changed yet? What have you been up to?"

He explained that he was on the phone and hadn't had time to change out of his uniform. Tracy then asked him who he talked to; Eddie explained that he spoke to Vivian Parkman from the day before.

"Did you reassure her that her father is okay?"

"I did," he said curtly and then added, "I will tell you more about our conversation later."

He then got up from his chair, and as he passed by Tracy, he mentioned that he was going to change.

A few minutes later, Eddie reemerged from his bedroom dressed in a pair of Wrangler jeans and a button-down flannel shirt, which he tucked neatly into his waistband. He then walked into the kitchen, and saw that she had already made both of them fried bologna and cheese sandwiches. Eddie picked up the paper plate that held his lunch and, with his free hand, grabbed a bag of potato chips. Then he proceeded over to the couch.

Tracy followed his lead, and she too took up a seat on the sofa but waited for him to finish his silent prayer before she started to eat. In between bites, they exchanged their thoughts on solving the remaining parts of the poem. When they finished eating, Eddie collected the paper plates and napkins. He deposited them into the trash can in the kitchen. Then he came back and took up his seat once again.

Without saying a word, Tracy picked up the copy of the *Annapolis Book of Seamanship* and placed it on her lap. She quickly found the page where she left off and resumed reading a particular passage that caught her eye earlier in the library. Meanwhile, Eddie picked up the 1926 Midwest High School yearbook and again looked at the photograph of Arthur Daniels. He looked so young, Eddie thought. He then set the school yearbook aside and began reading all of the newspaper and magazine articles. As he read, he jotted down notes. At one point, Eddie looked up to let his eyes adjust, and he noticed that Tracy, too, had taken some notes as well.

An hour and a half later, Eddie stood up and stretched his back. Tracy looked up at him and asked, "did you find anything interesting?"

He smiled at her and responded, "yes, do you want to hear about it?"

Tracy set her book and notes down on the coffee table and then sat back and folded her legs one over the other.

"Okay, I am ready."

Eddie discussed Arthur Daniels' life, his profession mostly, and about one of his passions, sailing. Arthur Daniels was the son of the Standard Oil Company executive in charge of operations in the Salt Creek Oil Field. He was the oldest of two siblings, both sisters, and was an honor roll student in Midwest. After college, Daniels moved to Hammond, Indiana began his career at Standard Oil-Indiana Division. When not at work, Arthur loved to sail, and his sailboat moored in nearby Michigan City, which is on the shore of Lake Michigan. Interestingly, his boat bore the name *Black Gold*.

He also explained that Arthur was married once briefly, from 1936 until 1940. From then on, he remained a strident bachelor for the rest of his life. Arthur had no children, and when he died, he left his amassed fortune to his three nieces to split amongst them.

Tracy nodded that she understood but then asked, "that is all good information, but it doesn't explain why he would write a poem to lead people to a treasure, does it?"

"I was just getting to that."

Then Eddie further chronicled that one magazine article covered another one of Arthur Daniels' hobbies, orienteering. He described that the activity started in Sweden and became popular in the United States after World War II. Arthur had joined a club in Gary, Indiana, in the early 1950s. Lastly, he summarized that the object of orienteering was to take a detailed map, a compass, and a set of written clues to find all the objectives from start to finish.

Tracy interceded, "so, this was an outside activity, like in a State Park or something like that?"

"Yes, precisely."

"But that still doesn't answer my question. Why would Arthur bury something near Midwest?"

Crandall reached over to the stack of printouts that sat on the coffee table, and he pulled out an article. He informed her that in the report that he held, Arthur Daniels often spoke at municipal groups and various Chamber of Commerce meetings about the values of the word *community*. Additionally, he pointed out examples where Arthur orated that his sense of community comes from his hometown in Wyoming.

"But he doesn't name Midwest specifically, does he?"

Eddie nodded but clarified, "Arthur did, but it was in a small riddle of a sort. I quote, 'my views of what a community means here in the Midwest comes from Midwest,' end quote. That is the only mention of anything with direct ties to this area." After a short pause, he asked, "what did you find?"

Tracy smiled and then instructed him to stand up from the couch, which she did the same, and they exchanged places. She told Eddie to sit on the end of the sofa and extend one of his legs down the cushions to the other end. Next, Tracy sat down on the other end couch before him with her back toward Eddie. Lastly, she asked him to extend out his arm and keep it raised horizontally.

She explained further, "Eddie, picture the couch as a boat. Behind you is the stern, and the other end is the stem. The left side is called the port side or just 'port,' and the right side is 'starboard.' Your arm then is the tiller to the rudder."

Tracy looked back over her shoulder, grabbed his outreached arm by the wrist, and explained further. "So, Eddie, if we want to turn the boat to the starboard side, I have to push the tiller toward the port side. Do you understand now?"

Finally, she let go of his hand and moved over to the end of the couch, where she turned and faced him. Meanwhile, he remained in the same position with his arm extended until the intimation hit him.

After a few seconds, he dropped his left arm and said, "I get it now," and he reached over to the coffee table and picked up the poem again. He read aloud the line, "*MANAGE PORT TILL POINTING THE CRAFT.*" Then after a short pause, he continued, "What this tells me is that Dan Pruitt ended up where he did because he didn't understand the terminology. He wasn't to turn left; instead, he should have turned right or starboard. Is that what you determined?"

Tracy nodded. However, she confessed that the following line confused her: *INTERSECT THE LIP NOT SLOWED BY DRAUGHT.*

"I don't see how we can decipher it because the clue is talking about the depth of the water, is it not?"

Eddie shook his head. "It is not that confusing at all. So, imagine we are driving up Highway 259 toward Midwest, and we see the *OASIS.* We then turn right. So, what is before us away from the *OASIS*?" He paused briefly, then explained further, "the Rimrocks, which is an escarpment, or a *LIP.*"

He then abruptly stood up and rhetorically asked aloud, "what is another word for *DRAUGHT*? It is old English for a draft of beer. Now let me rephrase the clue. At the Oasis, turn right or away from the bar, and go over the Rimrocks. That has to be where we need to look."

"Excellent, but what about the rest of the poem?"

Eddie shrugged. "I dunno. I guess we will have to go out there and kind of wing it from there."

Tracy shook her head in disagreement and said, "No. I don't want to wing it. I want you to sit back down, so we can try to figure this out together."

He nodded and replied, "okay."

Around 3:30 p.m., someone knocked on the front door, and Eddie got up from the couch to answer it. Bill Crooks entered and gave them both a puzzled look, which was apparent because they were each in civilian attire and not in uniform.

"What are you two up to? Is this your day off?" Crooks asked.

"We're not up to much, Bill. What began as a slow day ended up with us getting suspended with pay by Sheriff Doan, that is all," Eddie said facetiously.

"Suspended for what?"

"For improper conduct between two deputies while in uniform or something. Doan had hired someone to follow us to Colorado, and the investigator took some photographs of us that could become construed negatively and completely out of context."

Crooks nodded that he understood, and after he stroked his beard, he replied, "it seems to me that Sheriff Doan is pretty desperate to pull a stunt like that? What do you have on him?"

Tracy suddenly got up from the sofa and excused herself to use the bathroom.

When the bathroom door closed, Eddie whispered, "I don't have anything on him. The suspension came out of the blue."

Crooks shook his head. "Man, that guy is a coward and a bully."

Eddie's head snapped around, and he grabbed onto a specific word of Bill's. Then he remarked, "that is the second time I have heard the term 'coward' applied toward him in the last two days."

In the minutes that followed, Eddie quickly briefed Crooks on the details of the conversation he had with Vivian Parkman. Then, he stressed to the teacher that he needed to run down the facts in the story to see if anything had any merit.

Once again, Crooks stroked his beard, and then he asked about how the suspension went down. He explained that they responded to a call from the County dispatcher to assist him (Bill) at the ruins of the Salt Creek township. Then he recounted how Sheriff Doan disclosed the pictures, culminating in the Sheriff demanding he and Tracy resign to save their reputations.

Lastly, Eddie said, "thankfully, I had the presence of mind to record the whole conversation on tape using my micro recorder. Do you want to listen to it?"

Crooks held his hand up and shook his head. Then he whispered, "no, not right now. But I do think you need to store that tape somewhere safe just in case."

Eddie protested, "in case of what, Bill, how could he know?"

The teacher shrugged. "That man is a loose cannon and is unpredictable. Think about it, Eddie, he's acting desperate, and I wouldn't put it past him to have someone break into your place to look for more evidence to hang you with."

Crooks spun on his heel and looked out the front window, and placed his hands on his hips while he thought. Then, he turned back around and faced Eddie.

"Give me the tape. I will keep it. Sheriff Doan would never think to look toward me, though Chief Traynor, yes, but me, no."

Eddie knew Bill was right, and he reached into the right breast pocket of his flannel shirt with his left hand and took out the microcassette, and handed it over.

The teacher placed the cassette in the inside pocket of his down vest, then he added, "I will keep it with that business card we found in Dan Pruitt's wallet. Speaking of which, I am running that to the ground through some other channels. I don't want anyone within this County to know what I am doing. But by tomorrow, I should have some hard facts to go with my theory."

Eddie started to reply, but Bill Crooks warned, "listen to me, be careful, my friend. Sheriff Doan is a bully, and bullies always shame their victims, just like what he tried to do to both you and Tracy with those photos."

"About those, let me explain," Tracy pleaded as she ran back into the living room.

Crooks held up his hand with the palm forward and stopped her plea in midsentence.

"None is necessary. I am sure they are completely out of context. I might add that neither of you strikes me as the kind of people that would rush into a romantic interlude either, so I believe you."

Tracy nodded that she understood, and on the inside, she felt a little of her anxiety release.

Suddenly, Bill Crooks looked down at his wristwatch, which indicated: 3:52 p.m. "Dang, we are burning daylight."

Eddie and Tracy exchanged glances at one another since neither was utterly sure what Crooks meant.

Crooks continued, "the reason why I am here is that I got a call from my BLM supervisor. He wants me to go out behind the Rimrocks and look for a guy who has set up a camper on an oil well location on BLM property. I was hoping you would both provide me some backup because I am getting too old to walk upon people who may or may not be heavily armed. What do you say? Would you help me out? I mean, like, us leaving in a few minutes.?"

Eddie was confused, so he asked, "but don't you need a Sheriff Deputy? We got suspended, remember?"

"Oh, that doesn't matter much to me. I want someone who can handle a weapon and watch my back. I am not asking you to do anything in a law enforcement capacity." The teacher looked down at his watch again and then pleaded, "so, will you help me? I want to get out there and back before the sun sets at 4:54 today."

Eddie was a little apprehensive, but then Tracy suggested, "If we have any time left over, we could look around for the last few clues in the poem? Again, the job takes us behind the Rimrocks after all?"

While Eddie mulled the offer over, Bill Crooks interjected. "Yes, please, do solve that poem so those yahoos stop coming around."

Finally, Crandall replied, "okay, but give us a few minutes to grab our gear."

"Thanks, Eddie, and you too, Tracy. I appreciate it."

* * *

30

Minutes later, Eddie drove his 1978 Ford F150, which he inherited from his father a few years before. Ahead of him was Bill Crooks in his conspicuous 1960 Willys Jeep pickup that always sounded like it badly needed an exhaust system overhaul. As they motored out of town limits, Tracy reported her progress to Eddie about the book *Friday Night Lights*. She adeptly associated the unifying chant of "MOJO" in Odessa, Texas, with the "OFT" chant used around the Salt Creek community.

Concerning the moniker, *Oil Field Trash*, Tracy opined that it was similar to something that happened at Grand Forks, Air Force Base. In particular, she pointed out that one missile maintenance specialty was nicknamed the "Buttcracks" by other maintainers. She explained that the "Buttcracks" handled the tasks that other maintenance teams disparaged, like diesel engine work, air conditioning, and electrical, to name a few. Instead of taking the term derogatorily, the "Buttcracks" adopted the name as their motto in a show of unity.

Eddie listened carefully, and he agreed on the similarity of taking a negative term and spinning it around with positive psychology. Although, he had only received a trace of Tracy's musings. Instead, he focused more intently on the thick gray clouds that had moved in and blotted out the sun. He recalled the morning news telecast that forecasted Central Wyoming was entering a Winter Storm watch, but that wasn't supposed to start until the next morning.

"There it is!" Tracy exclaimed, which interrupted Eddie's thoughts on the weather. "There is the *OASIS*," she said and pointed to it.

As expected, Crooks soon turned his pickup to the east and onto a heavily used oil field road a few hundred yards south of the Castle Rock Bar. In some places, huge ruts demarked the edges of the trail. Unfortunately, the grooves also served as a reminder that the land turned into a soupy clay mess anytime the ground got wet in the area.

Advancing easterly, Crooks made a few successive turns onto other roads. Soon, they climbed over the southern shoulder between the Rimrocks and the lone sentinel, Castle Rock. Within minutes, they ventured down the slope behind the Rimrocks and had crossed over the Salt Creek. Then they climbed uphill away from the stream over a small hill. On the other side, in a small bowl lined with sagebrush, they spotted a modern Chevrolet pickup with a 1960s, pink and white, Shasta Compact camper still hitched to the bumper.

Bill Crooks stopped 50 yards from the camper, and when he got out of his truck, he asked Eddie and Tracy to take up positions far right and far left of him as he approached. Then, seconds later, Crooks rapped authoritatively on the door, and a man who looked to be in his late 60s opened the camper. Crooks identified himself as a law enforcement officer and then assertively instructed the man to pack up and move his unit out of the oilfield and suggested that he go back into Casper. The man didn't complain, and within a few minutes, he had moved out and drove past both pickups.

"That was easy enough," Crooks stated, and he continued, "this is a State School Section of land, but the guy shouldn't have been out here camping anyway since state law does not allow it."

"I agree, Bill. But if I had opened the door to find you, armed, and in your mountain man garb, I think I would have fled too," Eddie joked.

The teacher roared an enormous belly laugh as if he had stored it up for a month. "Okay, folks, thank you both again. I need to head home."

But when Crooks turned to walk away, he stopped and came back to where Eddie and Tracy still stood. Then, he asked, "are the two of you going to stay and look around a bit?"

Eddie nodded.

The teacher squinted his eyes slightly as he looked at both Eddie and Tracy for a few seconds. Then he instructed them not to waste much time out there because it would soon get dark, and by the look of the clouds, snow would start falling too.

Crandall then assured him, "don't worry, Bill, we will be a few minutes behind you. I want to make out a few landmarks so that we can come later to explore further."

Crooks turned and walked back to his truck, and without turning around, he raised his right hand and said, "see ya."

As they walked back to the pickup, Eddie grew wary of Bill Crooks' warning about the weather. The temperature felt like it had dropped another ten degrees just in the last minute or two. He looked up at the sky, and it did look and feel like it was going to snow at any second.

They climbed back into the truck. After Eddie started it, he executed a three-point turnaround on the road. Then they began backtracking the route back toward Highway 259. Finally, however, after driving over the low water bridge that spanned Salt Creek, Tracy spoke.

"What stream is that, Eddie?"

He looked to where she pointed and said, "that is Salt Creek believe it or not. The headwaters start many miles southeast of here, and it kind of snakes its way along. It almost runs into Edgerton before bending to the west and going past Midwest to the south. Then it turns to the north where it dumps into the Powder River near Kaycee."

"Why is it called Salt Creek?"

He explained, "The creek receives its name for its salty taste. To me, it tastes like a brine that you make to soak a turkey in before cooking it."

They rode in silence as Eddie negotiated his truck around a bend in the trail that came precipitously close to a sizeable sandstone boulder on the west side of the road. Meanwhile, Tracy continued to scan the area, and then she saw another stream.

"Eddie, was stream is that?" she asked as she pointed south and east of the road.

He quipped, "that is Teapot Creek."

Within a microsecond of his utterance, another idea hit him. He immediately pulled off the road to his left and onto a sparse patch of prairie grass, where he came to a stop.

"What are you doing?" she asked.

"Pull out that poem again and do it quick!" he demanded.

Tracy dug out the poem, and Eddie excitedly snatched it out of her hand. He scanned down the lines until he found it.

He then read aloud: "*NEIGHBORLY TEA STEEPS INTO BRINE.*"

Tracy didn't follow the implication as indicated by her furrowed eyebrows, but Eddie caught her expression.

He further explained that Salt Creek is the *BRINE,* and Teapot Creek is the TEA. Eddie further proclaimed, "it was so apparent that I almost missed it."

Tracy smiled and reached over to Eddie and took back the poem. Then, she read aloud the following line: "*GUAGE A CRYPT ALONG THE SPINE.*"

Then they simultaneously stepped out of the pickup and looked around. He instinctively knew that the *SPINE* was referring to a rock formation. To the south and east, Eddie only saw the flat drainages of the creeks. He then looked back to the sandstone boulder next to the road a half-mile to his north, but it too did not look like a spine. Finally, Eddie looked west and above the massive sandstone rock and saw an enormous domed-shaped hill.

Up until that point, he assumed the domed hill was part of the Rimrocks. Then he spied not one sandstone spine, but three of them, and all of them with a rock shelf facing south. The only problem was getting up to them since they would have to hike up one of the steep sagebrush choked ravines to access the sandstone outcroppings.

Eddie pointed and said to Tracy, "up there, one of those rock out-croppings has to be the *SPINE*!"

"Do you want to go up there?" she asked.

"Yes, I do, but if we are going to do it, we need to do it now. We are running out of daylight."

Tracy started to walk away toward the hill when Eddie called out to her to return. Instead, he gave her the backpack that she had prepared earlier then donned his own.

She immediately protested, "Eddie, it is ridiculous to carry this thing. I mean, we are only going to walk, what, a half-mile from the truck?"

He abruptly replied, "yes, but you have to remember that being even a mile from town out here can become a dangerous situation at a mo-ment's notice. Just take the bag. It is better to have it and not need it than to need it and not have it. Besides, we may have to dig out our flash-lights if we get caught out here after sunset."

Next, Crandall adjusted one of his straps, looked up at Tracy, and asked, "are you ready?"

She nodded in reply.

He led the way up the southernmost sandstone topped ravine. At first, the walking was easy until they ascended to the start of the sand-stone outcropping. The angle of the slope they mounted increased the higher they climbed alongside the spine.

"Eddie," Tracy asked, "what are we looking for so I can help?"

He looked over his shoulder and said, "the next line of the poem said something about a *CRYPT*, so I take that to mean a small cave or some-thing."

"Okay!" she shouted in return against an ever-increasing wind.

After a few minutes, they had hiked the entire length of the first rock face until it faded out into a rounded hilltop. Next, they scrambled over the dome and began descending the second of the threes sandstone topped ravines.

Suddenly, the clouds broke and snow started falling with just a cou-ple of flakes at first, but then a few seconds later, a hundred of their ice crystal friends joined in the dance. The storm hit so suddenly and with such force that visibility dropped to just a few yards within an instant.

Tracy, however, managed to walk closely behind Eddie and followed his steps along the sandstone wall. "Eddie, I can't see anything in this snow. Are you sure we can find the truck when we get to the bottom?"

Eddie stopped and placed his back against the sandstone wall. He pulled off one of his gloves and wiped his face, and then looked up at Tracy.

With numbed lips, he said, "I hope so, I am not sure where this ravine comes out exactly along the road, but I know we will turn right once we hit it. If this snow doesn't let up, though, we could walk right past my truck and never see it."

"So, why don't we find some shelter here along the rock wall or something and wait until the snow stops? I don't think we have a choice, don't you think?" she asked.

He nodded but suggested, "how about we keep following this outcropping down to the bottom. Maybe the snow shower will be a quick one."

Crandall led off again, and it was arduous slogging with each step. The inch of snow underfoot turned the soil beneath their boots into a slick and sticky mess. First, Eddie slipped and fell, then Tracy did as well.

Five minutes after the snowstorm started, the wind increased to over 30 miles per hour, yet the duo only covered 75 yards. Also slowing them down were the gusts of wind hit them so hard that it felt like waves of body blows. Plus, the gale bit their exposed cheeks with needle-sharp teeth.

Once again, Eddie stopped, but instead of putting his back against the wall, he knelt to one knee, dislodged a sizeable tumbleweed, and released it into the wind. Tracy marveled that the tumbleweed disappeared within a second due to the wind-driven snow

"Tracy, here!" he exclaimed. "I found a small cave that is big enough for the two of us to climb into and get out of the wind."

She didn't protest and quickly followed behind him into the recess. The opening to the fissure was only three feet wide and three feet high, but once inside, they found it opened up slightly. While the cave height remained about the same, the width doubled to about six feet. The overall length was around six feet as well.

The back of the cave ended with a pile of sandstone and earth rubble. But between the top of the rockpile and the ceiling, a small dinner-sized porthole indicated that another chamber existed beyond, albeit a small one. The tiny alcove was quiet inside except the torrent wind howling just a foot or two beyond the opening.

The cramped conditions also made it challenging to wiggle their arms out of their backpack straps. Tracy stifled urges to laugh when Eddie kept bumping his head against the low ceiling. Finally, after a lot of frustration, he pulled the pack off his back and placed it between them.

Tracy finally asked him, "so, are we just going to wait out the storm here? Is that what you are thinking?"

"Honestly, I don't know. I just knew that we needed to get out of the wind before we both froze to death."

"I wonder how long it will be before we can leave?"

"Again, I don't know, sorry."

Eddie moved his body around so that both he and Tracy could lay parallel to one another but with their heads on opposite sides so they could see each other's faces. He then inhaled and let out an exasperated breath. But something alerted him.

Meanwhile, Tracy focused on the storm raging outside the cave into an increasingly darkening wall of snow. The sun must be setting, she thought silently.

"Tracy!" Eddie said, trying to get her attention.

She turned her face from the opening and cast her eyes upon him. "Sorry, I was looking at the snow."

He nodded and asked her, "do you smell that?"

She sniffed the air, and from the look of her face, it seemed puzzling to her as well. After a few seconds, she surmised, "it almost smells like cucumbers, like in a salad. Is that what you detected too?"

"Yes," but it continued to puzzle him as to the source of the strange scent.

* * *

31

At 8:30 p.m. that night, Bill Crooks had finished grading a stack of quizzes from his Civics and American History classes. It pleased him that every one of his students had passed. Like all teachers in Midwest, Crooks cared deeply for his students and wanted them to succeed, not just academically but in life afterward. But, most of all, he did his level best to equip his students to be an informed constituency and take the task of electing government officials very seriously.

The telephone rang in the kitchen, which broke up his musings.

Lois called out from the master bedroom, "Bill, can you get that?"

"Sure, honey!" Crooks replied, and he pushed away from the dining room table and walked over to the kitchen to answer the phone.

"Hello?"

"Hey, Bill, this is Dr. Gaines," the caller said.

"What's up, Doc?" Crooks replied with a chuckle.

"You are hilarious, Bill. The reason I called to tell you is that school is closed tomorrow and probably Friday as well due to the storm."

Shocked by the news, Crooks commented, "wow, I didn't know it was that bad outside. I have been grading papers since supper and haven't looked outside."

"Yep, it is a pretty big storm. That warm-up a few days ago brought up a bunch of moisture from the Gulf of Mexico and combined with an Arctic clipper. As a result, we now have blizzard conditions. But, Bill, I need you to do me a favor?"

"Sure, whatever you need, Doc."

"Great, can I give you a list of teachers to call and let them know about the school closure tomorrow? I would appreciate it. It will also keep me from being on the phone all night."

"No problem, Doc. Who do you want me to call?"

Dr. Gaines provided Bill Crooks the names of 10 teachers, all of which lived in Midwest. Crooks also made a specific mental note to remind the three first-year teachers to stay at home and ride out the storm. Dr. Gaines again expressed his gratitude and ended the call.

When Lois heard her husband hang up the phone, she asked, "Bill, who was that?"

"That was Doc Gaines, honey. He said that school is closed tomorrow because of the storm. Doc also asked me to call some of the other teachers."

"Okay," she replied, but then asked him, "Bill, before you make those calls, can you take the trash out before it gets any worse outside. Oh, and can you bring in some meat from the freezer in the garage? I want the kitchen freezer full, so we don't have to leave the house?"

"Yes, darling," Crooks replied.

Crooks then walked to the back porch, where he stepped into his boots and donned a well-worn canvas Carhartt coat. When he opened the back door, he had to push hard against the storm door to move a two-foot-tall snowdrift off the back step. Once outside, he looked out into the yard and listened to the howling wind, but he could not see anything. So, he turned on the backyard flood lamp. The brightness of the light reflected off of the heavy snow that blew sideways from the wind. From the looks of it, it was indeed a blizzard.

As Crooks trudged his way to the garage, he couldn't see anything more than four or five feet in front of him. Instead, he scraped his right boot along the ground to feel for the concrete sidewalk, which he knew would lead him directly to the garage twenty yards away. When Crooks arrived at the building, he extended his hand and felt his way to the garbage cans located on the east side. After depositing the trash bag, he returned to the small garage door, opened it, and stepped inside.

In the brief respite from the storm inside the garage, Crooks made short work of filling a paper grocery sack with Elk sausage, burger, and a couple of roasts to take back inside. But before he left, he reached up to one of the rafters and pulled down a 70' foot coil of rope. He opened the small door and tied one end of the cord to the clothesline post. Next, Crooks picked up the sack of meat, and he slowly retraced his back to the house, and again, scraped a boot along the sidewalk with each step. Finally, he set the bag of game meat just inside the backdoor and went back out outside, and tied the other end of the rope to the handrail on the stoop.

It was then that he saw his wife, Lois, standing there after stepping back inside and onto the back porch.

"Thanks, Bill; it is pretty bad out there, huh?"

Crooks replied with an incoherent grunt as he took off his coat and boots. But, when he stood up and turned around to face his wife, she broke out into laughter. While out in the storm, the snow had impacted his signature overgrown beard. It was so frozen that he couldn't move his lips.

Lois reached up and scratched tiny snowballs out of her husband's beard until it was clean and moist. Then, she looked out the window again and asked, "why did you string a rope to the garage?"

"I did that so we can find our way to the garage during the storm if we have to go out there for other supplies, like our camping gear, if the electricity goes out."

She patted him on the shoulder and said, "good thinking."

Later, while Lois put the sack of meat away in the refrigerator freezer, Crooks pulled his list of faculty phone numbers out of their antique bureau. He diligently called each one of the teachers on the list that Dr. Gaines provided him, though turning a rotary phone dial had started to annoy him. Crooks thought it was time to give up the relic for a modern pushbutton variety. He smiled at the thought that he and only one other person he knew of still had a rotary telephone. But, when he thought of that other person, his smile dropped suddenly, "Eddie," he thought to himself, "I wonder if he made it back home before the storm?"

Crooks walked back to the kitchen and picked up the phone again. He dialed Eddie's number, and he waited while it rang. When Eddie didn't answer, he hung up and called Tracy, and still, no answer either. So he hung up once more and dialed Chief Wyatt Traynor, and listened for the call to connect.

On the second ring, Traynor answered. "Chief Traynor, how may I help you?"

"Wyatt, it is Bill. I will make this short. Did you happen to see if Eddie's pickup was parked in his driveway before you left the office?"

Traynor paused briefly and then answered, "no, I can't say because I didn't think to look. So what is going on?"

"This afternoon, just before the storm hit, I asked Eddie and Tracy to serve as armed backup while I ran off a guy who set up a camp behind the Rimrocks."

"I don't understand, Bill. Didn't you hear that they were suspended this morning? Why did you ask them?"

"Come on, Wyatt, of course, I knew about their suspension, and I wasn't asking for the Sheriff's Department assistance. All I needed was them to support me in a show of force to get the squatter to leave."

"What time did you get home?"

"I don't know the exact time, but I pulled in the driveway just as the first wave of snow began to fall, so, maybe 4:45 or so."

"I see, but you didn't see them follow you out of there?"

"No, I did not. But what I do know is that Eddie and Tracy had made some more sense of that silly treasure poem, and from what they explained to me, the supposed cache was somewhere on the backside of the Rimrocks. Eddie also promised me that they would finish looking around get out of there before sunset."

Traynor took a deep breath and exhaled. "Do you think that they are still out there behind the Rimrocks?"

"That is exactly the fear I have, since neither one of them is answering their home phones. But, if they are out there still, I hope they got back to Eddie's pickup. Perhaps they found a place to hole up out of the wind."

"Well then, all we can do is wait until the storm abates before I can go by Eddie's place to verify that he is missing. But from there, I don't know how we could mount a search with the roads surely drifted closed with all this wind."

Bill Crooks thought silently for a few moments, and a plan started to formulate in his mind. "I have it. We could call around the area to get people with snowmobiles to help."

Traynor nodded. "I like it, but why don't we call the Sheriff's Department to handle it? I mean, Eddie and Tracy are still Sheriff Deputies, are they not?"

Crooks vehemently opposed the idea. "Yes, they are still employed, but do you honestly think Sheriff Doan will expedite the search? No, Wyatt, he won't. He will tell us that once the roads open up, he will send his people out here. But, how long will that take, Wyatt? By the time Doan gets off his butt, Eddie and Tracy could become popsicles. The wind chill has to be -minus 40 degrees out there, and people can die from hypothermia within minutes!"

"I know that, Bill, but I would be grossly negligent in my duty if I didn't report it or ask for assistance."

"Fine, make the call, and when Doan denies it, get back with me."

"Okay, in the meantime, Bill, start making some calls and watch the television for weather updates. Maybe we can get lucky and have a few hours between the waves of this storm." But then Traynor added, "don't worry, Bill, Eddie is pretty capable, and I am sure Tracy is too."

"Okay, Wyatt, I will try not to worry. I will get back to you later with my plan," Crooks said and hung up the phone.

He then walked over to the television and turned it on. Sure enough, it was wall-to-wall coverage of the storm. The newscasters were already calling it the blizzard of the century.

"What's wrong, Bill? Why do you look so worried?" Lois asked.

He craned his neck around to make eye contact with his wife. "I think Eddie Crandall and Tracy James got caught in this storm, and I have to try to figure out how to get to them. I am afraid that we are in for a long night."

"No problem, I will put a pot of coffee on. What else can I do to help?"

Crooks pointed over toward their antique 9-drawer Victorian bureau in the living room and asked, "can you hand me the stack of topographical maps in the top right drawer for me? Thanks."

* * *

eanwhile, Eddie and Tracy sat in a small cave five miles away. They huddled close around a survival candle that he had removed from his backpack. The tiny flicker emitted enough illumination for both of them to see each other, but not in great detail. Most importantly, the candle provided enough heat to survive.

After entering the cave and before the ambient light faded at sunset, Eddie and Tracy made an inventory of their things. They each had a spare pair of jeans, t-shirts, wool socks, a couple of sweatshirts, two 36-hour survival candles, matches, two flashlights with extra batteries, and four energy bars between them. They placed the extra clothing on their legs to help retain body heat since neither Eddie nor Tracy had worn long underwear. He was also forced to part with his black cowboy hat because it kept bumping up against the sandstone walls around him, so he set it aside, crown down next to his leg. Next, Eddie fashioned a cap of sorts out of an extra t-shirt and wrapped it around his head. Lastly, he lit the candle and placed three flat sandstone rocks in a tee-pee around the canister to reflect heat.

"Boy, am I glad you made us bring those backpacks. Who would have thought that we would get stranded five miles from town and a half-mile from our truck," Tracy stated.

"Yep, it was a good thing."

"How long do you think we will be in here?"

"I dunno. I guess it just depends upon when the storm will let up, which may be tonight, tomorrow, or the next day. But there is no guarantee we could get out of here if the road snowed shut."

"Wow, thanks for the optimistic outlook," she teased.

He moved his cramped legs and tried to find a more comfortable position, but the cave walls restricted him from finding one.

She sensed his unrest and suggested, "I bet you wish you had a cup of coffee now, don't you?"

He teased back, "ya, I do wish that, but I would have to be constantly crawling over you to go outside and pee. That wouldn't be fun, would it?"

Tracy shook her head but doubted he could see her gesture. "No, that wouldn't be fun."

After a few seconds of silence, she added, "since we don't have any water, we could eat small handfuls of snow. But we will have to be careful since too much could lower our body temperature."

Eddie nodded. "Yep, I thought of that, too. Good call." But then a thought occurred to him, and he suggested, "I think it would be best if we stay awake or sleep in shifts to make sure the candle doesn't go out. If it does, this cave will get super cold quickly."

Tracy guffawed loudly and said, "again, there you go with the party popper stuff, come on, Eddie, let us keep a little more positive."

"I am acting practical, though I have faith we will get out of here," he argued.

Before she could retort, he realized the harshness of his tone and said, "I'm sorry."

She reached across the candle and patted him on the knee, and said, "it is okay. I am a little anxious too. That is why I am getting a little chatty. It's what I do when I am stressed."

Eddie nodded and then pulled up his coat sleeve and uncovered his wristwatch from under his flannel shirt. Then he pressed a button on the side of the watch. The digital display illuminated to indicate it was 10:50 p.m., which was still just under eight hours from sunrise.

He smiled and looked over at Tracy and said, "here is something positive. In eight hours and forty minutes from now, we will have been together for two whole weeks."

Tracy was surprised by his comment as that thought hadn't occurred to her. She replied, "I know, Eddie, two whole weeks, but do you know something? I have a strange feeling like I have known you for a long time, like a year or something."

"I know what you mean. Maybe it is from all the time we've spent together during those days."

She nodded. "True, but I get the feeling it is something else."

"I think why it feels so long is because of all the talking we have done in that short time."

Tracy guffawed and quickly retorted, "you think we talk a lot? Are you kidding me? Oh, you can talk at length about historical stuff, but not when it comes to personal stuff. When I first met you, watching you put your sentences together was challenging because you wanted to say everything correctly and by the book. It was like watching a mason construct a brick wall, you know, piece by piece."

It was a good thing that Eddie couldn't see Tracy's hands mimicking a mason building a wall, or he might have taken offense. However, her words resonated with him, and he knew that communication, especially with women, was always difficult. Though he wanted to do anything other than have a long, drawn-out personal conversation, he also knew it was the best way to keep them both awake and alive.

"So, what do you want to talk about then?" he asked.

"Seriously? You want to talk?"

"Yes, I do. So, ask, ask me anything, and I will tell you."

She shifted her legs slightly and said, "okay, let me think, tell me... about your parents?"

Talking about his family ranked in the top three topics that Eddie abhorred. However, his family wasn't necessarily embarrassing; instead, there were just too many hurts and resentments.

Tracy preempted Eddie's thoughts when she said, "come on, Eddie, you are stalling. You said, 'ask me anything, and I will tell you.' So, get started."

Eddie broke his silence and told Tracy about his lifetime. He was born in a Casper hospital and grew up in Glenrock. He was the oldest of just one other sibling, Wendy, who was two years his junior. Eddie also told about how his dad worked in the oil field around Glenrock, where he drove Vac trucks and operated backhoes. His mother worked nights as a bartender in a place that no longer existed.

When he paused, Tracy asked, "tell me about them. I mean, what were they like?"

After another brief pause, he revealed, "my mom and my dad were never around the house, and when they were, they fought like it was their favorite sport. Now, I am sure you must have heard your parents argue, but nobody could do it like my folks. So whenever they fought, I always had to reassure my sister that everything was going to be alright."

"What did they fight about?"

"Money sometimes, but mostly it was because they were both raging alcoholics. It was so bad that when my sister graduated high school, she left for Colorado and vowed never to come back."

The story shocked her somewhat, but she still wanted to know more. "What happened to your parents? Do they still live in Glenrock?"

"Nope," he said abruptly. He took a deep breath, cleared his thoughts, and told Tracy the rest of the story.

"My mom died of breast cancer in January 1984, just after I arrived in the Salt Creek area. My dad..." Eddie said and started to choke up, though he quickly regained his composure. "My dad passed away a year and a half later from the effects of his liver shutting down from cirrhosis. He moved in with me in that old trailer I had in Edgerton, and I watched him decline daily over his last two months. Then one morning, I found him dead in his bed. The doctor told me that he had a heart attack because his heart was so overworked in trying to push blood through his stiff liver."

"Oh, Eddie, I am so sorry. I didn't mean to bring up something so tragic."

"It is okay. It is what it is. But there was one good thing that came out of that."

"What was that?"

"After my dad's funeral, Walter Merino came over to see how I was doing. I know he didn't have to, but he wanted me to know that people in the community cared for me. So, I started going to church for the first time since I was in the fourth grade, and the change inside of me has been nonstop ever since. I don't harbor the resentments of my childhood. Instead, I can see my parents as just broken people, which we all are in varying degrees." Then, after a momentary pause, he added, "does that answer your original question?"

"Yes, and again, I am sorry."

"So, tell me about your family, Tracy?" Eddie inquired.

"Well, there is not much to tell. My mom and dad met in college at the University of Wyoming, and they moved to Cheyenne, where my dad worked as a State employee. My mom stayed home raised my two little brothers and me until my ninth-grade year. Then my mom went to work at a hospital on the eastern end of town. My parents rarely argued, and we used to go to church as a family at the First United Methodist Church. Then one day, my parents sat my brothers and me down and told us that they were getting a divorce."

"That must have been hard on you, was it not?"

"It was, and it caused me a lot of discomforts," she said.

"Discomfort, why?" he asked.

"It just did, Eddie. I mean, my mom got remarried ten months later to a male nurse, and then my dad got remarried too a year later to a geologist who worked for the State. My parents, who never fought, could no longer not stand to be in the same room together. I felt like I had to mediate everything between them, and that was just too much to ask a teenager to do. For instance, I had to go to two houses on birthdays and listen to one parent openly gripe about the other. I felt caught in the middle, and maybe it was then that I started distrusting people. Come to think of it, I never trusted any of my boyfriends, and the few girls I knew turned out to be backstabbers."

"Wow, I am sorry too for picking a scab. So, tell me about your Air Force days instead?"

Tracy sighed deeply. "That is another mixed bag. I loved deployment, and I loved being at work. What I hated was downtime in the dorm."

"Why?"

"I don't...I mean, I don't want to talk about some things, okay."

"Okay, I respect your privacy."

They sat in silence for what seemed like an hour though it was probably closer to five minutes. In the quiet, they stared out of the cave's small opening and into the dark abyss. Occasionally, the torrent of wind blew a stray snowflake inside, but they remained dry.

Suddenly, Tracy turned toward Eddie and broke her silence. "Do you like women, to date, I mean?"

Eddie partially choked at the question but managed to say, "Wow, that was bold. Why do you ask?"

"I don't know. I am just trying to figure you out."

He studied her facial expression in the dim light. Then answered, "yes, I do like to date women."

"Have you ever been married?"

Eddie wiped his mouth with his sleeve and said, "no, I have never married. I was engaged twice, though. The first was right after high school graduation from Glenrock since she was my high school sweetheart. The second one was a woman I began dating in Douglas when I went through the state law enforcement academy."

"What happened to them?"

"My first fiancée broke my heart by going out on me with my former best friend. The second one broke my wallet when she skipped town with a brand new $1500 engagement ring that I bought her."

"Sounds to me like you didn't choose very wisely, no offense."

"None was taken because I came to that same conclusion myself. I can see where you are going with this line of questioning, so let me pre-empt your next set of questions."

"What questions, what did you think I was going to ask?"

"I know you better than you think I do, Tracy, so, okay, ask me that follow-up question."

She hemmed and hawed and then said, "well, it isn't that I have a question. It is more like a few observations. I mean, not once since we started working together have you hit on me or even said anything with a sexual connotation to it. But, then, when we were in Steamboat Springs, Deputy Tombrello practically threw herself at you, but you didn't make a move. So it is just weird, that's all."

Eddie calmly replied, "I decided a long time ago that I had to get myself right with the Lord first. Only then could I be an equal partner to the woman I marry."

"Gosh, Eddie, I was talking about your dating someone, not marrying. First things first, dude."

He shook his head in disagreement and said, "well, I don't want to date anyone that I am not ready to marry."

"Aren't you putting unrealistic expectations on yourself?"

"No, not at all. I also won't date a woman unless she too has an ongoing relationship with the Lord."

Tracy shook her head in disbelief. "Come on, Eddie, you are a man, and every man I have ever known only wanted one thing and one thing only."

"Are you implicating every man that you know? Is that what you are saying?"

The retort made her pause briefly. "Well, no...but like when I first joined the Sheriff's Department, guys looked at me like fresh meat or something. Those pigs, McKinney and Peck, were the worse since they always hit on me and dropped multiple sexual connotations around me. They even put condoms on my desk with a note that told me where to meet them to cash them in!" she shouted, and again, the sound reverberated within the small enclosure.

"That is textbook sexual harassment, and you should have reported it."

Tracy vented her frustration, "I did report it! I went directly to Sheriff Doan, and he told me that 'boys will be boys.' Then he ignored my complaint."

Eddie had listened patiently and carefully, so he asked, "did that kind of stuff happen to you in the Air Force too? I mean, harassment?"

Tracy quickly replied, "harassed, no. At my first duty station, I met a guy, we went out and did some things, you know. Anyway, I told my friend about it, and she told her boyfriend, and before I knew it, every unmarried guy in my unit wanted to get with me. Then the same thing happened at my next duty station."

He took it all in and understood the unfair juxtaposition between the reputations of young men and young women. It might have explained why he made a pact with himself years before always to treat women with respect. But, there within the silence, another question came to mind to ask Tracy.

He asked, "why did you also call Sheriff Doan a pig this morning? Was that because of his inaction on your complaint, or did he harass you too?"

* * *

33

Thursday, January 16, 1992

It was after midnight when Tracy began unfolding her story. One month ago, she attended an informal Sheriff's Department Christmas party at the Pumpjack Bar. The party itself was festive, and she recalled speaking to several department employees that she had never met.

Around 10:30 p.m. on the night in question, Tracy said that she became tired and wanted to leave since most of her other co-workers had already gone home. However, when she grabbed her coat and started to put it on, Sheriff Doan stopped her. He encouraged Tracy to have just one more drink with him because he wanted to talk to her. When she insisted that she didn't want any alcohol, he suggested having a Coke or something. Finally, she consented to his request, took her coat off, and then excused herself to go to the restroom.

On her return, she had spotted Deputies McKinnon and Peck playing a game of pool in the back room. She also noted that only two other patrons were present. One had his back turned and watched television while the other slept in a booth. Tracy then found Sheriff Doan waiting for her at the end of the bar. When she sat down next to him, a Coke in a tall glass awaited her.

Tracy also recollected that Sheriff Doan was friendly and handled himself as a gentleman. She also remembered that they mainly talked about things that the Sheriff liked. But then, a little while later, she started to feel woozy. That was Tracy's last memory until mid-morning the next day.

Eddie asked, "were you drunk or sick or something? Did you have a hangover? That is what I am getting at?

She began to sob. It astounded Eddie to see her express so much emotion and pain, and he regretted asking her the question in the first place.

"It is okay, Tracy. You don't have to say anymore."

"Stop!" Tracy shouted. "Stop placating me, please," she said in a much softer tone. Then she added, "I just want to get it all out, and I need you to listen, please."

"Okay, I will just listen."

Tracy wiped her face with the spare shirt that rested on her lap, then took a couple of deep breaths and continued. "The last thing I remembered was being at the bar and nothing else until I came to my senses. I later woke up in my bed, naked, which is weird because I never sleep that way." She then paused and looked over to Eddie. "I think he raped me!"

The word "raped" hung in the deafening silence inside the cave. Eddie searched his thoughts as to what he could say, but he allowed the pause to continue. He reminded himself that his job was to listen.

Once again, Tracy looked over to Eddie in the dim light. "I know what you're thinking, Eddie. How could I know that a rape occurred without me remembering anything? But a woman knows her body, and I woke up with an incredible dull ache in my, umm, you know...down there."

"What did you do then?"

She shrugged. "I woke up my roommate and asked her how I got home the night before, but she said she didn't get back to our apartment until about 3 a.m., and I was already in bed."

"Did you ask Sheriff Doan?"

Tracy nodded. "I did. I went to see him the next Monday in his office, and he said that he gave me a ride home when I didn't feel well. I asked him if he had taken me inside, but he denied doing so. But the weird thing was he then stated that I threw myself at him and begged him to fulfill my needs. But I swear to you, Eddie, I know I didn't do any of those things. Do you believe me?"

"I do believe you. But I have one more question."

"Sure, ask."

"Why is Sheriff Doan the 'pig' that you called him?"

Tracy then explained that a few days after she met with the Sheriff, Deputies McKinnon and Peck became even more overt in their sexual comments to her. She witnessed them telling another deputy about a small tattoo of a strawberry on her hip just below the panty line. Tracy stressed that there was no way that those two men could have ever known that. She also added that nobody in Casper could have known that either.

Once again, she wiped her face. "So, I filed a complaint with our human resources officer that I was sexually harassed and assaulted. Then, the next day, Sheriff Doan called me into his office and told me that he would fire me if I didn't drop the charges. When I told him that I wouldn't, the Sheriff told me that he already excused the charges and told me that he was sending me out to Midwest to train with you."

In the silent pause then ensued, Tracy picked up the spare t-shirt and blew her nose into one of the sleeves. She then turned her head and looked out into the dark abyss just outside the small opening to the cavern. Next, Tracy dropped her left hand down along her side and located her flashlight. Turning it on, she pointed it out of the opening and saw snow still blowing sideways. However, it wasn't as heavy as hours earlier. But before she turned off the light, she quickly panned it over to Eddie, and she spied that he quietly watched her every move.

Tracy turned off the flashlight and said to Eddie, "thank you for listening; it feels good not being condemned."

"Don't worry, I believe you. Want to hear my theory?"

"Sure."

Eddie cleared his throat. "I think it was Rohypnol in your drink, you know, roofies. There was a state-wide bulletin recently on date rape drugs, and loss of memory and feeling woozy like you said are classic indications."

Tracy started to protest, but he continued.

"I think that at an opportune moment, Sheriff Doan placed something in your drink, and if I may sound so crass, he then took you home and had his way with you.

"You do?"

"Yes, I also think that when you complained of the assault, Doan sent you out here to hide you and get you discouraged enough to quit."

"Eddie, that doesn't make sense."

"Sure, it does. If you hated it enough out here to quit, and then you furthered your complaint, Doan would paint you as a disgruntled former employee."

Tracy listened carefully and allowed it all to sink in for a moment. She then commented, "that's a pretty thin theory, but it does make sense."

Eddie shifted his legs slightly and then proclaimed, "I promised you that I would listen, but now you have to trust me. When we get out of here, there will be a reckoning, count on it."

"Thanks, I know where your heart is, but no. I don't have any proof other than my testimony, which doesn't count for much since I have no memory of leaving the bar."

He pursed his lips and then speculated aloud, "I wonder if there is a security camera behind the bar that captured that night in question? Perhaps it could show you and Doan together and maybe him slipping something into your drink?"

She shook her head in disbelief. "No, I am sure that even if a security tape existed, it is certainly long gone by now."

Undeterred, he offered one last thing for her to consider. "I don't think this is the first time Sheriff Doan has date-raped someone. Do you remember Vivian Parkman, Mr. Sprenger's daughter in South Dakota?"

Suddenly, Tracy sat up straight. "I do. Vivian's father is that grumpy old man in Edgerton."

Eddie cleared his throat again and said, "let me tell you about Vivian's daughter, Melanie."

Meanwhile, Bill Crooks' sat at his dining room table inside his residence on Ash Street in Gas Plant. He studied every known trail and elevation line on a topographic map of the area where he last saw Eddie and Tracy. On the wall above him, Lois' antique Black Forest Cuckoo Clock chirped two times, and he lifted his eyes off the chart and leaned back into the wooden dining room chair.

As he rubbed his tired eyes, he hoped that his impromptu rescue plan would work. The best-case scenario was finding Eddie and Tracy sitting safely in Eddie's pickup. However, the worst case was that his friends were out in the elements, which in all probability meant they were dead.

Before formulating his plan, Crooks had confirmed that Eddie and Tracy were missing. Earlier that night, he called a teacher who lived at #7 Navy Row. He instructed her to step outside and look across the street at Eddie Crandall's place and report what she saw. When the teacher called Crooks back, she stated that Eddie's house was dark and his truck was not in the carport. Then, a little while later, Chief Traynor called Crooks again. As he predicted, Sheriff Doan had declined to send out Sheriff's Deputies from Casper to assist due to the storm.

But oddly, as word spread of Eddie and Tracy's disappearance, area residents began calling both Crooks and Chief Traynor to offer their help in a rescue mission. One of the volunteers was Pat Conrad, the Wyoming Department of Transportation supervisor that lived in Midwest. Pat proposed that he and one of his men, Doug Hanson, could plow Highway 259 to the Castle Rock Bar for an ambulance crew if needed. Crooks was thankful, nonetheless, but he questioned the foreman about using State equipment without authorization. Pat informed him that he would ask for forgiveness later than to ask for permission first. However, the man also insisted that it was the right thing to do regardless of approval.

Crooks also marveled at the list of other offers like Walter Merino, Pete LaRoche, and Joe Proctor, who wanted to be a part of the search and rescue team. Additionally, Steve Otten offered to retrieve Eddie's truck with his backhoe once the storm ended. The last person to offer help, and most surprising of all, was Clare Olsen. Clare had recently purchased the junction store and wanted to donate all the gasoline for the rescue effort.

The whole plan hinged precipitously upon the weather. Since the local news channel seemed to be of no help, Crooks called the National Weather Service office near the Casper-Natrona County International Airport. He spoke directly to the meteorologist on duty. The forecaster was pensive about talking to him at first and suggested watching one of the news channels. However, Crooks managed to change the meteorologist's mind after he explained the situation involving a potential rescue. He then asked for a comprehensive forecast of the storm. Specifically, he wanted to know if and when the snowfall would abate long enough to begin a rescue mission.

Then, an hour later, the meteorologist called him back and predicted that snow would gradually taper off starting at midnight and stop altogether by six in the morning. The forecaster warned, however, that the deadly wind chill factor would remain in the area. He also cautioned that the next leg of the storm would bring another 8-10 inches of snow and more blizzard conditions to begin around noon.

The rescue plan comprised three elements. Phase I consisted of Crooks, Pete LaRoche, Walter Merino, and Joe Proctor meeting up at the junction store at 6:00 a.m. on their snowmobiles and riding out from there. Though Chief Traynor insisted on being on the advance team, Crooks thought he should coordinate the effort via handheld radios from the junction store. From there, Crooks anticipated it would take the search team about 30 minutes to make their way to the backside of the Rimrocks, where he hoped to find Eddie and Tracy stranded in his truck.

Phase II would involve Pat Conrad and Doug Hanson plowing a single lane south on Highway 259, beginning at daybreak. Pat assured Crooks that he would snowplow the road to Casper if needed to do so.

Phase III would then require the Midwest ambulance crew to meet the rescuers on Highway 259 if either Eddie or Tracy needed medical assistance. Then, if needed, the ambulance would transport Eddie and Tracy to the helipad on the north side of Midwest and wait for the Flight for Life helicopter. The hardest part now for Crooks was the wait.

* * *

34

Back at the cave, Eddie and Tracy had each napped in turns while one slept, and the other made sure the candle stayed lit. Eddie was relieved when Tracy fell to sleep. He knew she needed it after the emotional toll of revealing her darkest secret. Plus, he added to her emotional fatigue when recounting the story about Melanie Parkman.

Melanie's story started in 1963 when she was a senior at Midwest High School when she attended a New Year's Eve dance at the American Legion Post on Second Street in Edgerton. During that party, she met a Casper police officer in his mid-twenties named John Doan. How and why Doan received an invitation to the dance was unknown.

But as the night went on, Melanie became enthralled by the dashing young man. Then around midnight, Doan coaxed her out of the building to join him in his 1960 Chevrolet Impala parked around the corner. First, he tried to get her to drink some bourbon from a pint that he hid in his glove compartment, but Melanie refused. Next, Doan wanted to kiss her but again was thwarted. Finally, when Melanie tried to exit the vehicle, he suddenly reached across her torso and handcuffed her right wrist. He then connected the other end of the handcuffs through the hole of the armrest on the door.

Eddie had left out the brutalizing details of what happened next but picked up with the aftermath. When Melanie returned home that night, she told her parents what happened to her, and they called the local Sheriff's Deputy to file a report. Melanie presented physical evidence of the attack, such as the cut marks on her wrist from Doan's handcuffs, a black eye, a bloodied lip, a torn dress, and the fingernail scratches on her inner thighs.

When the investigator interviewed Doan, he spun the accusation into a "he said, she said case" and vehemently denied even meeting Melanie. He also went so far as to mention that the people in Edgerton were trying to frame him simply because he was a Casper policeman. He even told Vivian that he never wanted to hear from her or her oil field trash daughter again. When Eddie finished retelling Melanie's story, Tracy wept once again.

Somewhere in the silence that ensued, Tracy managed to drift off to sleep. Meanwhile, Eddie remained vigilantly on candle watch. Occasionally, he picked up his flashlight and reached across Tracy to shine it out of the entrance to look at the storm. With every movement, though, he tried not to wake her.

After another hour had passed, he once again shined the light outside. But, this time, there wasn't a reflection off of many snowflakes at all. Though he still heard the wind blowing up a gale. He pulled his arm back that held the flashlight, and then he rechecked his watch, which the digital display read: 5:00 a.m., and then shut it off.

Moments later, Eddie felt annoyed about a rock that had somehow rolled up against his leg within the last hour. While trying to alleviate his discomfort, Eddie bent his left leg and dragged the heel of his boot toward his buttocks when it happened.

BANG! Something struck his pant leg that sounded with a dull thud, but then Eddie felt something move. He turned on his flashlight, and to his horror, a three-and-a-half-foot prairie rattlesnake slowly writhed while it tried to pull its stuck fangs out of Eddie's jeans.

Eddie screeched a blood-curdling yawp, and he grabbed the snake by the head with his left hand. He jerked the snake off of his pant leg and then flung the biter through the cave entrance and into the wind and snow. Tracy had startled awake at Eddie's shriek, and she watched in wonder at the sight of a snake fly past her nose.

Tracy lunged toward Eddie to see if he was alright, which caused her to knock over the candle. But worse, she also bumped her head in the process. Finally, Tracy turned on her flashlight and illuminated the horror-stricken face of Eddie, who was desperately trying to pull up his pant leg.

"Eddie, listen to me; you have to calm down. Now lie back and let me look at your leg."

She pulled up his pant leg and saw only one small needlelike red prick on his shin halfway between his knee and his ankle.

"What do you see?" Eddie asked impatiently.

"It looks like one fang might have got you, but who knows if any venom got in. Does it hurt?"

"No, I don't think so, at least not yet."

"Want me to cut it and suck out the poison?"

He shook his head. "No, that is the worst thing to do. Instead, take my extra t-shirt and tear a piece of it into a long strip. Then I want you to tie it around my leg under my knee tight enough to slow down but not cut off blood flow."

She then pulled the pocketknife out of her backpack and made a long ligature out of the shirt, and tied it around Eddie's leg as told. While she pulled his pant leg down, she heard him say, "I am so stupid."

"Why are you stupid, Eddie?"

"That cucumber smell. Rattlesnake dens smell like cucumbers. That is why I am stupid."

Tracy grabbed her flashlight and turned it on. She told Eddie to stay still, and she then shined the light toward the dinner plate-sized hole in the rear of the cavern. She carefully drew her legs up underneath her and gently stepped over Eddie to look into the hole. To do so required her to tilt her head and place her ear against the sandstone ceiling.

"What do you see?"

"Oh, man. You are not going to believe this!"

"What more snakes?" Eddie asked nervously.

"Of course, there are hundreds of them in there, but guess what is in there also?"

When he didn't respond, she replied, "I see a small metal box. I think it is the treasure, Eddie."

"Fine, it can stay there. I should have told you in all of our talks that I hate snakes more than anything in this world."

"That's okay. I hate spiders."

While she continued to look at the mass of snakes, Tracy asked, "I thought snakes hibernated in the winter and can't move. How come that one came down and bit you?"

Eddie explained, "first of all, snakes don't hibernate. Instead, they enter a period of slowed animation called brumation. Second of all, rattlesnakes can sense or see heat signatures. I think the snake fell next to me trying to get warm, and when it did, it must have been warm enough to strike."

"Man, it smells like cucumbers up here; I will never forget that smell," Tracy surmised aloud.

"Do me a favor?"

"Sure," Tracy said while still looking inside the den.

"Go outside and scoop up some snow, and then use it to block that hole. The snakes won't cross that cold barrier, no matter how warm we seem to be to them."

While she worked, Eddie opined that *VIPERS HISS FROST* in the poem's last line was appropriate since the box rested in an active snake den. Hence, only in the wintertime would it be remotely possible to retrieve the strongbox safely.

Tracy made short work of plugging the hole, and when she had finished, Eddie re-lit the survival candle.

Then a few minutes later, he said from the shadows, "Tracy, my leg is starting to hurt. I know I got a dose of venom."

Worry shot through Tracy's veins like an electric pulse, and she asked, "what are we going to do?"

Eddie calmly explained, "if the storm has abated at dawn, you will have to descend the hill to the truck and call for help using my CB radio."

She disagreed by shaking her head at him.

"Tracy, it is the only way," he insisted.

They sat in silence for a long stretch, and they each took turns looking out of the entrance for the trace of first light. Finally, it seemed to them that the storm had paused, and when Tracy shined her flashlight to the south, she thought she saw sagebrush on the other side of the ravine.

Eddie startled her when he spoke, "it should be first light soon. My watch indicates it is 6:15. So I think you could probably see okay by seven or so."

She nodded. "Alright, Eddie, sit back and relax as much as possible. I don't want that poison pumping through your veins. Do you want me to tighten that cord on your leg?"

He thought for a moment and then replied, "no, if it is any tighter, it might cut off all the blood supply, and then I will lose my leg."

They ceased talking and listened instead to the wind. It, too, had calmed down a lot like the snow but still coursed about 20 miles per hour.

Fifteen minutes later, Eddie started to feel sick to his stomach. He motioned for Tracy to move away from the entrance, and he crawled out the opening and tried to vomit, but nothing voided.

Instead, he reached down and formed a tiny snowball with his hand and brought it to his mouth. Eddie then took a small bite of snow, but his attention caught sight of something that he thought could be the onset of delirium. He could have sworn that he saw lights reflecting off of the hillside adjacent to the cave, but then again, he reasoned that it was just the poison messing with his mind.

When Eddie slowly inched his way back into the cave, he looked up at Tracy and said, "Okay, time for you to go. It is light enough to see out there. When you get to my truck, the keys are in the ashtray. So, start it up first, turn on the heat, and then raise someone on the CB radio. Keep calling out and changing channels until someone responds."

"I got it, but I hate leaving you alone," she insisted and hoped that Eddie had changed his mind.

"Go. It may be our only hope of getting out of here, but promise me something?"

"What is that?"

"Do not tell anyone about the metal box in the back of the cave. I want the two of us to come back up here later after figuring out what to do with the snakes. But, above all, I don't want anyone else to get hurt."

"Deal," she said while she gathered up her backpack in one hand and zipped her coat up to her chin with the other.

When readied, she placed the flashlight in her teeth and crawled out of the opening. Unfortunately, Eddie could only watch her descent for about 10 feet due to his view from inside the cave.

After Tracy disappeared, a Bible verse from the book of Philippians came to his mind. It was the same one that he always turned to when facing problems: *Don't worry about anything; instead, pray about every-thing.* So then Eddie prayed silently and alone.

* * *

35

Phase I of the search and rescue launched at 6:10 a.m. from the junction store in Midwest. Despite the bitter cold temperatures and unplowed streets, twenty-five of the area's residents gathered and cheered on the snowmobile team when they left.

Twenty minutes later, Bill Crooks stopped his snowmobile at the top of the saddle slope between the Rimrocks and the monolithic Castle Rock to the south. As his machine motor idled, he turned around to make sure the other men of the search team were still with him. Within seconds, Joe Proctor came to a stop to the right of Crooks, while Pete LaRoche and Walter Merino, who also towed rescue sleds, filed in behind.

From atop their perch, they could begin to make out objects below to the east in the pale blue predawn light. Lucky for them, the snowfall subsided at 2:00 a.m., and now only a steady wind remained. The brief break was needed and appreciated by the men. Their snowmobile ride from Midwest down Highway 259 was uneventful. Much of the road was clear save for some monstrous snow drifts across the pavement. However, their journey became more challenging once they turned off the highway and onto the snaking oil field roads they currently traveled. At times, it was hard to see where the route existed at all.

Heavy snow combined with high winds filled the ditches on either side of the road to a level plain. Once, Crooks' machine bogged down in deep snow, and at another time, Joe Proctor's did too forcing the rescuers to stop and dig each other out.

Crooks stood up and dismounted his machine, and he motioned for Joe Proctor to do the same.

"Joe," Crooks said, "I last saw them there," and he pointed to a spot in the valley ahead of them. But, he continued, "keep your eyes open for that red Ford Eddie drives as we go down there."

"Got it," Joe said and closed his visor.

After revving the engine of his snow machine, he edged forward over the pass. The snowdrifts on the eastern slope were immense. The snowmobiles plunged through pristine drifts of champagne powder, which slowed the rescuers' progress down to a steady crawl.

Once the foursome reached the bottom of the valley, Crooks led the team northeasterly along Teapot Creek. Everywhere the team looked, the landscape offered binary colors of white snow and dark shadows. But then a flash of a red stood out in stark contrast to the two-tone surroundings. Spotting the flash of color, Crooks sped up in the direction of what he saw.

The team came to a stop alongside a red 1978 Ford F150 that everyone recognized as Eddie Crandall's. The truck was found in four inches of snow and not in a snowdrift as Crooks had feared. Instead, a thin layer of powdered snow covered the front windshield and side windows of the truck entirely. Crooks flipped up the visor on his helmet and jumped off of his machine. He reached up and wiped off a circle in the snow covering the passenger door window and peered inside. He saw nothing. Fueled by a sudden surge of adrenaline, Crooks lifted the handle and threw open the door, which validated his initial finding.

He turned to the other men, who had already crowded around the truck, and said, "they are not here."

While Crooks unslung his backpack to retrieve his binoculars, Walter Merino climbed into the cab. He looked into Eddie's usual hiding place for his keys, the ashtray. "Bill," he called out, "I found the keys; I don't think they made it back."

He nodded and then instructed the team, "start scanning the hillsides because that is the only place for cover anywhere around here."

Pete LaRoche took off his helmet and looked at the domed hill to the west, as did the rest of the men. But, unlike the other men, Pete did not use binoculars. It wasn't that he didn't have a set; instead, Pete possessed extraordinary eyesight. As a result, he was often known to spot things that were impossible for other humans. While most hunters mounted a scope on their rifles, Pete's eaglelike vision allowed him to see in uncanny clarity at any distance over his iron sights.

When Tracy had left the impish cavern in the sandstone ridge, she carefully sidestepped down the slope. She knew she needed to reach the pickup safely; otherwise, her life and Eddie's would be in peril. With each step, her feet pushed out waves of snow that fell below her in micro avalanches. Steadily, she made her way to her goal: the bottom of the ravine, where walking would be less arduous.

Tracy was halfway down the slope when the wind carried the sound of a high-pitched machine, but she strained to pinpoint the source of it. She scanned the flats below, near Teapot Creek, but saw nothing. Tracy then shook her head and dismissed the sound as merely wishful thinking. Instead, she focused back on her task, and two steps later, she heard the whining sound again and looked up.

Her face stretched into a gleeful smile when she spotted four snowmobiles coming to a stop in the open ground to the east. Tracy jumped and waved, but none of the riders seemed to notice.

As a matter of survival, Tracy knew that she needed to make contact with those snowmobile riders. Seeing no other option, she sat down her backside, lifted her feet, and slid down the slope. The large sagebrush in the drainage basin stopped her skid, and Tracy scrambled to her feet. From her new vantage point, she could see Eddie's pickup along with the four snow machines alongside it.

"Help! Over here! Help!" she screamed as she trotted down the wash.

While the other men panned the countryside, roads mostly, Pete focused on a place that he would seek shelter if he needed to get out in the elements. He reasoned that the only place out of the wind was along the sandstone outcroppings. He had been up there amongst the rocky spines once a few years ago while hunting deer, and he found many places to stop and watch the game trails in the breaks.

But so far, Pete's brief search had covered the entirety of the first ridge but found nothing. He then scanned down the second spine when he thought he saw a large snowball roll to the bottom. Pete looked away from the draw and rubbed his eyes because he thought he saw the snowball sprout legs and stand up, then it grew arms that waved frantically at him. When Pete looked again, he said, "I've got her! I see Tracy!"

Without being ordered to do so, Joe Proctor started his snowmobile and raced out to recover her. Meanwhile, Tracy continued slogging through the snow as fast as she could toward the fast-approaching snowmobile. When the machine stopped, she pleaded with the driver to help Eddie first because he was hurt.

Proctor comforted her and said, "it is okay, Tracy, we will get him. But, first things first, let's get you safely down the hill. Come on, climb on back."

Joe then returned quickly to the pickup truck with Tracy on the back of his snowmobile. When the machine stopped, Bill Crooks helped her step off the seat and up into the passenger side of Eddie's pickup. Then Walter Merino stepped forward and handed her a water canteen and instructed her to take a drink. To that point, none of her utterances made any sense and Crooks, and the others desperately wanted her to reveal Eddie's whereabouts.

When Tracy lowered the canteen, she said, "Eddie is up there," and pointed toward the hill. "He is in a cave and has a snakebite."

"I'm on it," Pete stated, and he swiftly started his snowmobile and sped off up the hill. Crooks followed him, but not before he instructed Joe and Walter to watch over Tracy.

While she watched the snowmobiles climb up the gradient, Walter walked around to the driver's side of the truck. He started the motor to generate some heat inside the cab. Then Joe removed his helmet and took the opportunity to introduce himself to Tracy. After the greeting, he assured her that she was amongst family and Eddie would receive all the help he needed.

Meanwhile, Pete made a course up the north side of the spine, which was grass-covered. He and Crooks stopped their machines about halfway along the ridge and above the rock ledge. After jumping off his snow machine, Pete went to the edge of the sandstone wall and scanned the snow-covered slope below. When Crooks asked him what he was doing, Pete indicated that he was looking for Tracy's tracks, which they could trace back to the cave entrance. Crooks understood him and walked uphill along the short cliff.

A few seconds later, "over here," Crooks called, and Pete ran up to meet him.

The sandstone overhang was only about six-foot-tall, so Crooks held Pete's arm as he slid over the edge. He then watched from above as Pete found the cave entrance and squatted and crawled out of sight.

When Pete emerged, he flung Eddie's backpack up to Crooks and then disappeared from view again. This time, when Pete materialized, his arms held Eddie. As soon as Crooks saw his friend's red hair, he laid down prone on the ground and reached down with both arms. Together, Crooks and Pete lifted Eddie up and over the ledge and then sat him down on the back of Crooks' snowmobile.

"Thanks, guys. I need to get to the hospital," Eddie said.

Crooks nodded at him and said, "we will, and soon. Where are you hurt?"

"My left shin, rattlesnake bite."

Crooks reached down and lifted Eddie's pant leg while Pete maneuvered behind to get a better view. The wound was there, all right. It looked like a bruise about the size of a donut with a single red pinprick in the center. The teacher then checked the ligature below Eddie's knee for tightness and determined that it was still in place but not too tight to stop all blood circulation.

"Okay, Eddie, how about we get you out of here. Do you need a sled, or can you ride behind me?"

"No, I am okay. I'll ride."

Bill Crooks remounted his machine, and Eddie slid in behind him and hung on.

When they went down the slope and stopped at the truck, Tracy sprung from her seat and ran over and hugged Eddie. Meanwhile, Crooks asked Joe for the handheld radio and queued the microphone.

"Wyatt, this is Crooks; how copy?"

"I got you, Bill. Did you find anything?"

"I got both Eddie and Tracy, and they are alive. Execute Phase Two because Eddie needs a hospital ASAP."

"Roger, start bringing them out, and we will meet you on the highway."

It took the four snowmobiles about 15 minutes to retrace the trail they blazed just an hour before. The machines tracked well in the packed course, but the wind became a factor. On the ride into the backcountry, the wind was at the riders' backs. Now, the biting wind hit them on their fronts. Even Crooks had to painstakingly ignore the tiny stings of cold air that managed to push through even the smallest of gaps in his clothing.

Soon afterward, the rescue crew exited out of the oil field and spilled onto Highway 259. Chief Traynor was already there with an ambulance, and a host of others waited patiently. Finally, when he spotted the machines coming, Traynor got out of his Ford Bronco and reached Bill Crooks when the snow machines slowed to a complete stop.

"Bill, there is no flight for life, too dangerous to fly,"

"How are we gonna get them to the hospital?"

Traynor smiled and said, "don't worry, Pat Conrad and Doug Hanson are way up the road and have already snowplowed a single lane to I-25 and have started toward Casper. So, stop gabbing and help me get these two into the ambulance."

* * *

36

Two hours later, inside Casper's hospital, Tracy sat in an outrageously uncomfortable chair next to Chief Traynor in the surgical waiting room. When they had arrived at the hospital's emergency room, the professional staff gave Eddie a dose of antivenom but then grew concerned with the bite wound itself. The doctor recommended removing the affected flesh since snake venom breaks down the victim's tissues around the bite. Tracy, too, was treated for mild frostbite on her toes, but she was in surprisingly good health other than a bit of dehydration.

She recalled that their ride in the ambulance into town was slow since the driver followed Chief Traynor and the snowplow in front of him. Nevertheless, it was a quiet ride inside the ambulance. Coupled with the warmth inside the compartment, both Eddie and Tracy catnapped.

But unbeknownst to Tracy, at exit 191 north of the city, Chief Traynor called over the law enforcement mutual aid channel to request assistance. When they exited Interstate 25 at Center Street, two Casper patrol units and a city snowplow met them and escorted them to Sacred Heart Hospital.

Suddenly, Tracy lifted her head and stood up. When she spun around, she bet over at her hip and said to Traynor, "we need to talk, now. But not here, too many ears."

Traynor immediately got up and led them away to a small nook of a spare nurse station at the end of the hall. Once there, Tracy didn't parse words. She quickly revealed her secret regarding what happened to her with Sheriff Doan, which up to this point, only Eddie knew. Chief Traynor listened intently and refrained from commenting or judging. She then told the story of Melanie Parkman.

When Tracy finished revealing her and Eddie's theory about Sheriff Doan, the Chief said, "I am not surprised. Man, what a scumbag. But now I want you to let me handle it. I have a buddy that is beyond Doan's reach and will see to it that justice prevails."

"Fine, I want this to end. Thank you, Chief."

Their discussion was interrupted when they heard a repeated call from someone down the hallway.

"Deputy?" called out a nurse.

"Yes," Tracy said, and she walked toward her with Chief Traynor following closely behind.

"Deputy, this is Doctor Underwood. He operated on Sergeant Crandall," the nurse said.

Tracy turned and asked the doctor, "Is he okay?"

"Yes, Deputy, he is doing fine, and he is in the recovery room. You can see him soon, I assure you."

"How bad was it, Doc?" Traynor asked.

"He had a lot of dead or dying tissue from the venom, so I removed it. Don't worry. He will be fine in a few weeks."

"Thanks, Doctor," Tracy replied.

Dr. Underwood started to turn but then looked at Tracy. "Before I forget, your placing that crude rope above the bite wound probably saved his leg, good job."

"Doc, you can tell him yourself, it was his idea; all I did was tie it."

A half-hour later, another nurse from the surgical ward informed Tracy and Chief Traynor that Eddie had left recovery to a private room on the fourth floor. As they navigated the hallways, it seemed that every hospital staff member they encountered acted oddly toward them. Specifically, she noted a mixture of both smiles and stares.

When the elevator door opened and they stepped in, Tracy and Traynor felt a sense of relief from the gauntlet of attention. Then, just before the elevator door shut, a petite hand jutted through the gap, which caused the closure to reopen. The hand belonged to a doctor, and when she entered the car, she sized up Tracy and Traynor with a glance.

Without turning her head, the doctor mentioned, "you both are famous, you know?"

"Why is that, ma'am?" Traynor asked.

"Your story is all over the news about the daring rescue of two sheriff deputies. And the story is about how the whole community came together to save two of their own. It is quite touching, I must say because we don't see much that here in Casper."

The elevator door stopped, and the doctor exited and said over her shoulder, "turn on the news; you'll see."

"Thanks, Doc," Traynor said.

The elevator door closed again, and they rode in silence up to the next floor. From there, Tracy and Chief Traynor found Eddie's room at the end of a quiet wing near the emergency stairwell exit.

When they entered Eddie's suite, he sat awake with his left leg elevated by a sling. An intravenous bag hung above him, and a length of tubing connected the container down to his left hand. The television on the wall displayed a local news crew with a live video feed outside of the same hospital. Eddie looked over to his visitors, and, instead of greeting them, he held his right index finger against his lips and motioned for them to listen to the news story.

One community, One harrowing rescue...County Sheriff's Department Sergeant Eddie Crandall and Deputy Tracy James miraculously survived last night's blizzard in a make-shift shelter. However, the Sheriff's Department has declined comment on why the deputies were in the Salt Creek Oil Field remote area late yesterday afternoon. When the deputies' disappearance was noted, community leaders from Midwest and Edgerton joined forces. They organized a thrilling rescue involving snowmobiles and snowplow drivers.

Let's go to our certified meteorologist, Amy Holcomb, for an update on the storm...

"How about that? We are famous," Eddie said.

Tracy walked up to the side of the bed and slid her left hand into Eddie's right. Then she asked, "how are you feeling, Sergeant?"

He smiled. "I told you, my name is Eddie." Then, after giving her a quick wink, he continued, "I will be okay; how did you make out? Any frostbite?"

"Just some minor stuff on my feet. Nothing to worry about."

Traynor walked around the other side of the bed and smiled down at his friend. "Really," Traynor quipped, "a snakebite Eddie? In winter? It gives a new meaning to the name, 'biting wind,' doesn't it?'

"Very funny, Chief." Then he added, "if it wasn't for Tracy, you, and the others, I might not be here."

Traynor smiled. "You are welcome. But it was a community effort just like the tv reporter said."

The television screen flickered on the wall, and it drew Traynor's attention. To the Chief's disdain, Sheriff Doan stood in front of the camera in full uniform, complete with his pristine gray Stetson that rested snuggly atop his head. It was widely known that the only time Doan wore that specific cowboy hat was when he met with reporters.

"Shhh, I want to hear how he will claim credit for this," Traynor quipped.

Sheriff Doan spoke directly into the camera as if he talked to each viewer at home. He stated that his Deputies were in stable condition, and both would be back to work very soon. Doan went on to say that his departmental training regimen was responsible for the survival for his two deputies. He also extended a special thank you to the Wyoming Department of Transportation drivers for risking their lives to plow an emergency path into the city in-between the torrents of the storm.

Traynor went numb and said in complete resignation, "I don't know why I am expecting that guy to change."

Tracy grimaced. "I agree."

A few minutes later, Traynor turned and looked at Tracy and then said he would go down to the cafeteria. He offered to bring something back to the room, but she declined.

In the Chief's absence, it was the first time Eddie and Tracy had been alone since the cave. She continued to sit next to him and hold his hand, which surprised her that he hadn't rejected the affection. She closed her eyes for a second and thought back to the long talks they had the night before. Her thoughts were then interrupted when a hospital maintenance man suddenly appeared at the door and quietly asked to enter to fix the light above the bed. Eddie waved the man in, and he set up a ladder at the head of the hospital bed. The man ascended the steps, made a quick repair, and exited just as fast as he arrived.

When Chief Traynor arrived back in Eddie's room, the television was still on. But both Eddie and Tracy were asleep. He thought that the duo deserved a little rest and walked back out of the room. Instead, the Chief walked down the hall and stopped at the nurse's station, where he asked where he could find a payphone. A nurse informed him that there was a telephone room, and she pointed toward the opposite end of the hallway from Eddie's suite.

As Traynor walked away, the heels of his boots clicked on the freshly waxed floor. It reminded him of when he was at Marine Corps basic training and of his drill instructor walking down the center aisle of the barracks in the middle of the night. Drill instructors wore taps on their boots that made a distinguishable click sound on the floor. Traynor also remembered how everyone in his platoon feared the sound of the taps stop suddenly, which meant to him and other Marines that the instructor had found a violation. He smiled at one specific remembrance when the bunk bed next to his toppled over with two trainees still in it. The infraction? One Marine's footlocker was left unlocked.

He soon found the small room, as described by the nurse, and it contained four payphones. Traynor sat down at the nearest phone, placed coins in the slot, and dialed the number. Instead of hearing the sound of a ring, he was surprised by an automated message. It said: "*The number you have dialed cannot be connected. Please refer your number and try again.*" Instantly, Traynor realized his mistake of not dialing the complete number to call from Casper to Crooks' place in Gas Plant. Nevertheless, he was successful on the second attempt.

Bill was glad to receive an update on Eddie's condition, and he promised that he would spread the word through the pipeline. But Crooks detected something amiss in Traynor's voice.

"What is it, Wyatt? What are you not telling me?"

"I feel so bad for her, Bill?"

"Who?"

"Tracy, who did you think I was talking about?"

"I don't know. You weren't making any sense. What about Tracy?"

Traynor cuffed the phone with his hand and took a quick peek out of the door to make sure that nobody else was listening. When he lifted the receiver back to his ear, the Chief retold the story that Tracy had shared with him. He continually stressed that this wasn't a gossip thing throughout the reveal, but he wanted to do something about it.

When Traynor finished the story, Crooks said, "don't worry, buddy, things are already in motion regarding Sheriff Doan."

"Okay, who is running it?"

"I will let you know soon. Oh, before I forget, I-25 has closed again. So you will have to find a place to bunk for the night."

"Gee, thanks, any more good news?"

"Ya, call your wife. She keeps calling my house wanting to know when you are coming home."

Traynor hung up the phone and called his home phone, and talked to his wife. Of course, she was upset, but then again, anytime his work interfered with their home life, Debra would always get sideways with him.

The Chief hung up the receiver after the call and walked out of the telephone lounge and back toward Eddie's room. As he passed by the nurse's station, a nurse's assistant called out to him. The assistant passed on to him that an anonymous person left a message that there were two pre-paid rooms at the River Hotel, one for him and one for Tracy. Suddenly, Traynor's gloomy outlook on the prospect of sleeping in a hospital waiting room vanished. Though he wanted the rest, he would let Tracy determine when to leave and not rush her.

Once Eddie started to nod off to sleep again, Tracy and Chief Traynor decided it was an opportune time to go to the River Hotel. The hospital was empty at that time of the night since most visitors had left hours before. When they reached the lobby, the news crew had long since vanished, and only a security guard remained, who uttered a simple "goodnight" as they walked by him.

Once outside the turnstile glass door, the wind and cold blasted Tracy again and reminded her that winter was still in full force. When Traynor egressed the door behind her, he zipped up his coat and gently grabbed Tracy's arm, and steadied her down the snow-covered sidewalk.

The emergency room parking lot seemed inexplicably dark when they approached the Midwest Police Department Ford Bronco sitting all by itself. Traynor also noted that three parking lot lights were out and made a mental note to mention them to the maintenance staff in the morning.

He then took out his keys, unlocked the driver's side door, removed two long-handled ice scrappers from under his seat, and handed one to Tracy.

While Traynor stretched across the hood to brush snow off of the windshield, he suddenly heard the muffled sounds of footfalls closing in fast behind him. Before Traynor could turn around, the assailant managed to wrap his arms around Traynor's upper body from behind. Instinctively, Traynor recalled a wrestling counter move from his high school days. He heisted his hips outward and created an angle to counter the aggressor.

The masked assailant was a much younger and bigger man, but the Chief now had the leverage. In a flash move, Traynor grappled for control and executed a textbook suplex. The attacker's head struck the frozen pavement, which knocked him out.

Meanwhile, on the other side of Bronco, Tracy, too, had been alerted to someone rushing up from behind her. But, unlike Chief Traynor, Tracy had the time to turn around.

When her attacker closed within three feet, she aimed for the throat and jabbed the long-handled ice scraper into the would-be attacker's windpipe. Then, while the hooded assailant grasped his throat in pain, Tracy grabbed the man by the jacket, jerked his head forward, and then thrust the crown of her skull upward under the man's chin. Next, she stepped back and swung a vicious knee upward into the assailant's crotch, which disabled him.

"Tracy, you okay?" asked Chief Traynor.

"Yes, Chief."

"Good, grab my extra set of handcuffs out of the glove box, and put them on your attacker."

After Tracy tightened the restraints over the attacker's wrists behind his back, she grabbed him by the ankles. She then dragged him over the snow around the other side of the Bronco. There, she propped him up against the rear wheel next to the other assaulter.

"Ready to see who these punks are under their masks?" Traynor asked.

"Sure," and she reached out and snatched off a ski mask. "Deputy Peck!"

Traynor reached up and pulled off the mask of the other man. "Deputy McKinnon."

Chief Traynor stood up and said to Tracy, "watch these two turds while I call it in."

While the radio squawked between exchanges, Tracy tried to figure out why they were the target of Sheriff Doan's lackeys. Then it hit her.

She screamed out, "Chief, nobody is watching Eddie!"

A few minutes earlier, Eddie was fast asleep in his hospital bed. It was the first deep sleep for two days aside from a few brief naps. After Tracy and Chief Traynor had left, the nurses assured that they would only check on him sparingly so he could rest. It took him a little while to completely dose off because his mind created micro dreams, and all of them included rattlesnakes. Though, finally, he did sleep.

Eddie awoke abruptly and looked down at his wristwatch, which indicated that it had only been 13 minutes since Tracy and Chief Traynor had left. But, to him, it felt much longer than that. A small click of a cowboy boot heel drew Eddie's attention toward the partition curtain near the door.

"Who is there?" Eddie asked.

"Oh, just an old friend," a familiar voice said.

Eddie watched as a male body stepped out of the shadows and stopped at the foot of his bed.

"What's up, Sheriff?"

"I come to see my favorite employee. At least, that is what I will say if anyone sees me here."

"What do you want, Sheriff?"

"My, Eddie, you are so direct. What I want is for you and Miss Tracy to go away, for good."

"Why? I don't...."

"Eddie, you and Tracy should have just resigned to save me the hassle of what comes next."

"What's that?"

"Oh, I will get to that later, but first, I want you to tell me where the treasure is?"

"How did you...."

"I had your place bugged when you were in Colorado. I heard all about you, and Tracy deciphered that treasure poem. You found it, didn't you? Want to tell me where it is?"

Eddie refused to reply, but he repeatedly thumbed the call button to the nurses' station under the covers.

Sheriff Doan shook his head at Eddie and said, "it is okay. I will find it later. By the way, I disabled the call button, so you can stop trying."

Crandall then tried to sit up but found himself restrained by nylon straps that Doan must have placed on him while he slept. When Eddie tried to shout to get one of the nurse's attention, Sheriff Doan pulled a small cloth from his pocket and shoved it into his mouth. Doan then quickly secured the rag in place with two wraps of tape around Eddie's head. He tried again to scream but could only generate a muffled and barely audible noise.

"Don't worry, Eddie, both Tracy, and that rent a cop friend of yours is being dealt with as we speak," Doan said.

Meanwhile, the Sheriff walked over and methodically removed two latex gloves from the box that hung on the wall next to the door and donned them. The Sheriff then moved around to Eddie's left side and stopped next to the IV stand. With his left hand, the Sheriff removed a small glass ampoule and a syringe out of his pants pocket. Panic struck Eddie, and his eyes danced wildly between the needle and Doan's face, and he jerked against the restraints with every ounce of strength. Finally, the Sheriff reached out and rubbed the top of Eddie's head with his right hand in a feinted attempt to calm him.

"It's okay. It won't hurt; instead, you will feel euphoric initially before you finally go to sleep, forever."

Sheriff Doan pressed the needle into the small vial, drew back on the syringe plunger, and filled the barrel with an unknown substance. Then, oddly, Doan turned and looked at Eddie.

"In full disclosure, you know too much about me. But know this before you go to sleep: both Tracy and that tramp Melanie got exactly the thing that they begged me to give them, and so did all the others."

Doan reached down, picked up the IV tubing, and held the port with his left hand, while with his right, he stabbed the rubber seal with the needle.

Suddenly, the room exploded with the sound of bodies rushing in, and Eddie watched in horror as Doan managed to push down the entirety of the syringe plunger, which emptied the contents into the IV tubing. Instantly, Eddie felt light-headed, and his world went dark.

* * *

Saturday, January 18, 1992

Casper, Wyoming

9:00 am

Eddie opened his eyes, and he looked around at the unfamiliar surroundings. He had a dull headache, and now his left shin throbbed in pain as well. Eddie jerked back the covers on his bed, and he spied his leg bandaged. Only then did the memories of the snake, Tracy, and the blizzard roar back to him like a March Wyoming wind.

As Eddie flung the covers back over his leg, he spotted a man sitting quietly in the corner of his room. He recognized the man's face and asked him, "are you here to fix something?"

The man smiled, stood up, and walked over to the side of his bed. Then the man asked, "do you remember me, Eddie?"

He nodded. "Yes, you fixed the light above my bed last night."

However, the man shook his head and said, "No, I am not a maintenance man. I am Ken Hopkins from the Wyoming Department of Criminal Investigations."

"What is DCI doing up here from Cheyenne?"

"Well, that is a long story, Eddie. But first, how about I go get the doctor to let him know that you are conscious and responsive."

Fifteen minutes later, immediately after the doctor left his room, Ken Hopkins and Adam Riley entered the door. Eddie smiled at his friend and shook both of their hands. But in his mind, he questioned why the men were in his hospital room.

"What is going on, gentlemen? Am I under suspicion of something? Where is Tracy?"

Agent Hopkins sat down next to Eddie and said, "don't worry, you are not a suspect of anything. You are our star witness."

"A witness to what?"

The agent then carefully unfolded how Sheriff Doan had been under surveillance for nearly a year after DCI had received a complaint alleging a sexual assault that happened in 1979. Since the initial charge, DCI had received two other anonymous calls as well.

Hopkins also added, "that is where Adam Riley comes into the picture. He provided me the particulars of Tracy's complaint back in December."

Eddie rubbed his eyes while trying to connect what the agent was insinuating. But, before he could ask a question, his friend Adam Riley picked up on the story where Agent Hopkins left off. He explained that the main thing in three out of the four witnesses was their lack of memory of the sexual assault. Riley further revealed that Undersheriff Witten asked for an investigation into Sheriff Doan's abuse of power and creating a hostile work environment.

"How does any of that apply to me?" Eddie asked. But, suddenly, his memory of the events from two nights before came back. He then looked up at the two men.

Both men nodded at him, and Agent Hopkins asked, "what do you recall from that night?"

"I dunno? I think Doan said that I know too much. But after that, all I remember is hearing a bunch of people rushing into this room before everything went dark."

Riley leaned forward and asked, "do you remember Doan saying that both Tracy and Melanie Parkman got what they wanted?"

"Yes, he did say that! But how did you know?"

Agent Hopkins informed him that he was used as the bait to lure Sheriff Doan out. The agent further explained that he dressed up as a maintenance man and placed a tiny camera and a microphone in the light fixture above Eddie's bed. Thus, not only did they hear Doan's threats, but they also captured his actions on camera as well.

Then, unexpectedly, Hopkins handed Eddie a clear plastic evidence bag with a small glass ampoule inside it.

Eddie turned the bag until the drug name: *Flunitrazepam,* read on the label. He then asked, "what is this stuff?"

"Eddie, that is the intravenous form of 'roofies,' and Sheriff Doan tried to give you a lethal overdose of it. Thankfully, your friend Riley here had the presence of mind to yank the IV needle out of your hand as soon as we stormed the room. He probably saved your life."

Eddie sat back in his bed to take in the various elements of the story. He also thought back to the night in question, and then he recalled the rest of that last verbal exchange with Doan.

He abruptly sat up and asked, "where is Tracy? Doan said something about her and Chief Traynor being neutralized!"

Adam Riley smiled and assured him, "both Tracy and Chief Traynor are fine. However, deputies McKinnon and Peck are in custody for attempting an assault on both of them."

Agent Hopkins laughed and added, "ya, Tracy and the Chief made short work of those two guys."

It was a lot of information for Eddie to process, and he again rubbed his eyes while trying to make sense of everything.

"It is okay, Eddie," Hopkins said. Then after a moment, he continued, "Sheriff Doan won't politic himself out of this situation. Once he becomes convicted of all the charges, Doan will spend the rest of his life in prison."

Eddie nodded and quipped, "I hope you guys have talked to Bill Crooks too. He has the wallet of Dan Pruitt, you know, the man we found froze to death. Anyway, I want to know why the wallet had Sheriff Doan's business card inside of it?"

Agent Hopkins nodded and replied, "yes, I am aware of that too. But, at this point, I don't want to burden you with all the charges. I want you to get better."

Riley added, "that is right, and, by the way, acting Sheriff Witten has removed yours and Tracy's suspensions and has purged your records."

"Thanks, Riley. I won't know how to operate without fearing that Doan is scrutinizing everything I do."

Agent Hopkin's face pinched together and asked, "you don't know, do you?"

"Know about what?"

"About why Sheriff Doan hated you from the very first day you started with the department, Eddie," Riley added.

Before he could speak, Agent Hopkins leaned closer and said, "Doan's first accuser, the one from 1979, was your sister, Wendy. So maybe Doan always suspected that you knew about it somehow, and that is why he transferred you out to the Salt Creek area in the first place."

Eddie didn't know what to say other than to repeat, "my sister?"

Riley placed his hand on Eddie's shoulder and said, "Yes, your sister. By the way, she flew in last night from Denver after Tracy called her. So she is out in the hallway with Tracy and a whole host of others waiting to see you."

"So, let me get this straight. Doan thought I knew about what he supposedly did to my sister?"

Riley nodded. "Yes, I think that back in 1983, he sent you to Midwest-Edgerton with hopes that you would get frustrated enough to quit. But when you flourished in that community, I believe Doan continued harassing you to keep you in your place."

"So, Doan then sent Tracy to me either hide her or frustrate her, right?"

"Exactly," Riley confirmed.

At the break in the conversation, Agent Hopkins thrust out his right hand, and Eddie grasped it in a tight grip. Then the agent said, "we are going to leave now and allow you to see your friends. But, promise me that you will call either one of us if you remember any other details about the case that we aren't aware of?"

"Deal."

As soon as the investigators left Eddie's hospital room, Tracy led Eddie's sister, Wendy, followed by Chief Traynor, Bill Crooks, Steve Otten, and four others. First, Traynor recalled the details of his and Tracy's encounter with Deputies McKinnon and Peck. Next, Steve Otten gladly reported that he had recovered his pickup, and it was back home safe in the carport. Then Bill Crooks recounted the news stories detailing all the criminal charges levied on John Doan. Meanwhile, Tracy remained quiet and held Eddie's hand. At the same time, everyone told and retold the last few days' events, primarily the community rescue effort.

By late afternoon, all the visitors except Chief Traynor, Tracy, and Wendy had left the hospital and returned home. For Eddie, it was nice to see everyone. Still, at the same time, it was also delightful to enjoy the relative quiet once the cacophony of voices had ceased.

A little while later, the conversation in the room centered more on the future than the past. Then the doctor entered the room and asked everyone to leave, though Eddie convinced her to allow Tracy to stay. The doctor examined him and found him healing well. On that news, Eddie begged the physician that he wanted his discharge so that he could finish recovering in the comfort of his own home.

"I don't know, Eddie. With you being single, I worry about you having a support system?" the Doctor asked.

"Doc, I assure you, I have a community of folks who would look out for me. But, more importantly, I have a partner," and Eddie looked at Tracy and winked at her.

The physician shrugged her shoulders and obliged his discharge request. She said that it would take about 30 minutes to get all the paperwork ready, though, in the meantime, he could get dressed.

At 5:30 p.m., Eddie begrudgingly sat in a wheelchair while impatiently waiting for Tracy to pull up to the front door of the hospital. He had complained all the way down from the fourth floor that he was capable of walking on crutches. Still, dutifully, the nurse's assistant softly rejected his overtures.

When Tracy finally drove up the patient pickup driveway, Eddie was pleased to see his familiar department Blazer come to a stop in front of him. Only then did he smile. Then, with help from the nurse's assistant, Tracy helped Eddie into the passenger seat. Meanwhile, Wendy scrambled into the backseat with the agility of a child.

It was a quiet ride through Casper until Tracy merged onto I-25 north. It was then he turned his head toward the backseat in the Blazer and made eye contact with his sister. "What happened?" he asked Wendy.

She intuitively knew what her brother wanted to know. So, she took a deep breath and exhaled slowly. Then Wendy told him about one particular night in the summer before her senior year in high school. On that night, she had driven to Casper to meet up with friends at the Central Wyoming Fair. They all had a good time, but while driving home to Glenrock, her car broke down eight miles east of Casper on Highway 26.

Wendy then described that a man in his forties had stopped and offered her a ride home. She had initially refused the offer, but, still, the man identified himself as Undersheriff John Doan, so she accepted his gesture. Once inside his car, Doan had asked her what her name was and her age and seemed friendly. But instead of going straight to Glenrock, Doan turned north onto Cole Creek Road and went over the bridge that spanned the North Platte River. Then he pulled into the fishing access parking lot on the other side.

"Stop!" Eddie said suddenly, "I don't want to hear every gory detail of the rest of your story."

Wendy calmly replied, "Eddie, Doan did try to have his way with me, but he wasn't able to do everything he wanted."

"Why not?"

"Because I managed to kick him in the mouth, and he stopped."

"What happened then?"

"He shoved me out of his car, and I walked the rest of the way home. But it was what he said that I remembered most. He called me an, I quote, 'oil field tramp,' and then he took off."

"Why didn't you tell anyone like Mom or Dad?"

"I did tell Mom, Eddie, and she told me I had it coming because of the way I dressed...I have never forgiven her for that."

"So, that is why you left when you turned 18 and never came back, isn't it?"

"Yes."

Tracy drove silently and listened to the entire exchange. She didn't want to seem rude or insert herself into a family discussion, but a thought bothered her. So she asked, "so, why did you come forward and call DCI?" Then she watched in the rear-view mirror and could see Wendy's bright teeth even in the darkness.

Wendy then quipped, "a few years ago, I drove up to Cheyenne with a few girlfriends of mine from Loveland, Colorado, to take in a concert at Frontier Days. When we were at our hotel, I turned on KTWO news to see what was happening up here in Casper. That was when I saw Doan give an interview, and a flood of suppressed emotions came up. That's how."

Eddie looked over his shoulder again at his sister and said, "I am sorry that happened to you, and I wish I would have known, or I would...."

His sister cut him off and finished his sentence, "I know, you would have never taken the job. I appreciate that, brother, but now I am glad I hadn't told you."

"Why?"

"Because, Eddie, you would not have become such fixture in the Salt Creek community. That's why I am glad. I sat there in the hallway and listened to all these people come up and tell me about how much they adore you. I am glad I didn't take that away from you."

The department Chevy Blazer fell quiet inside as Tracy deafly exited off I-25 and onto Highway 259. In the cloudless night sky illuminated by a bright half-moon, Eddie easily made out familiar landmarks against the blanket of snow. First, to the west, he saw the pine tree-covered hill that folks referred to as the "amphitheater," then he saw East Teapot Creek.

Lastly, he spotted the rock of twenty-nine's bane itself, Teapot Rock. As Tracy drove up and over 40-mile hill, Eddie sat up so he could perhaps spot the same oil field road that took them over to the backside of the Rimrocks and the small cave. Though in his anticipation, he spotted something else.

Instead, he saw a light similar to a camping lantern on a hillside that he knew was uninhabited like everywhere else in the oilfield. But, to him, the illumination was different in a couple of ways. First, its color was odd and glowed in a slight greenish tint. Secondly, the light didn't seem to reflect against the snow underneath it. While they drove closer, the anomaly took on the shape of an orb. It continued floating down the hill and up toward the highway. Then the greenish-white ball of light vanished when the Blazer's headlights cast upon it.

Eddie looked over to Tracy who's face expressed that she too had just seen something extraordinary.

Then he leaned over and whispered to her, "you saw that, didn't you?"

"I did."

Wendy sat forward between them and asked, "saw what?"

"Nothing, sis. It was just something in the oil field, that's all."

When they reached the junction of Highways 259 and 387, Tracy turned left off of the highway and drove over the cattle guard and onto Lewis Street. Wendy remarked from the backseat that she had never been in Midwest before. Yet, after she looked around, she commented that the houses looked like those in Glenrock.

When she drove up Ellison Avenue to the intersection with Navy Row, Tracy looked out of the driver's side window and across the empty lot toward Eddie's house.

"Look, Eddie!"

He looked up and saw his house decorated with white Christmas lights. The bright lights reflected against the snow and the faces of at least 50 townsfolk that braved the cold night to welcome him home. Tracy then pulled into the empty stall of the carport next to his red Ford pickup. With Wendy's assistance, she helped Eddie onto his crutches.

Eddie looked around in delight at the lights, the shoveled walkway, and all of the smiling faces. Even the reclusive Reed had made a rare public appearance. Then he spotted two of the smallest of faces, which belonged to Wes Corbin and Stu Jenkins.

Next, he motioned for the boys to come closer, and when they did, he bent over and asked them, "guess what I just saw, boys?

* * *

Saturday, February 1, 1992

East of the Rimrocks Near Midwest, Wyoming

It had been two weeks since Eddie arrived home from the hospital. His physical recovery was a short one, and he had discarded the crutches within a few days. His sister, Wendy, stayed for a couple of days before returning to her home in Colorado. It was a pleasant visit, and the siblings promised one another that they would see each other more often.

The day after Wendy left, Acting Sheriff Witten drove up to Midwest unannounced to visit with Eddie. He quickly warmed to his new boss' cordial manner. Witten then inquired about his injury and recovery. He insisted that he felt well enough to return to full-time duty.

Though Sheriff Witten appreciated Eddie's plucky nature, he ordered that he and Tracy take two full weeks of non-chargeable vacation days. The Sheriff felt that both of his employees needed the time to recover mentally from their ordeal. When the visit ended, Eddie suggested that the Sheriff drive around Midwest and Edgerton and stop to talk to people. He further implored Sheriff Witten that the simple gesture of saying "Hi" to people in the community would also help him separate himself from the defrocked former Sheriff.

The ever-present wind blasted against Eddie and Tracy as they sat on the seat of a snowmobile parked above the same sandstone ledge that bore their infamous cave. A little over a week ago, Eddie had contacted Roy Wahl, an acquaintance of his who lived in the small town of

Glendo. Roy was an expert rattlesnake handler. He collected wild specimens to milk them of their venom, which made lifesaving anti-venom serum.

"Roy, are you about done yet?" Eddie called out.

"Yep, give me a few more minutes, then it will be all clear."

"How many did you get?"

Roy responded, "I got 152 rattlesnakes, 14 bull snakes, and even six little garter snakes. I have seen some big dens, but this one is incredible."

Eddie turned to Tracy, and she raised both of her hands to him and shook her head in protest.

"No way, Eddie, I am not going in there!"

"Tracy, we talked about this already, and you agreed."

"Can't Roy just stick his hand in there and grab the container?"

Eddie started to get impatient and said, "okay, then I will go down there; how about that?"

"Come on, Eddie, I don't think your leg is strong enough for you to descend the rock face, let alone crawl inside that cave."

"Then what choice do we have?"

She shook her head from side to side, and then sighed heavily. "Fine. I will do it, but you owe me."

"Owe you what? I thought you were okay with snakes; it is spiders that you don't like?"

Tracy looked back at Eddie with a stern look and said, "you owe me," and then she knelt, grabbed the rope, and lowered herself down the small cliff. Roy helped her repel the last couple of feet, and Tracy turned toward him.

"It is all clear, but, don't worry, they won't harm you. They are more worried about the bags and cold than you," Roy explained.

"Thanks," Tracy said while she knelt to crawl inside the cave.

The small chamber smelled heavily of cucumbers. Notwithstanding, Tracy gingerly pushed past the pile of 20 bulging gunny sacks stacked against the left wall. Even though each bag held the snakes, it still made her nervous. She took out her flashlight, turned it on, and peered through the dinner plate-sized hole at the rear of the cave. The beam of light confirmed no more serpents, but it also illuminated the side of a metal-sided box.

She reached through the hole and grabbed the container, and tugged at it. Surprisingly, the metal carton broke free from the rocky soil beneath it. Tracy struggled for a minute to pull the box close enough to grasp it with both hands due to its sheer weight.

When Tracy emerged from the cave, she handed the metal container up to Eddie, and then he helped her ascend back up the little rock face.

After opening the lid to the container, they were delighted to find ten stacks of $1000 bills. Eddie quickly computed the math in his head. Then he said aloud, "if each stack contained 100 notes, then the sum of the cache would be precisely the $1 million promised by Arthur Daniels."

"Eddie, are these real?"

"It looks like it. I mean, Grover Cleveland is pictured on the front. Plus, the series date predates when these taken out of circulation in 1969."

"So, if they are out of circulation, are they still legal?" she asked.

"Yes, they are still legal tenders."

Their discussion was interrupted when a gunny sack filled with empty bags landed in front of them. Then a tug on the rope beneath Eddie's feet alerted him to step forward to help Roy up the wall. Eddie reached down and grabbed the back of Roy's coat since one of his hands was on the rope, and the other one carried a gunny sack that sagged with the weight at the bottom.

As Eddie assisted Roy, he asked him, "are those what I think they are?" as he pointed to the sack.

Roy held up the bag and smiled. He said, "yes, I have six nice-sized ones here to take home with me. But the others are safely back inside that massive den. You know, some snake dens get used for hundreds of years if they are safe and provide good shelter. I am pretty sure this is one of those too."

He nodded at Roy's comment and then reached down and untied the rope from the sidebar of the snow machine and coiled it. Then, from behind him, he heard Roy start up his snowmobile, and Eddie started his engine as well.

They drove up through the snow-choked ditches when they left since most of the road was completely void of snow, but was still un-driveable in a slick muddy mess.

Thirty minutes later, Eddie and Tracy rode together in the cab of Eddie's pickup with Bill Crooks' snowmobile secure in the bed.

Tracy asked, "so, now what? We got the money, but what do we do with it?"

Eddie looked over at her and replied, "I was just thinking about that."

"Ya, what are you thinking?"

"I think that after we count the amount of money in the box, we should arrange for a press conference this upcoming Monday and hold it at the school."

"Okay, why at school?"

"I was thinking of the irony that we found the money on a State school section of land, though I don't think that was just a coincidence. I think that was Daniel's plan all along."

"So, then what, we turn the money over to the State?" she asked.

"Sure, we do exactly that, but with pre-conditions. Like we demand that some of the money goes to restore the swimming pool at Midwest High School."

"Yes, and maybe some money can go toward a bike path or something between Midwest and Edgerton. I hate thinking about community kids having to walk or ride their bikes on the side of Highway 387. There are just too many trucks, and somebody is going to get hurt."

Eddie grinned. "I agree," but also suggested, "plus, the town could use some money to finish building the park across from my house and south of Navy Row. But, then, Edgerton could use a nice park too."

Tracy agreed, but another thought came to her mind.

"What if the state officials disagree with us and say they will decide how to spend it?"

Eddie smiled back at Tracy and said, "then I will threaten that we will put the money back there inside the snake den. Then they can take their chances on getting it out."

Tracy laughed, and then she smiled back at him and said, "I like your plan."

They rode in silence for a minute or so when Eddie suddenly turned his head toward Tracy and said, "I have one last request now that this case is solved."

"What's that, Eddie?"

"I would like to take you out to dinner to celebrate our one-month anniversary as partners."

The request hung in the air, and she kept him waiting for an answer long enough for him to feel uncomfortable.

"Tracy, if I, uh...."

She guffawed. "I'm just playing with you, Eddie. I would like to go out to dinner with you, platonically, of course."

"Yes, platonically. But you get to choose. Is there anywhere you want to go?"

"Really, wow! Let me see; there are so many choices...umm, how about you decide?"

"Okay, that's easy. There is a café on the west side of Casper on the Shoshoni Highway that serves hamburgers the size of a supper plate."

"It sounds like our kind of place, Eddie. I can't wait."

THE END

AFTERWORD AND ACKNOWLEDGEMENTS

This novel is a work of fiction. The names, characters, and exploits are the product of the author's imagination and are used fictitiously. Any resemblance to actual persons, living or dead, businesses, and companies are entirely coincidental.

The Wyoming towns of Midwest and Edgerton depicted in this story are real. They are the last townships within the Salt Creek Oil Field that once held the World's Largest Light Oil Producing Field title. Another truth is that Midwest High School was the first high school to host and play in a night football game under a lighted field. Additionally, the small towns of Crook and Iliff, Colorado, portrayed in this work are also real and represent yet another resilient community.

The author sends a special appreciation to long-time Midwest resident Karen Bays for providing a trove of additional historical background information.

Photos: On the covers, the author thanks his father, Gene LeMaitre, for using his image of Teapot Rock taken from Highway 259 south of Midwest. Additionally, the author thanks his daughter, Lilly LeMaitre, for her photo editing skills. The author's photo depicts him sitting on the porch of his childhood home at #10 Navy Row in Midwest, Wyoming.

Lastly, the author thanks his wife, Nancy, for inspiring him to write his first book, *SALT CREEK*, and for her continual support throughout all projects.

Follow phillemaitreauthor.com to receive the latest news relating to future works.

OTHER WORKS BY THE AUTHOR:
SALT CREEK: A Novel
EARLY DAWN: A Salt Creek Novel

Phil LeMaitre is a former resident of Midwest, Wyoming, and graduated from Midwest High School in 1986. LeMaitre is a 29-year active-duty veteran of the U.S. Air Force and now serves as a Christian Life Coach. Other works include SALT CREEK: A Novel and EARLY DAWN: A Salt Creek Novel. The author lives in Florida with his wife and their three youngest children.